What People Are Saying About The Distant Shore

"Adventure, mystery, and romance on Florida's wild Merritt Island of 1904 will capture your heart.—a beautiful story of love in all aspects of the word."~ **Ruth Carmichael Ellinger**, author of *The Wild Rose of Lancaster*

"Imaginative writing and vivid word pictures will sweep you into this climactic story of a young girl whose life is turned upside down."~ **Suzanne Woods Fisher**, author of *Copper Star*

"You will grow to love Emma-Lee in this suspenseful, inspirational story that delights to the very end."~ **Sheila Cragg**, author of *A Woman's Walk With God*

"I was thrilled to discover such an enjoyable, clean, even educational story. I'm always glad to catch my daughters reading. We need more books like *The Distant Shore* to offer girls today." ~ **Lisa Whelchel**, actress, national speaker, founder of MomTime Ministries, author of numerous books including *The Facts of Life and Other Lessons My Father Taught Me.*

"*The Distant Shore* captivated my attention from the very first page...enjoyable for girls of all ages." ~ **Haven Cauble**, age 14, daughter of Lisa Whelchel

"*The Distant Shore* is as magical as any movie you'd find featured on the Disney Channel." ~ Reader Views

"A story richer with characters is hard to find these days. I thoroughly enjoyed this story; it touched my soul." ~ Coffee Time Romance, 5 cups (top rating)

The Distant Shore
Debora M. Coty

Vintage Romance Publishing
Goose Creek, South Carolina
www.vrpublishing.com

Debora M. Coty

ISBN: 978-0-9793327-6-0
PUBLISHED BY VINTAGE ROMANCE PUBLISHING, LLC
www.vrpublishing.com

Dedication

For my beloved husband, Chuck,
and our precious children,
Christina Coty Boyer
and
Matthew Coty

You are my inspiration and my wings.

"May the God of hope
fill you with all joy and peace
as you trust in him,
so that you may overflow with hope
by the power of the Holy Spirit."
Romans 15:13, NIV

Chapter One

Emma-Lee Palmer managed to keep a brave face, showing Papa only a few sniffles before she boarded the train with the help of the white-haired conductor. When she settled on the scratchy, burgundy seat with Sarah's hand-me-down trunk under her feet, she stretched her trembling body as tall as she could to see out the half-opened window tinged with coal dust.

There stood Papa on the platform, his broad shoulders drooping and a strange, sad look on his face as he stared at the snorting, hulking iron beast that was taking his daughter away. He looked like a crumpled photograph of the strong, ramrod-straight Papa whose hardened expression always hinted at barely-concealed anger.

Emma-Lee couldn't hold back any longer. Deep sobs racked her quivering body as she reached for the man who represented her entire life—everything she had ever known and loved. *It's all a terrible mistake*, she thought. *He'll come back for me any minute. He'll take me home to Mama, my sisters, and brothers, and the nightmare will be over.*

A shrill whistle blew, and Emma-Lee's hands flew to her ears to mute the horrible sound. The smokestack of the enormous black engine began billowing out thick smoke that stung her eyes and made the inside of her nose burn. When the coach lurched forward, chugging and jerking with loud clanging noises, Emma-Lee knew it was too late. Papa wouldn't be coming after all.

The scream of an infant behind her on the train seemed to come straight from Emma-Lee's own heart. She couldn't stop crying, even when the conductor came for the ticket Mama had pinned to her dress collar. The old man waited patiently while her trembling fingers fumbled with the pin. He continued sneaking glances from beneath his black hat bill while he punched the ticket and handed it back.

"So, miss, are you from Miami?" he asked, the ends of his fuzzy, white mustache tilting up in a smile.

Emma-Lee nodded.

"And would this be your first train ride?"

"Yes-s-s sir," she managed to say over the enormous lump in her throat.

"How old are you, if I might be so bold?"

"Nine-and-a-half." She always added the half, but at this moment, somehow it didn't seem so important.

"Well, you're a mighty lucky young lady, if I may say so. Not too many gals of your stature have the good fortune to be a passenger on the most advanced locomotive in the 1904 Florida Seaboard Coastline Railway. And you're headed off to an adventure, I'll wager. What's your name?"

Emma-Lee reached into her traveling satchel and took out a delicate, white handkerchief embroidered with pink, curly letters, *ELP*. Mama's initials. She wiped her eyes and thought of Mama quietly tucking the folded cloth into her bag after her tearful goodbye in the kitchen of the Victorian frame house on Flagler Street.

"Emma-Lee Palmer," she told the conductor as loudly as she could, although her voice was hardly above a whisper.

"I see you're going to Eau Gallie, Emma-Lee Palmer," the conductor said, studying her ticket, his deep voice smooth as warm molasses. "Are you visiting relatives there?"

Emma-Lee dabbed at her nose before speaking. "Yes sir. I'm going to stay with Aunt Augusta on Merritt Island." Her voice quivered and rose crazily in pitch as she gave her brief explanation, but the gentleman kindly overlooked it.

"Ah, what a paradise, that island! You're not going to believe your eyes—beauty not seen anywhere else on earth." His eyebrows arced like tiny rainbows as he gently patted her shoulder. "A very lucky young lady, indeed."

He turned and moved down the aisle, his body swaying left and right as the train's rhythmic clackety-clack settled into a regular pattern.

Emma-Lee's eyelids grew as heavy as her aching heart with the motion of the coach rocking back and forth. She closed her eyes and pretended it was the wind blowing her cradle in the treetops, like the song Mama sang when she was little and curled up in her lap in the big rocking chair on the front porch. Mama used to smile and sing so pretty back then...

The next thing she knew, the conductor was tapping her arm. "We're here, little lady. The train is pulling into the Eau Gallie station."

* * * *

Emma-Lee looked for Aunt Augusta as the conductor carried her trunk down the train steps and placed it on the platform, but she was nowhere to be found. Fast moving people hurried by left and right, but not one of them was Aunt Augusta.

She dragged the trunk half as big as herself to a vacant bench and climbed up. She sat and waited, carefully studying the face of each middle-aged woman as she passed. Five minutes crawled by...ten...twenty.

Emma-Lee squirmed on the splintered wooden bench in the prickly August heat, fighting back tears. The bright, central Florida noonday sun beamed through the filter of oak leaves framing the waiting area of Eau Gallie's train depot. She could feel sweat beading on her forehead under her sunflower-colored traveling bonnet and the damp cotton petticoat sticking to her ribs beneath her matching yellow dress.

The crowd thinned out and the ear-splitting whistle shrieked its warning as the train began pulling away from the station. The conductor gave Emma-Lee a quizzical backward glance from the metal steps of the train car as he lowered the guardrail.

Still no Aunt Augusta.

Maybe I've forgotten what she looks like, Emma-Lee thought. *It's been quite a while since she visited us in Miami.* But the image of the rows of tiny wrinkles around Aunt Augusta's mouth, all pointing like little arrows toward the thin lips she kept clenched into a tight line sprang clearly to mind.

No, she was sure she would recognize Aunt Augusta—the "sensible" old fashioned hats she wore atop the tight bun that reminded Emma-Lee of a knotted tree root (Aunt Augusta was quick to criticize the "ridiculous uselessness of stylish hats nowadays"). There was no forgetting the sharp gray eyes that missed nothing, the beak-like nose that seemed too big for her face, and the rapid steps that propelled her slight, five-foot frame ever forward, allowing no room for "dilly-dallying" from dawdling nieces and nephews.

Something about Aunt Augusta always made Emma-Lee think of the black wasps that hovered around their papery nest beneath the kitchen window sill—dark, leggy creatures with sharp angles and a big stinger. Although small in size, they were enormously scary to have flitting about.

Emma-Lee's feet, clad in her ivory, button-top traveling shoes, dangled above the platform as she shifted positions on the hard depot bench. She untied her bonnet and used it to fan herself. Damp tendrils of thick red hair curled around her ears and stuck to her neck.

Where can Aunt Augusta be?

She peered through the open depot door at the half dozen people trying to talk to the ticket agent at once and twice as many milling about inside the station.

Didn't she know I was coming on the morning train?

Papa had said everything was arranged. Yes, she remembered every one of Papa's words on that terrible Sunday afternoon he'd made the shocking announcement to the family in the parlor.

He'd called everyone together and ordered them to sit down. He stood in the doorway, his face hard and his eyes distant.

"In two weeks, Emma-Lee will be leaving. She'll stay with Augusta on the island and help her in whatever way she can during the following school year. All arrangements have been made. There will be no further discussion about it."

In the tense silence that followed, Emma-Lee's eyes darted first to Mama, who had a pained expression on her face as she held the baby tightly against her chest and rocked back and forth in a chair that wasn't a rocker. Papa fidgeted with his pocket watch, dropping it into his coat pocket and pulling it right back out again once, twice, three times for good measure.

The other children looked stunned. Sarah, the eldest and almost always cheerful, looked as if she was about to cry. The three boys stared at each other in surprise, speechless for the first time Emma-Lee could remember.

She'd wanted to scream out, "Why? What terrible thing have I done that you're sending me away?" But she knew silent obedience was expected—no, demanded of her—so she swallowed hard, pushing down the bitter lump of hurt and fear clogging her throat and remained mute.

Only later in the privacy of Sarah's bedroom could she finally ask the haunting question that echoed in her brain: "Why don't they want me anymore?"

"It's not that they don't want you, dearest," Sarah had said. She seemed so grown up for a fourteen-year-old. She'd enveloped Emma-Lee with her soft arms and gently stroked her waist-length red hair with her fingertips, struggling for words.

"It's just that...there are some things...well...sometimes things happen that you can't understand...not until you're older. Even then, it's hard. For now, you must be a brave girl and accept this as what's best for you."

Emma-Lee's thoughts were snatched from Sarah's comforting embrace and returned with a jolt to the train depot by two large, dusty boots that planted themselves in front of her bench. Her misty eyes followed the vertical line of the black boots all the way up the tall figure to where the glaring sun was blocked by a black hat. The man's eyes were shaded by the wide brim as he looked down from his towering position above her.

"You named Palmer? Emilene Palmer from Miami?" The man spoke slowly, drawling the words with his gravelly voice, pronouncing her hometown, "My-am-a."

"I'm Emma-Lee." She reached up to wipe away the drop of sweat tickling her nose. Or was it a tear?

"Your aunt has taken ill. She is recovering at my house. Gather your things and come with me."

"What do you mean? What's wrong with Aunt Augusta?" Emma-Lee felt that now familiar sensation of hot fear bubbling up from her belly.

"This is your trunk?" the man asked, ignoring her question and reaching for the leather handles on the trunk beside the bench.

"It's my sister's trunk," Emma-Lee answered honestly.

His eyes narrowed, and he shook his head ever so slightly as he lifted the case and turned to walk away, leaving Emma-Lee to jam her bonnet back on her head, collect her traveling bag, and shimmy down from the high bench. The stranger's back was already disappearing around the corner of the building as she gained her footing.

Mama always told me never to go anywhere with strangers, she thought, clutching her satchel to her chest with both hands. *I don't know this man. Can I believe him? Is he really taking me to Aunt Augusta?*

Her eyes sought out the nearest adults—inside the train depot—where business went on as usual, no one paying attention to the goings on outside. It occurred to her there was nobody on earth to help her if she did indeed need help on that fine summer morning.

Nobody at all.

Emma-Lee's heart ached for Mama.

"What's keeping you, girl?" boomed a deep voice attached to no face that she could see. Emma-Lee knew it belonged to the man who had taken the trunk containing her every possession. Although she shook all over, she saw no other choice but to follow.

"If you're there, God, please help me," she whispered toward heaven as her feet found wings, and she flew around the building toward the frightening unknown.

Chapter Two

The tall stranger loaded Emma-Lee and her trunk into his black, horse-drawn buggy. The lumbering trip through the muddy, pot-holed streets of Eau Gallie passed in stony silence.

Emma-Lee yearned to ask questions—so many questions—but Emma-Lee Palmer had been raised with proper manners and knew children should not speak unless spoken to. One look at the stranger's tight face told her that this was not a man who carelessly used words, and he had no intention of wasting any on her.

As they pulled up in front of a two-story, white frame house with navy blue shutters and a matching door, the man in the black hat looked at Emma-Lee for the first time since the train station.

"Your aunt is very ill. I suspect it was her anxiety over your arrival that's triggered one of her sick headaches. You can go to her room and tell her you're here, but don't stay more than a few minutes. She needs to rest."

With that, he climbed down from the driver's seat. Wordlessly, he swung Emma-Lee down to the ground, heaved her trunk from the buggy, and carried it up the three front steps. He placed the trunk on the wide front porch before disappearing through the door freckled with peeling blue paint.

Emma-Lee figured she was supposed to follow him inside, but by the time she entered the house, the man in the black hat had disappeared. There was no one anywhere to be seen, and the only sound she could hear was the ticking of the big grandfather clock in the parlor to her left.

She pulled the front door closed behind her, and the loud *click* as the latch fell into place made her jump as if a gun had fired.

The parlor looked clean and orderly but not as well appointed as the Palmer parlor in Miami. The purple velvet curtains were shiny in places, and the settee and stuffed armchair appeared frayed and worn in the sitting places.

Emma-Lee took slow, careful steps down the hallway toward the staircase, looking this way and that into every room—the library, sitting room, dining room, and kitchen. Nobody stirred. She couldn't understand where the man in the black hat had gone or why he hadn't told her where to find Aunt Augusta.

He must not have any children, Emma-Lee thought. *There are no toys or picture books lying around.* The place had a stuffy, grown-up feel about it.

She came to the foot of the stairs and looked up, straining to hear any sounds coming from the second floor that might give a hint as to the whereabouts of Aunt Augusta. Hearing nothing, she tentatively climbed the first three steps and paused, listening.

Well, if Aunt Augusta is the only person here, I guess it won't bother anyone if I go looking for her, Emma-Lee thought, feeling a little braver as she mounted the remaining stairs. Her stomach made a loud rumbling noise. She hadn't had anything to eat since she left the breakfast table that morning in Miami, and her stomach was quite empty. Mama had made her favorite— blueberry flapjacks—but she was so upset, she could barely swallow the few bites she took.

There were two closed doors down each side of a short hallway to the right of the landing. Emma-Lee approached the first door on the right and lifted a tentative hand to knock. No answer.

Spreading her small fingers on the large, tarnished brass doorknob, she twisted and pushed. The door stuck. Seldom-used hinges squeaked their protest as she shoved the door open and took a step inside. It was a storage room of sorts. Emma-Lee could see lots of boxes stacked along the walls and white sheet-covered furniture piled in the center. Dusty pictures of a beautiful young woman in a riding habit and a smiling couple in wedding attire hung askew on the walls.

Something indefinable about the darkened room made Emma-Lee feel sad. The pungent smell of cedar hung heavy and nauseating. As if bearing testimony to the demise of hope itself, two long, narrow hope chests, each draped with a flowing white cloth like a funeral casket, flanked a white-curtained window.

The window must have been opened a crack, allowing just enough breeze to send the thin white fabric softly rolling and billowing like a ghost floating in mid-air.

Emma-Lee shivered, although the room was hot enough to melt butter.

Turning toward the west side of the room, her heart lurched! There, upright in the shadowy corner, was the motionless body of a headless woman!

Emma-Lee felt the blood rush from her face, and her mouth drop open as a scream gathered in the back of her throat. Her hands flew to cover her mouth as she backed away and turned to flee from the frightful figure. Out of the corner of her eye, she noticed pins sticking out of the woman's dress and saw that half the collar was missing. Suddenly, the image of another headless woman tugged at her mind.

Where was it?

The attic? Yes, it was the attic at home.

Oh, it's only a dress form in a blue shirtwaist! Memories of the leather dress form that Mama used to sew dresses for herself and Sarah popped into her mind. It was shaped like a woman's body with no head. The decapitated lady wasn't real. She was like a big doll that had lost her head. Emma-Lee remembered her doll, Eloisa, after Archibald had ripped off her head and stuck it on the fence post. Half her collar was missing, too.

Emma-Lee took a deep breath to calm her catapulting heart. She thought she could hear it ricochet off her chest walls. *Why am I so afraid of everything?* For as long as she could remember, she had escaped frightening circumstances by taking refuge beneath her four-poster bed. Her brothers constantly reminded her of her shameful cowardice. Archibald's favorite taunt struck up in her brain:

'Fraidy cat, imagine that! Run and hide, you 'fraidy cat!

"I *am* a 'fraidy cat," Emma-Lee muttered in disgust.

Quickly backing out and shutting the door behind her, she studied the other three doors in the hallway. The fringe of a throw rug was peeking from below one of the doors. She'd try that one.

Her timid rap on the door brought the same silent response, but this time Emma-Lee lingered in the hallway while she swung the door open. The room, obviously a bedroom, was unlike any she'd ever seen. The unmade bed was heaped with sheets rumpled and tossed about recklessly. Men's socks, belts, shirts, and trousers scattered about the floor and bed. More were draped across the back of the wooden chair at the desk by the window and across the stuffed armchair beside the bed. A strange odor lingered in the air. It smelled a little like Papa's pipe tobacco but not quite the same.

She took a few steps into the room and looked around. She had never seen such a mess. Mama was an immaculate housekeeper, and the Palmer children were never allowed to leave their rooms in such disarray.

Books were stacked everywhere—on the floor, the desk, the bedside table, even a few on the pillow. Big, thick volumes with long words on the covers that Emma-Lee couldn't pronounce littered the room. One nearby lay opened to a picture of a young boy with a huge, bloody gash on his left ankle. There was a lot of writing above and below the picture, but Emma-Lee couldn't understand many of the complicated words. The picture on the opposite page showed the same boy on crutches, standing on his right foot with his left pants leg tied below the knee.

She stared at the picture for a long moment trying to figure out what was odd about it. Then it struck her. The little boy no longer had a left foot! Emma-Lee reeled in horror and fled into the hallway, panting hard and feeling sick to her stomach.

A tiny sound like a kitten mewing drew her attention away from her quavering stomach to the second door on the left side of the hallway. It must be Aunt Augusta! Emma-Lee felt so relieved, she didn't even stop to knock before rushing into the room.

Heavy drapes covered the windows, and it took a few moments for her eyes to adjust to the dim light. The room was dark and musty although a slight breeze from the open window fluttered the drapes.

The first thing she could make out was a heavyset woman in a white nurse's uniform, sitting in a chair, her arms crossed and her chin drooping down to her chest. Short, whinny-like snores were fluttering from her open mouth, and she jerked her head up a few inches every time her chin touched her immense bosoms, which inflated like balloons with every intake of breath.

Another mewing noise came from the bed beside the nurse's chair. Someone—Emma-Lee couldn't tell if it was a man or woman, boy or girl—lay there beneath a light bedspread. The slight form barely made a lump beneath the covers. The upper face was obscured by a folded white towel exposing only parched lips and two flared nostrils.

Could that poor person be Aunt Augusta? Emma-Lee wondered, tip-toeing to the side of the bed opposite the nurse and craning her neck to see over the covers. *The man in the black hat said she was sick, but I didn't think she was nearly dead.*

Emma-Lee placed both hands on the edge of the bed to raise herself higher for a better view of the patient's face. As she did, the weight of her body depressed the mattress, causing the patient's head to roll in her direction. An oversized hooked nose slipped out from beneath the towel, and a pathetic moan filled the silent room. The nurse choked in the middle of a whinny and awoke with a start.

"Wh...what is it?" the nurse sputtered to life. Her eyes shifted from the patient to Emma-Lee standing on the other side of the bed. She blinked to focus on the little girl in the yellow bonnet, barely visible above the bed covers. "Who in tarnation are you?"

"I'm Emma-Lee." Her voice sounded loud in the tomb-like room. "I'm looking for Aunt Augusta."

"Shhhh," the nurse said, putting a finger the size of a plump sausage to her lips. "You could wake the dead."

The figure on the bed stirred as if to prove the nurse right, and a white, claw-like hand slowly made its way from beneath the covers to the head, where it dislodged the folded towel from across gray eyes narrowed into two slits. A nest of scraggly, coffee-colored hair became visible, bunched on the pillow beneath the head.

The corpse was beginning to look a little like Aunt Augusta.

"Quiet, child," said a weak voice coming from the cracked lips. It was beginning to sound like Aunt Augusta, too. She moved as if to sit up but stopped with a moan and sank back onto the pillow, her hand rubbing her forehead above one eye.

The nurse leaned forward to retrieve the towel, which had slid down behind Aunt Augusta's left ear. "Ah, yes, the niece from Miami," the pudgy nurse whispered. "Your aunt came over early this morning by fishing boat to meet you, but she was struck ill."

She dipped the towel in a basin of water on the table beside the bed and wrung it out. "You need to leave her be so she can sleep it off." She waved her hand at Emma-Lee as if she was shooing away flies. "Away with you now."

"But...what do I do? Where do I go?" Emma-Lee asked, looking from the nurse to Aunt Augusta and back again.

Aunt Augusta's lips moved but no sound came out. Emma-Lee had to lean forward to hear her faint, staccato words.

"Sit–on–the–porch–and–wait."

Even in her deathbed condition, Aunt Augusta's orders held authority, and Emma-Lee backed toward the door as the nurse replaced the towel over her patient's face.

A full hour later, she continued to wait. As she sat wilting on the stiff wicker porch chair of a house she'd never before seen in a town she'd never before visited, she recited the words she'd often heard from Papa.

"You've jumped out of the frying pan and into the fire."

He frequently used the phrase when Archibald wouldn't own up to his most recent wrongdoing, like breaking Mama's vase or stuffing the cat up the chimney. The glaring evidence of his crimes—his baseball bat lying among the shards of broken glass, or the streaks of black soot marking a trail on the furniture from the fireplace to the corner where poor Kitty was frantically trying to lick herself clean—didn't matter. Archibald never admitted guilt, even with the persuasion of Papa's leather strap. He spent days in his room in isolated punishment still proclaiming his innocence.

Emma-Lee didn't know what crime she'd committed, but the punishment felt harsher than she could bear. The porch held little interest for a nine-and-a-half-year-old, and she quickly became bored watching the carriages and wagons that lumbered by on the road in front of the house. The grandfather clock in the parlor struck two *bongs*, and she knew why her stomach felt as though it was scraping her backbone.

Although she hadn't seen the man in the black hat since her arrival at the house, his buggy had disappeared while she was looking for Aunt Augusta upstairs. She considered searching the kitchen for something to eat, but decided in the end it was better to go hungry than risk disobeying Aunt Augusta.

Another fifteen minutes passed, and her porch purgatory became more and more like the place of eternal fire and brimstone she'd heard about in church last Easter. The prickly chair grew harder and stiffer, and sharp pieces of wicker jumped out of nowhere to torture her dangling legs. Mosquitoes did a nasty business on her bare arms below the short sleeves of her summer dress, and trickles of sweat down her back made it itch in places she couldn't reach to scratch.

A tiny breeze wafted by every few minutes, but it wasn't enough to actually cool off, just enough to keep her from melting into a puddle and disappearing between the floor boards.

She watched a furry, black spider spinning a web in the corner of the eves. Slowly, ever so slowly, bits of shiny thread lengthened and overlapped to form an intricate pattern.

"The man in the black hat will probably come along tomorrow with a broom and ruin all that hard work in one swipe," Emma-Lee said aloud to no one. She shook her sweat-dampened head.

The bleakness of her situation and the hopelessness of the future seemed to collapse around her shoulders like a burning barn. Salty tears spilled over her eyelashes and dripped down her face. She tried to cry quietly so not to disturb Aunt Augusta.

As she reached for Mama's handkerchief with trembling fingers, she pictured Mama's dear hands folding the precious square of cloth—it was the handkerchief she used only for special occasions. Those same hands had lovingly caressed her cheek and calmed her fears so many times in the past. What happened? Hard, hot sobs suddenly gushed unbidden from Emma-Lee's deepest parts.

How could Mama and Papa send me away? Why don't they want me anymore?

She covered her face with the handkerchief and tried to stifle her sobs. Instead, she caught the faint whiff of Mama's lilac scent within the folds of cloth, and it brought a new wave of raw emotion crashing over her.

I want to go home! I want to go home! She thought her head would burst with the weight of the words, and before she could stop them, they flew out of her mouth in a wail.

"I want to go home!"

"Can you keep it a bit quieter down there?" A voice descended from the open second story window, blocked from view by the porch roof. "Your aunt is having her own set of troubles, and it's not helping her to hear you out there carrying on."

Emma-Lee had no idea how to respond. Her first thought was to reason with the round-cheeked nurse who must be standing at the window in Aunt Augusta's sickroom. Maybe she could help. She was the only choice.

If I could just make her understand...

Emma-Lee ran halfway down the front walkway toward the street and turned expectantly toward the window. The flap of drawn drapes greeted her. The nurse was gone. As she stood there alone and forlorn, something inside her turned hard.

No one cares. No one at all. I'm on my own. I have to take care of myself now. Without a single thought of the consequences, she simply started walking.

Chapter Three

At the end of the stone walkway, Emma-Lee turned right, blindly bounding down the rutted street past tidy, white picket-fenced houses that gradually made way for busy store buildings fronted with crowded timber walkways. She turned again onto a cross road and was instantly attracted to the sparkle of sunlight dancing on the deep blue waters of the Indian River straight ahead.

Turning left onto the street bordering the wide river, she marched as if on a mission. Emma-Lee had no idea of her destination. She just knew it was *away* from where she'd been.

It must have appeared strange to anyone happening to notice a determined young girl in her best traveling frock and bonnet, venturing alone into the most unsavory part of town. But Emma-Lee had no fear, for she felt invisible. If she couldn't be seen, she couldn't be harmed. The coarse-talking sailors and rough men who peopled the wharf were no threat to her. She walked right through them, untouched by curious glances and comments shared by boatswains and mates in low tones behind her back.

Feeling numb and completely emptied in every way, she stopped in front of a pier. Tied to the pier was a white freighter filled to the water line with crated oranges. Emma-Lee stared at the cargo, her stomach growling and rumbling in spite of the pain in her heart.

I wonder—would anybody notice if I took just one? The tangy citrus smell of the largest oranges she'd ever seen made her mouth water. She licked her dry lips. She could almost feel juice dribble down her chin and taste the sweet pulp between her teeth.

But it's not right to take one. That would be stealing. Papa had once beaten Archibald for stealing an apple from the peddler's cart.

She moved a step closer to the fruit-laden boat and craned her neck to see if anyone stirred on board. There was no movement. With hands clenched together in front of her, she took another step forward, trying to weigh the options in her mind, but she couldn't think clearly. She couldn't take her eyes off those beautiful oranges. The breeze carried the tempting, sweet aroma to tease her nose and curl around her tongue. The longing was unbearable...

The high-pitched tune of a popular sea-faring song broke into her consciousness and grew louder with the *clump-clump* of approaching footsteps on the platform behind her. Startled, she turned to meet the twinkling, sea-blue eyes of a burly man in a battered seaman's cap and a faded red shirt. His hands were stuck into the pockets of worn gray breeches, patched at one knee, and he was whistling a jaunty tune as if he hadn't a care in the world.

"Ahoy, ma'am, and a glorious mornin' to ya,'" he said, tipping his cap. A pleasant lilt in his voice bespoke of Irish ancestry. "I see you're admirin' my boat." He smiled and indicated the white freighter with a nod of his head. "She may not be a ravin' beauty like some, but she sure gets the job done, don't ya' say so?" He paused to allow Emma-Lee to respond, his bushy mustache separated from his full brown beard flecked with white by a row of straight, pearly teeth with a friendly gap between the front two. But she could only stare back at him, deeply afraid that he had somehow read her mind and knew the dastardly deed she had been about to perform.

He gave no indication that he suspected any foul play afoot, or that he found it unusual for an unchaperoned young girl to be standing on a dock in the middle of a workday, gawking at a boatload of fruit.

"Captain Cornelius Stone at your service, ma'am." He held out his hand, bowing gallantly. "And what lovely name would you be known by?"

Although she had often been told her behavior was mature beyond her years, no adult had ever introduced themselves to her as if she was a lady before. Taken by surprise at Captain Stone's act of chivalry, she solemnly shook his hand, muttering in a barely audible voice, "Emma-Lee Palmer, sir."

"Very pleased to make your acquaintance." He stood erect and tapped his pointer finger on his hairy jaw.

"Miss Palmer, is it? Well, you're in the right place, yes, indeed. A 'Miss Augusta Lemstarch' booked passage for herself and a young lady named Palmer to be transported across the river to the island tomorrow morning." He smiled broadly and pointed to his boat. "You and your aunt are to be my passengers on the Verily. How clever of you to come down to survey the premises. Is your aunt here, too?"

"No, sir," she replied. *I wonder how clever he'll think I am when he finds out I've run away.* "Aunt Augusta's sick."

"Ah, I'm terrible sorry to hear that." He cocked his head slightly to one side. Then he slowly took off his cap and ran one hand through dark curls highlighted with strands of white as he studied the forlorn figure before him.

Like an irresistible magnet, the scent of luscious oranges drew Emma-Lee's attention back to the Verily.

The good captain followed her line of vision. "Mighty, aren't they? Most are four to five inches across. Fetch a pretty penny in big city markets. Are ya' hungry then, lassie? Have ya' eaten?"

She shook her head.

"That won't do a'tall, no, siree, it won't." He plopped his cap back on his head and addressed her formally with one hand bent behind his back and a debonair expression on his face. "Miss Palmer, would ya' do me the honor of allowin' me to escort ya' to dine at the Eau Gallie cafe?"

"Really?" Her eyes lit up at the prospect—she had never eaten in a restaurant before. But then her good sense took over. "Oh, no, sir, I couldn't," she said, her shoulders sagging as she spoke. "I should wait until Aunt Augusta feels better."

"Now, beggin' your pardon, but I don't think that's the right thing to do in this case, Miss Palmer. To be sure, a body has to eat, and only the Good Lord knows and He ain't telling how long it'll be 'til your aunt's feeling frisky again."

Her eyebrows shot up at the thought of Aunt Augusta *ever* feeling frisky.

"Tell ya' what, the café is just down the street, and it won't take two swipes of a gator's tail for us to grab a bite. Then you can tell me where your aunt's staying, and I'll take you back there myself. How does that sound?"

It sounded better than heaven itself. Emma-Lee nodded with a smile on her face for the first time in weeks.

Ten minutes later, a weathered sea captain holding the hand of a little red-haired girl entered the Eau Gallie café. No one noticed the pair of dark eyes that had been watching them since they left the docks.

* * * *

Julius Duckett pulled his cap down over his eyes and tried to look nonchalant as he slouched against the post supporting the front porch of Mitchell's Mercantile. The tall, pimply-faced adolescent stole another glance across the street as the door of the café closed behind Captain Stone and the little girl he'd picked up at the dock.

Probably another of his strays, the sullen boy thought. During the three months since he'd left home at sixteen and hired on as a crew hand for the Verily, Julius had seen Captain Stone collect a number of "strays," like the dogs his grandfather used to take in off the street back home in Atlanta.

Captain Stone never kept the lost people but usually gave them a bed to sleep off a hangover, fed them, or even slipped them a few dollars before sending them on their way with a "God bless ya' now."

Julius could not, for the life of him, understand why Captain Stone would go out of his way for these people he didn't even know. They weren't just down-on-their-luck strangers, but losers who had gotten themselves into the messes they were in.

"Life has a way of giving you what you deserve," his pa had always said. Why should Captain Stone help people who wouldn't even help themselves?

It just don't figure, Julius thought, shaking his head and pushing his cap back in place atop his stringy, shoulder-length brown hair. He crossed the street, pausing to let a wagon loaded with barrels of whisky and ale pass, and stepped onto the wooden walkway in front of the café. Sauntering over to the front window, he scanned the room until his eyes fell on the big seaman and the child sitting at a table in the corner.

This one's different. I don't remember him ever taking in a kid before. Now what's he gonna do with a lost kid? Maybe she's a run-away. Nah— she's dressed too uppity to be a run-away. She looks a far piece better than the captain there. His ratty clothes look like they oughta be on a drunk in the gutter.

He shook his head and jammed his hands in his breeches pockets. *I swear I'll never end up like that. One day, I'm gonna have so much money, I'll be the best dressed man in town, and people will stand when I walk into a room.*

Smirking, Julius turned away to follow the ale wagon to its destination at a seedy saloon on the wharf.

* * * *

It took two wrong turns before Emma-Lee was able to retrace her escape route to the home of the man in the black hat, whose name she didn't know. The scruffy, middle-aged seaman and heat-wilted young girl finally stood in front of the white house with the navy blue shutters and door. The scorching, mid-afternoon sun simmered behind a vast cloud the color of bruises.

"Aye, that'll be the house of Dr. Hartman," Captain Stone said. "Had a hard time lately, God bless him. His wife died of the fever last winter, and there was nothing he could do to save her. He keeps to himself now, doin' a bit of doctoring, but turning most of it over to his partner."

Captain Stone followed Emma-Lee as she walked the stone path toward the porch. "Your aunt is a mighty lucky woman to have Dr. Hartman look after her while she's sick. A fine man, he is, a godly man. Just has to find his way out of the iron grip of grief. A matter for prayer, I'd say. I'll see to it right away. Only the Good Shepherd can lead his sheep down that narrow path, out of the darkness and into the light."

Emma-Lee had never heard anyone outside of church talk about God like Captain Stone. Easter and Christmas were the only times Papa took the family to the big church in town with the stained glass windows. Mama listened to the children's prayers at bedtime, but they included God in name only. "God bless..." followed by a list of family members and friends. There was no more feeling involved than when reciting the alphabet. The Almighty was left out of normal, everyday conversation, as if God didn't exist except for those specific times when they addressed Him at their convenience.

But Captain Stone spoke as if God were as much a part of life as breathing. Emma-Lee found that thought strangely comforting.

The unlikely pair climbed the steps to the porch, and Captain Stone looked toward the blue door, appearing unsure of what to do with his new friend.

"I'd better stay here on the porch, like they told me, until Aunt Augusta is better," Emma-Lee said, tilting her head back to look up into the captain's leathery, sun-darkened face. "Thank you for lunch. I feel much better now."

The captain's eyes crinkled around the edges as he smiled down into Emma-Lee's round, blue eyes beneath the yellow bonnet. "Why, you're quite welcome, lassie. Most enjoyable dining companion I've had in many a day. You'll be all right now?"

She nodded and climbed into the porch chair to resume her solitary waiting vigil.

"Till tomorrow then," Captain Stone said, tipping his cap. He paused, wrinkling his brow in thought. "Maybe 'twould be best to keep our outing today our little secret, eh? God bless you, Emma-Lee Palmer, and keep you safe within His lovin' arms."

His loving arms...the words echoed in Emma-Lee's mind after the good captain had taken his leave. *Am I really in God's loving arms?*

A sharp crack of thunder split the air, and the first spatter of raindrops plinked the tin roof. Emma-Lee removed her bonnet and placed it in her lap.

God's loving arms. That sounded like such a nice place to be.

A comforting breeze blew through the porch like a cool hand during a feverish, summer night. The rain began drumming against the roof in a steady pattern, and Emma-Lee's eyelids grew heavy. Her small body slumped sideways, molding her right cheek into the chair's prickly wicker weave. She dreamed of that wonderful place called home.

Chapter Four

The Wednesday morning sun rose in a cloudless, turquoise sky. Aunt Augusta, now puffy-eyed but generally recovered from her debilitation of the previous day, shook the bare foot of the little girl sleeping on a cot in the corner of the spare room. Long, red curls spilled over the sides of the narrow bed. The child groaned ever so slightly, as if reluctant to face another day.

"Emma-Lee, get up now. We must be at the docks by nine o'clock."

Emma-Lee rose and dressed in her blue calico dress, which was on the top layer of clothes packed in her trunk. She searched the room for her hairbrush and found it on the dresser by the white porcelain pitcher and basin. That must have been where Louisa left it the night before when she'd brushed out Emma-Lee's damp, tangled hair after her bath.

Kind, smiling Louisa. Holding the brush and thinking about Louisa made the brick-feeling in Emma-Lee's stomach soften to clay. Dr. Hartman's young housekeeper had gently awakened her as she arrived at the doctor's house after the storm. She'd been visiting her ailing aunt on her day off work and acted shocked to find a sleeping child curled up on the front porch chair. She'd taken Emma-Lee and her trunk into the kitchen where she'd filled the metal washtub with water from the wood-burning stove to give her a warm bath and supper of stewed beef and buttermilk biscuits before tucking her into bed.

Emma-Lee yawned in the early morning light and did her best to twist her hair into a fat knot at the base of her neck as

Sarah had taught her last week. "It's the way all the stylish young ladies are wearing their hair these days," she'd said. Emma-Lee was proud Sarah had considered her a stylish young lady, too. At home, Mama usually braided it for her, but Emma-Lee had a feeling Aunt Augusta would not often be performing such a task.

She laced up her black, ankle-high everyday shoes and treaded downstairs. Aunt Augusta was seated at the kitchen table eating eggs, toast, and mango marmalade with Dr. Hartman, who seemed a bit more communicative than yesterday. He nodded as Emma-Lee entered the room and wandered over to the only unoccupied place setting. Louisa turned from the stove and gave her a bemused smile before placing a plate of eggs and sausage before her.

"Land sakes, child, what have you done to your hair?" Aunt Augusta asked as she glanced at Emma-Lee and then did a double take. "It looks ridiculous. Much too old for you. Who told you to fix it that way?"

"Sarah," Emma-Lee said, feeling a flush creep up from her chin all the way to the roots of her hair.

In her proper school teacher voice, Aunt Augusta said, "Well, eat your breakfast and then correct the problem. Dr. Hartman has kindly offered to take us to the boat this morning. We don't want to keep him waiting." Aunt Augusta nodded her head appreciatively toward the doctor, her tight lips stretching over her teeth in what was meant to be a smile.

Emma-Lee thought she looked more frightening than friendly.

An hour later, Dr. Hartman deposited Aunt Augusta and Emma-Lee at the pier in front of the Verily. Aunt Augusta stood straight as a fireplace poker in her black skirt and starched white blouse. A puff of wind nipped the single thin black feather adorning her sensible black hat. Emma-Lee gazed with anticipation at the familiar white freighter, absently twirling the dangling end of the blue silk ribbon that, thanks to Louisa, tied back her flowing red hair.

"Stop fidgeting, pleasssse," Aunt Augusta hissed. "I simply cannot abide fidgeting."

"Welcome aboard, ladies," boomed a voice from the galley below deck just before Captain Stone's head appeared in the stairwell. "Julius, could ya' help the ladies with their luggage and see to it that they're comfortable before we ship out? Oh, beggin' your pardon, I'm Captain Cornelius Stone and this here's my second mate, Julius Duckett. He'll take care of you while I finish up some things down below."

The captain tipped his cap and motioned for Julius to do the came. Julius ignored him.

Captain Stone paused on the stairwell to address his passengers once more. "You won't likely see Franklin, my first mate—he's busy in the boiler room buildin' up a head of steam so the Verily can run her course. She sets a right smart pace, she does—nigh on to five knots. We should be ready to cast off for the island within a quarter hour, so you'll be home in ample time for lunch." He grinned and winked at Emma-Lee before disappearing below.

Julius, with greasy hair tucked behind his ears and a scowl on his pock-marked face, secured their cases and showed them where to sit on deck, which was now cleared of its cargo of oranges. He skulked away without a good-bye.

Ever the teacher, Aunt Augusta cleared her throat to command her niece's attention. "I would like to take this opportunity before we get under way to tell you about our destination." She glanced down her beak-like nose to make sure her captive student was listening.

"Merritt Island is a sliver of land separated from the mainland by the Indian River, a very prominent source of commerce and trade in eastern Florida. The river is a mile-wide salt water sound with two inlets from the sea. Do you know what a lagoon is, Emma-Lee?"

Emma-Lee nodded.

"The river is very much like a deep, elongated lagoon," Aunt Augusta continued. "The island itself is long and tapered. The southernmost tip, Paradise Point, is parallel to the city of Eau Gallie, here on the mainland coast. See, it's right over there." She pointed across the blue plane of water.

Emma-Lee looked across the wide river at the piece of rocky land jutting out into the bay. Paradise Point? From here, it looked like a mound of shoe leather a dog had chewed and spit out.

"The island is accessible only by boat. It's bordered on the west by the Indian River and on the east by the Banana River, a much smaller river, very peaceful, and picturesque. A swatch of land nearly a mile wide stands between the Banana River and the Atlantic Ocean. That's the same ocean you've seen many times in Miami."

Emma-Lee had always loved the seashore. She nodded with as much enthusiasm as she could muster.

Aunt Augusta paused in the midst of her lesson and studied her niece. "Perhaps if you're good enough to deserve a reward, we'll hire a wagon to transport us to the beach one sunny day for a few hours. The road is no better than a footpath, really, rough and rutted, so the excursion takes most of the day. The shore is quite congested with coquina rocks formations, not like the flat white sand you're used to in Miami, but the water is pleasant enough for wading."

"Yes, ma'am. I'd like that."

"My cabin is on the outskirts of Tropic, a settlement a mile and a half north of Paradise Point. The school is another half mile beyond the cabin. The southern portion of the island is basically a strip of land about fifty yards wide between the two rivers. Tropic is located on the small piece that flairs into an expanse of one hundred and fifty yards then narrows again to fifty just north of the schoolhouse."

Emma-Lee frowned, her brow wrinkled in confusion.

"All right, child, picture a horse's leg."

"A horse's leg?"

"Yes. Picture how thin the leg is below and above the knobby knee. That is like the island. Tropic is located in the knobby part that flairs out like the horse's knee."

"Oh. Can you see both rivers at the same time?"

"Yes, indeed. In the southernmost areas the land is so narrow a man could throw a rock from one river to the other."

At that moment, the boat's steam engine started up, and Captain Stone came over to greet his passengers personally before casting off. He cordially shook Aunt Augusta's hand and welcomed her aboard his humble vessel.

"I've seen ya' from a distance during the three months I've been assigned the Tropic shipping route, ma'am, but we've never been introduced proper. I hear ya' do a whale of a job teachin' the wee folk on the island."

At that, Aunt Augusta looked even more pinched than usual and seemed at a strange loss for words.

The captain then turned to Emma-Lee and carefully acted as though he was meeting her for the first time. Only the gleam in his eye and the warm smile on his lips as he presented her with a juicy orange hinted at their previously formed relationship.

The Verily cut through the smooth, blue waters of the Indian River at a slow, steady pace. Magnificent flocks of snowy white egrets lined the sandy banks. Pink curlews, long-legged birds with red eyes and pink wing and back feathers, waded in the shallows. Ducks by the hundreds floated in huge flocks on the river teeming with fish, not disturbed in the least by the wake of the boat. A school of mullet, shining silvery in the sun, leapt out of the river beside the boat, splashing Emma-Lee with drops of warm, salty water.

A refreshing breeze blew strands of Emma-Lee's hair into dancing snippets around her face as white sea gulls with black-tipped wings squawked and swooped overhead. Brown pelicans v'ed low over the river like an airborne arrowhead. Emma-Lee turned her face toward the early morning sun, and copper-colored freckles that were spattered across her nose lit up like pennies in a fountain. She felt the calming warmth soak into her skin as she was drenched with light.

For one lovely moment, she forgot she had been sent away to face the world alone.

After the boat was tied to the longer of the two Tropic docks, Julius transferred the luggage to a wheeled, wooden cart which was pulled ashore by a young dockhand. Captain Stone reappeared to say good-bye. He politely tipped his hat to Aunt Augusta, then knelt and gathered Emma-Lee into his arms in a big bear hug. He pulled a small box of chocolate candy tied with a red silk bow from his pocket and handed it to her with an off-key "Ta-Da!"

"Is this really, truly a box of candy just for me?" she asked, drinking in the amazing sight.

"'Tis yours, really and truly," replied the grinning seaman. "And if it's agreeable with your aunt, I'd like to come by Saturday and take ya' with me to share the noon meal with my parents. I've a rare day off; usually Sunday's the only day I have free. They live a mile and a half a mile north of your aunt on the island. You'll like them—they're delightful folk. They adore their grandchildren, my sister's wee-un's, but they don't get to see them as much as they like, bein' they live up the coast near St. Augustine."

Emma-Lee and the captain gazed questioningly at Aunt Augusta.

Aunt Augusta looked from one eager face to the other. "Well, I suppose it would be all right, as long as she isn't gone long. We have lots of work to do in getting the classroom ready for the first day of school on Monday."

Emma-Lee waved good-bye over her shoulder to Captain Stone and followed Aunt Augusta down the long wooden dock. Aunt Augusta turned sharply to the right as they reached the landing and led the way down a road of sand, peppered with coquina seashells, toward a small, unpainted frame cottage about a quarter mile south of the docks.

This must be what the gates of heaven look like, Emma-Lee thought as she trailed Aunt Augusta down the road, gazing with awe at the tropical beauty surrounding her. Thickly fringed palm trees and bush after bush bursting with fragrant white flowers bordered the road. Lemon, orange, and grapefruit trees grew in neat rows on the narrow strip of land between the road and the Indian River; vines full of luscious, purple grapes hung on a low, wooden arbor on the side bordered by the Banana River. True to its name, the river was lined with clumps of banana trees, their long, feathery, green leaves swaying in the warm breeze from the rivers.

The air was scented with the heady aroma of confederate jasmine and sweet gardenia mingled with citrus tang and rich muscadine fragrance. Emma-Lee had never before smelled so many wonderful smells in one place.

They arrived at the cabin just as the dockhand was unloading their luggage from the pushcart to the small front porch. Aunt Augusta reached into her purse and extracted a coin, which she pressed into the young man's hand before dismissing him with a crisp, "Thank you, Albert; that will be all."

As Albert retreated with the pull cart down the road in a cloud of dust, Aunt Augusta turned to Emma-Lee. "Here, take the handle on this end and help me get this trunk into your room." Between the two of them, they managed to drag the old trunk through the doorway and into the tiny foyer.

Emma-Lee looked around in surprise. The cabin contained a mere three rooms. The first they passed through was a combined sitting room and parlor of sorts, a room meant to entertain company. Furnishings were extremely simple: a brown tweed settee, worn but clean, and a paisley wingback chair flanked by two bamboo end tables.

A black spinet piano and wooden stool stood against the side wall, which was adorned with only one picture—a small framed black and white daguerreotype of two children in frilly frocks standing in the front yard of a three-story frame house.

Emma-Lee stood on her tiptoes to examine the portrait.

"Come, child, you can look at the picture later. It's your mother and me at our home in Miami. That was long before...before the fire." Aunt Augusta's voice suddenly sounded strange, subdued. Her eyes didn't seem to be able to find a place to light. "Things continuously change, don't they?" She sighed heavily. "Such is the nature of life, I suppose."

Her voice found its edge again. "This is the kitchen, obviously. Many of the larger homes on the island have kitchens built separately from the house, so if there's a fire, the entire structure won't burn to the ground." An involuntary shudder seized Aunt Augusta as if cold, ghostly fingers had touched her. "But my small cabin is self-contained, so extreme care is prudent."

Emma-Lee's eyes were drawn to the sunny kitchen window overlooking the Indian River. Just below the window, a black wood-burning stove was wedged into the corner; a crate of pine, oak, and sap-rich lighter wood nestled by its side. There was no icebox like the one in Mama's modern kitchen at home. Emma-Lee's mental picture of an ice wagon making deliveries to the cabin on the remote island struck her as just plain silly.

A red gingham tablecloth covering a small table adorned with a jelly jar holding three wilted gardenia blossoms provided the only color in the room. By the schoolbooks stacked on one end of the table, Emma-Lee gathered that the table doubled as a work desk for Aunt Augusta when meals were not in progress.

"You've only one chair at the table," Emma-Lee observed. "Is there another for me?"

The lines around Aunt Augusta's mouth deepened as she pursed her lips. "I agreed to have you come here on the condition that I would accommodate you as best I could. Some concessions must be made. This is an island not a big city like

Miami. Hopefully, we can find an extra chair at the school to borrow. If not, a fruit crate and a pillow will suffice."

"Yes, ma'am."

"Now, I'm not one to make a fuss over food. Island fruit will serve for snacks. Meals will be nutritious but plain. Clam chowder and soda biscuits, or fried fish and soda biscuits, or whatever sea delicacy the fishermen returning to the docks provide the fishmonger each day...and soda biscuits. Variety is secondary to convenience, and soda, lard, and flour are always to be had at the Tropic mercantile."

"I like Mama's soda biscuits," Emma-Lee said, trying to be agreeable.

"Then you'll like mine, too. We learned to cook from the same mother, you know."

Emma-Lee hadn't thought of that. Maybe Aunt Augusta was harboring some other hidden quality that was like Mama, too. It sure must be buried deep.

"Supper will be served promptly at six o'clock each evening, and you are expected to set the table and be seated without me calling you twice. Your face and hands will be clean for every meal. The water pump is out back. We'll heat water for bathing twice a week on Tuesdays and Saturdays. I know most people on the island only bathe once a week, some of the children considerably less," her prominent nose twitched, "but I'm a firm believer in the old adage, 'Cleanliness is next to godliness.'"

"Yes, Aunt Augusta."

"Now, let's get this trunk into your room."

They passed through a doorway into a bedroom containing an iron-poster bed, a cane-backed chair, a wardrobe with peeling forest green paint, and a small oak armoire. Aunt

Augusta continued pulling Emma-Lee's trunk through another doorway draped with a thin brown curtain into a closet-sized cubicle.

"This will be your room," Aunt Augusta said, setting Emma-Lee's trunk down with a thud. "It's not as spacious as your room in Miami, but it will be adequate."

Emma-Lee looked around the tiny room, unable to speak.

"It will actually be good for you, teach you organizational skills." Aunt Augusta nodded emphatically. Emma-Lee watched the lone feather adorning her hat bob in the air above her head. It looked like a moth attempting to land on a rolling boulder. Emma-Lee felt an awful lot like that moth. If she quit moving, the boulder would crush her.

"A proper bed will be delivered next week, but in the meantime, you'll find the pallet I've prepared on the floor for you quite comfortable," Aunt Augusta said, indicating a quilt spread in the corner with a feather pillow placed at one end and a white cotton sheet folded at the other.

"Since space here is limited and I don't have another dresser, I've stacked three crates there against the wall in which you can store the things you use most. Leave the items you use least in your trunk and double its use as a night table."

Aunt Augusta looked at Emma-Lee for her reaction. Emma-Lee, however, was in too much shock to react at all. She just stared at the cubicle packed wall-to-wall with objects foreign to her. Objects that held no warmth or love or connection with the only life she had ever known. Home—would she ever see it again?

"Well, we can start this way, and if things are unsuitable, we'll sort it out as we go along." Aunt Augusta turned to leave the room and paused. She tentatively stretched out her right hand to touch Emma-Lee's slender shoulder.

"I'm not used to living with anyone else, as you know, and you're not used to being away from your mother. But we'll be fine, I think, if we both work at it." She retracted her hand and straightened her shoulders. "I'll leave you to unpack now."

Emma-Lee stared blankly out the bare window of her tiny cell, past the outhouse in the sloping backyard, past the rocky banks of the Banana River, past the entire island to an unseen place far across the sea.

Why did they send me away? Why? Why? The unanswerable question beat a burning hole in her mind like a pounding drum as her body gave in to the inner pain and she fell sobbing across Sarah's unopened trunk.

Chapter Five

Aunt Augusta tapped the ruler against her palm as she stood facing the lone student in the empty classroom Thursday afternoon.

"Emma-Lee, before we start preparing for the first day of school on Monday, there are some things you should know. As you may have noticed when we arrived, the school, which is actually an old fruit packing plant, was built so close to the river that, at high tide, you must keep to the planked walkway next to the building, or you'll get your feet soaked. There will be no going home to change shoes, so unless you favor sloshing around all day in wet shoes, you'd best take care."

Always the teacher, she paused, angled her head, and asked, "Can you tell me why the tides would affect the river?"

"No, ma'am. I thought the tides only affected the oceans," Emma-Lee answered, sitting up straight in her chair, trying hard not to fidget.

"The rivers surrounding the island are both fed by inlets of the Atlantic Ocean, so the tides are evident along the entire coastline of the island. You'll do well to remember that for future lessons."

"Yes, Aunt Augusta."

"You will address me as 'Ma'am' or 'Miss Lemstarch' in school. I wouldn't want the children to think I was partial because you're a relative."

"Yes, ma'am."

"Fourteen children will be attending school this term, some walking as far as three miles down the dirt road that snakes along the island coast. Most are the children of fishermen, dock workers, or fruit harvesters who live in wooden shanties near the river banks."

Aunt Augusta looked out the window and raised her chin high with an indignant sniff. "One wealthy shipping magnate and his wife who live in the northern-most range of our school district stated their preference to send their two daughters to the larger school at Lotus Landing eight miles north, which may be better equipped but *certainly* is not superiorly staffed."

The corners of her mouth curled in what could have been a wan smile or perhaps simple indigestion. "However, the authorities ruled that they would attend our Tropic School." She changed the distasteful subject with a "so that's that" nod.

"You will begin third grade studies along with one other child, and there will be two students each in the second and sixth grades. We have three fourth graders this year, one fifth grader, three seventh graders, and one girl completing her eighth and final year. The term is nine months long, and the school day starts at eight o'clock on the dot, not a minute later, and ends at half past three so the children can get home before the regular afternoon thunderstorms."

"I've already been introduced to the storms," Emma-Lee said, remembering her steamy afternoon on Dr. Hartman's porch.

Aunt Augusta turned away from the window and faced Emma-Lee, straightening to her full height. "Children are expected to mind their manners, do their work, and make the appropriate grades, or they are asked to leave school. No exceptions."

Emma-Lee understood clearly that she was not to be the exception.

"Now, there is much to do. Let's get to work."

Emma-Lee was given the task of washing the schoolhouse floor with a bucket of sudsy water and a stiff scrub brush. The pine boards were well worn, but an errant splinter found her shin as she painstakingly scrubbed on her hands and knees. She tried to picture all the feet that would soon be walking on this floor.

Would any of them belong to her friend? It would be nice to have a friend. Someone she could even call her *best* friend— someone like a sister with whom she could share the all feelings she had bottled up inside. She missed Sarah so much it hurt.

Friday, she was assigned a considerably more enjoyable chore: opening the boxes of new erasers and pencils and distributing them on each of the seven narrow tables set up in two rows of four and one row of three, two students to each table. There were also writing slates to pass out for working arithmetic problems, since paper was chronically in short supply.

Emma-Lee helped uncrate the schoolbooks that had been packed up the last day of school and returned them to the bookshelves. She opened the cigar box containing chalk and placed three stubby pieces near each of the two wall-mounted black boards and one on each table. But the best job of all was when Aunt Augusta asked her to pick wild flowers to place in an amber vase on the teacher's desk.

"A bit of the outside on the inside helps young minds stay fresh." Aunt Augusta said, picking up a crate of geography books and spellers. "Mind you, don't dawdle. We need to leave promptly in fifteen minutes to do our shopping and get home before the afternoon storm."

As Emma-Lee walked through the tall grass between orange trees, she could smell wild honeysuckle vines spreading their delightfully sweet aroma. She followed her nose to a thicket where delicate, white honeysuckle blossoms were intertwined with bright blue morning glories. She fashioned a beautiful bouquet, adding a half-dozen yellow buttercups that dotted the roadside and a feathery sprig of fern for good measure.

These flowers remind me of Mama's garden at home. Emma-Lee buried her nose in the fragrant blossoms. She had learned over the past two days that she needn't share her homesickness with Aunt Augusta or expect any consolation for her heartache.

With her usual blunt sensibility, Aunt Augusta had said, "You are not a baby any longer. You must learn to deal with whatever life hands you. Every tub sits on its own bottom, you know."

Aunt Augusta wasn't being cruel but was simply relating her own no-nonsense philosophy of life that had sustained her for thirty-eight years, most of them on her own. Emma-Lee tried to remember everything Mama had told her about her sister.

Augusta was the older of the two Lemstarch girls. Mama, younger by five years, was now her only living relative. Both their parents had died in a tragic house fire when the girls were in their teens, leaving them homeless and penniless in Miami. Neighbors had taken them in until Mama married Papa, a strapping twenty-four-year-old newspaper typesetter, two months after her fifteenth birthday.

A week after Mama and Papa's wedding, twenty-year-old Aunt Augusta had answered a magazine advertisement for a schoolteacher on remote Merritt Island and had moved to the romantic-sounding tropical paradise. She'd never married, but nobody in the family dared call her an "old maid" since Dexter got the wrong end of Papa's switch for uttering those forbidden words two years ago.

Aunt Augusta visited Emma-Lee's family for a week every Christmas. Even as a houseguest, she was serious and prudent and wasn't known for making small talk. Emma-Lee had once overheard Papa call her, "a capable teacher, no doubt, but a most incapable dinner companion."

Aunt Augusta did have a soft side, which she allowed to show briefly and only on special occasions.

Emma-Lee remembered the time she brought a wounded butterfly home she'd found on the ground. Aunt Augusta delicately stroked the beautifully colored wings with her long, tapered fingers. Her steel gray eyes softened to nearly blue. The hard lines around her mouth eased into what was almost a smile, and for a moment, she seemed approachable, even huggable.

But the moment was spoiled when Archibald ran by and knocked the butterfly out of Emma-Lee's hand. Aunt Augusta's face shriveled back into her usual disapproving expression and that was the last time Emma-Lee saw her with a countenance that didn't look like she'd just swallowed a spoonful of castor oil.

The rumble of distant thunder startled Emma-Lee out of her reverie. She hurried back to the schoolhouse.

As they began the long walk home, Aunt Augusta explained more about life on Merritt Island. "Routine is a way of life for the islanders. The fishing boats leave the docks every day at five a.m. and return at three p.m. The half-dozen market vendors and two fishmongers—three if old Toothless Jack manages to get his boat out—assemble at half past three like clockwork in the grassy 'square' between Sam Freeman's Mercantile and the clapboard building that serves as post office, bank, and city hall."

She paused to remove a pebble from her brown leather shoe as they approached the settlement. Emma-Lee was glad her shoes were ankle-high.

"The only other shop in Tropic is the blacksmith's hut, which sits across the square from the other two because of the noise and heat generated when Mr. Moses tends his fires and pounds hot metal on the iron anvil. Have you ever seen a blacksmith at work, Emma-Lee?"

"Sarah and me watched Mr. Logan make horseshoes once down by the stables."

"Sarah and I," the teacher corrected her with a razor-sharp glare. "We may not be in the city, but we can certainly speak like civilized folk."

With the shoe returned to its size five home, Aunt Augusta resumed her no-nonsense walk at an even faster pace. Emma-Lee trotted to keep up. "Town Square hosts the open-air market until the afternoon storms chase everyone to their homes. They never last long, but you don't want to be outdoors because of the lightning. The vendors display their baked goods, produce, or seafood and catch up on news and town gossip with the local residents who make the daily trek. I usually shop for supper on my way home from school, but during the summer and on Saturdays, I make a special trip. Naturally, everything is closed on Sundays."

They passed several cabins grouped around an inlet. The settlement was visible just beyond a stand of coconut palms.

"Ah, here we are now," Aunt Augusta said.

As Emma-Lee trailed her aunt into Town Square, a mixture of surprise and amusement appeared on the faces of the islanders milling about. *Aunt Augusta must not have told anyone I was coming*, thought Emma-Lee. *I wonder if she wishes I hadn't.*

Although Aunt Augusta got right to the business of selecting dinner items and participated in little socializing, Emma-Lee enjoyed watching the islanders engage in light-hearted bartering.

"Confound it! Twenty cents is highway robbery for a beefsteak, even if it is the last of your prize steer. I'll give you twelve cents and a fair wedge of my famous lemon pie."

"Tell you what, if you let me have a quarter bushel of that fine summer squash, I'll bring my stump-pullin' mule by and clear another quarter acre to expand your garden for watermelon season."

The island pace was relaxed and friendly, and many of the families had lived on the island for generations. It was the kind of place where everyone knew everyone else's business, good and bad, but chose to overlook the worst and get along anyway.

Aunt Augusta bought a fine, fresh mullet from Toothless Jack and then stopped at the bakery table to purchase a loaf of bread. Ola May Nesmith, the baker, gazed with curiosity at Emma-Lee, who was staring with longing at a platter of cinnamon buns liberally sprinkled with powered sugar.

Mrs. Nesmith was a squat pigeon of a middle-aged woman, happiest while roosting in her kitchen, sampling creations of coconut macaroons or sweetbreads. "Well, who is this, Augusta? A new teacher in training?"

"Of course not, Ola May. Emma-Lee is my niece from Miami. She'll be staying with me for a while." Aunt Augusta occupied herself by squeezing two crusty loaves of bread.

"Oh, a niece, is it?" The market's regular din of voices dropped a notch, and several heads turned in their direction. "I hope your sister's family is in good health." The noise level suddenly bottomed out at a low murmur, and a half dozen sets of eyes shifted toward the bakery table.

"Of course they are. I'll take this one," Aunt Augusta said in her most business-like voice as she handed a loaf of bread to Mrs. Nesmith and opened her handbag to extract her change purse.

"That will be fourteen cents, Augusta." The plump baker wiped her pudgy hands on her flour-smudged apron. She smiled at the red-haired girl whose shining eyes were glued on the pastry before her.

"Emma-Lee—my, what a pretty name. I'm Mrs. Nesmith. Would you like to pick out a sweet roll as a 'welcome to the island' gift, my dear?"

Emma-Lee looked up into the kind lady's face, nodding with such enthusiasm that her chin bumped her chest.

"No, thank you, Ola May," Aunt Augusta injected, counting out coins onto the table and pushing them toward the baker. "I'll purchase what we need, and today this is all."

The bobbing red head abruptly stopped.

"Now, Augusta, I was only trying to be friendly. Can't the child have a cinnamon bun as my treat? Every little girl needs a yummy treat once in a while." Mrs. Nesmith's doughy cheeks molded into two dimpled balls as she grinned at Emma-Lee.

"Thank you for your offer, but she is my responsibility. I'll be the judge of what the child does and doesn't need. Come now, Emma-Lee, we must be going."

The buzzing voices around them rose in muted crescendo, but Aunt Augusta ignored them all, squared her shoulders, and marched down the dirt road toward the cabin, holding her head high.

Casting one last mournful glance over her shoulder at the forbidden sweets, Emma-Lee scurried to catch up, oblivious of the heads shaking behind them.

* * * *

They arrived at the cabin just as the roiling clouds began to boil over. The sheer volume of the storm made Emma-Lee fight the impulse to hide beneath her aunt's bed. She ventured out of her closet-bedroom and was amazed to find Aunt Augusta sitting beside the open parlor window, lesson book forgotten in her lap as thunder claps split the air and spectacular lightning bolts zigzagged over the river.

Emma-Lee marveled at the wide-eyed awe and pleasure that passed over Aunt Augusta's face. She seemed to forget anyone else was there, becoming so engrossed in the magnitude of the storm that she transformed into a different person. Her eyes came alive, and her tense muscles relaxed. She looked ten years younger as she lifted her face to the cool breeze sweeping in through the window, ebbing as God's natural fireworks display moved south.

And then it was over. The transfiguration passed as quickly as the thunderstorm. She became Aunt Augusta again.

That night, as she had the two previous nights since she'd left home, Emma-Lee cried herself to sleep clasping her mother's handkerchief to her chest. She awakened every few hours, startled into consciousness by a recurring nightmare.

She was being abandoned at a strange train station, and a huge black locomotive pulled away from her, gathering steam as its shiny, metallic wheels churned faster and faster. She ran down the tracks in frantic pursuit, reaching, always reaching, screaming for the white-haired conductor to stop, but he sadly shook his head from the back steps as the train continued to pull farther away...

Breathing hard and pushing sweat-soaked hair out of her face, Emma-Lee rose from her closet pallet before dawn and tip-toed through Aunt Augusta's room and into the kitchen. She quietly let herself onto the back porch where she sat on the wooden steps and pulled her knees up under her chin.

Encircling her ankles with both arms and tenderly draping her mother's embroidered handkerchief across her knees as a pillow for her cheek, she gently rocked herself back and forth in the twilight before dawn. Loneliness welled up inside her and spilled out in a cascade of tears.

Her mind drifted back to a happier time—the family picnic back home at the Miami shore in June with Mama, Sarah, and her three brothers. The new baby, Nannie Mae, slept under the shade of a blanket stretched between two palm trees. Papa, as usual, was working at the newspaper office.

Everything had seemed so peaceful and *normal*...at least at first. They drank mason jars of fresh lemonade and ate the cheese and sourdough bread Mama had packed in the wicker basket. Archibald chased Michael and Dexter down the beach and left Emma-Lee lounging between Mama and Sarah on the white sand. As seagulls swooped overhead, the Palmer women sat silently gazing out to the horizon where no land was visible.

That was when Mama had said something strange, something that Emma-Lee would never forget.

"Can a woman ever reach the distant shore?"

She'd said it with sadness reflected in her face, such sadness that it reached into Emma-Lee's heart and gripped her with a hollow fear.

What did it mean? What distant shore was Mama talking about?

Sarah and Mama exchanged looks over Emma-Lee's head and then silently looked down at her upturned face.

Emma-Lee could see something amiss in Mama's troubled hazel eyes but couldn't understand what was wrong. Mama had been looking paler and thinner than ever since the baby was born in March. And those strange purple bruises had been appearing more often on her neck, their dark edges peeking above the high-collared, long sleeved dresses she always wore. She hardly smiled anymore, and she never, ever sang.

Emma-Lee's gaze shifted to Sarah, whose form now had filled out to become that of a lovely, young woman. Dear Sarah, whose strength she had always depended upon when the boys picked on her or when that frightening, stony silence descended upon the house during the darkness of the *angry* nights. The nights after Papa had finished shouting at Mama and the sounds of things crashing no longer echoed from behind their bedroom door.

"What makes Papa so angry?" Emma-Lee would whisper to Sarah as they huddled together on the floor behind her bed. There was never an answer. Just a trembling hug.

But on that sunny, glorious, summer day at the shore, there was a look on Sarah's face Emma-Lee could not interpret. Something about her eyes was so much like the look of the beautiful deer Emma-Lee had seen trying to escape hunters in the woods last fall.

Until Papa shot it dead.

A tear dripped onto Emma-Lee's hand as Sarah leaned across her little sister to drop her head into her mother's lap and cry. The three of them sat there like that, with Sarah's body stretched across Emma-Lee's as if to protect her from...what?

As Sarah lifted her hand to brush away a tear, Emma-Lee noticed four small, round purple marks on her underarm beneath her sleeveless swim dress. They looked like the fingerprints she'd left on the kitchen table after eating a bowl of blackberries. No one spoke as Mama stroked Sarah's head and Emma-Lee patted her back. Gestures of comfort for an unseen wound Emma-Lee could not understand.

The compelling fragrance of honeysuckle drew her back to Merritt Island in the present. The stillness of the pre-dawn enveloped her. Her quivering body gradually relaxed as the sobs ebbed to gulps and then to sniffles. She felt as though she were listening, waiting...

Are you here, God? Are you really holding me in your loving arms like Captain Stone said? If you are, sir, can you please hold me tighter? I'm so afraid.

A soft glow, the promise of light breaking through the darkness, drew her eyes to the banks of the Banana River. She looked through the trunks of tall, straight Royal Palm trees standing like sentinels guarding the rock-ledged river just as the sun began to peek above the horizon.

Shafts of sunlight sliced through the thin fog of early morning, beaming angles of misty light through the pointed, fan-shaped fronds of the saw-tooth palmettos growing along the banks. The throaty, trilling cries of a trio of gray Sandhill Cranes pierced the quiet dawn. Their vast, majestic wings beat a slow, rhythmic pattern as they swooped to a landing on the riverbank. The birds, two of them at least four feet tall, and the other half their size, gracefully roamed the river bank, the red swatches on their narrow heads reflecting daybreak sunrays like ruby crowns.

Emma-Lee remembered Sarah once telling her, as they observed a pair on the banks of the Miami River, that Sandhill Cranes mate for life and stay together as families until their baby birds mature enough to find their own mates. Watching the smaller, leggy bird standing close to its protective parents, she felt a searing blade of longing stab her heart. *They're a family. They have each other. God, if you're listening, I need a family, too. I'm so alone.*

As the sun ascended through lacy scallops of white clouds and bathed the island in dazzling light, Emma-Lee knew it was time to stop crying. It was a new day.

Debora M. Coty

Chapter Six

Captain Stone called for Emma-Lee shortly before ten o'clock Saturday morning. From the cabin window, she watched him saunter down the sandy road from the docks, his hands stuck in his pants pockets, cap pushed back on his dark, curly hair, puckered lips whistling "Sweet Adeline."

Strolling up to the front door, the captain knocked three short raps. Emma-Lee started toward the door but was surprised to see Aunt Augusta emerge from her bedroom wearing an ivory blouse and a pearl gray skirt instead of the usual faded, brown gingham housedress she wore around the cabin. The sapphire broach she'd purchased for weddings, funerals, and "important occasions" was at her throat. Her hair was brushed and carefully pinned into her usual tight topknot, but there was something different about her face. Could that be a bit of lip rouge?

Emma-Lee watched, amazed, as Aunt Augusta paused before the closed door to smooth her skirt and straighten her blouse. She removed her reading glasses and folded them neatly into her skirt pocket.

"A beautiful mornin' to ya' Miss Lemstarch." The captain's bass voice filled the cabin as Aunt Augusta opened the door, her right hand lingering on the doorknob. "And don't ya' be lookin' as lovely as the sunrise yourself, ma'am?" He swept the cap off his head and held it in front of him with both hands. "Is the little lady ready for our outing?"

Aunt Augusta's face colored at the captain's compliment, and she turned to find Emma-Lee's round eyes staring at her.

Aunt Augusta, looking as jittery as a cornered squirrel, pulled the doorknob so hard it popped off in her hand.

"Well, I'll be lambasted, will you look at that?" said the captain as Aunt Augusta stood glaring at the knob in her palm like it was a river rat. "Whale of a grip ya' must have there, ma'am. I'd be happy to fix that if ya' have a few tools handy."

With a horrified look on her face, her aunt wordlessly fled the room, leaving the captain and Emma-Lee staring after her. As if drawn by an invisible magnet, their eyes found each others.

"Do you reckon she's gone to fetch some tools?" Captain Stone asked in a subdued tone. He bent toward Emma-Lee and spoke behind his cap, as if sharing a deep secret. "I hope I didn't say anything wrong. Never did have a way with the ladies, no, siree, especially a fine, cultured lady like your aunt. Just can't fathom the way they think." He dropped his cap to his side and straightened. "What do we do now?"

At that moment, Aunt Augusta bustled back into the room carrying a small wooden toolbox, her angular cheekbones highlighted with crimson splotches. "These are all the tools I have, Captain Stone. I thank you for your kind offer to repair the doorknob. It's been loose for"—her eyes searched the ceiling—"quite a long time now. Why, a stiff breeze could have blown it off." She averted her eyes as she spoke and placed the toolbox on the floor.

That's funny, Emma-Lee thought. *I've been in and out that door a dozen times since I got here, and the knob didn't feel loose to me.*

"Yes, ma'am. I'd be happy to lend a hand." Captain Stone handed his cap to Emma-Lee and knelt on one knee beside the door. He extracted a screwdriver from the toolbox and went right to work. Within minutes, he had replaced the doorknob and seemed satisfied with its stability.

"There ya' go." He stood with the toolbox gripped in one large hand. "That should hold it. Would ya' like me to put these tools away, ma'am?"

"Oh, no, Captain, I'll take them," Aunt Augusta said in her schoolteacher voice as she held out her hands. He started to hand the wooden box to her but lost his grip and it slipped and nearly fell. As they simultaneously reached for the tools tumbling out of the box, their hands collided, and they both jumped back as if burned. Aunt Augusta's face flushed the color of ripe tomatoes as the tools clattered to the floor.

Emma-Lee found this incredibly funny, and for the first time in weeks, she laughed aloud as Aunt Augusta stood clasping and unclasping her hands, fretting, "Dear me, dear me."

Captain Stone rooted around on his hands and knees at her feet, gathering the elusive tools like they were wild rabbits trying to escape a hungry hawk.

* * * *

Ten minutes later, the captain and Emma-Lee walked down the road toward the docks, he shaking his head in befuddlement and she still giggling under her breath.

"Well, that was a right mess, wasn't it, lassie? Guess ya' can see why I never married. The sea, she's much easier to deal with than a woman. Even her wildest storms are more predictable. A man knows where he stands, yes, siree."

As they approached the docks, Captain Stone steered Emma-Lee to a wagon hitched to a horse standing beside a storage shed. The door to the shed stood open, and three-dozen burlap bags of onions were stacked in the bed of the wagon.

"I've asked Julius to give us a ride on his delivery run to Lotus Landing. He can drop us off at my folks' house and then pick us up again on his way back to the docks."

Julius staggered out of the shed with another bag of onions and heaved it on top of the others. He reached into his back pocket for a dirty blue bandana and wiped his sweaty face and the back of his neck. His greasy hair hung in clumps over his shoulders, and he ran his fingers through the damp hair in front, slicking it back from his pimply forehead.

"Julius, can ya' show the young lady some manners and say 'Good mornin'?'" the captain asked as he held out his hand to help Emma-Lee into her seat.

"Good morning," Julius responded in a flat voice as he cut his dark lash-fringed mahogany eyes toward the little girl hitching up her skirt to climb into the wagon. Emma-Lee thought he might have pretty eyes if they weren't always filled with such meanness. Julius closed the shed door and threw the wooden bolt.

"Good morning," replied Emma-Lee in a lilting voice. Somehow, her heart felt lighter than it had in weeks.

Julius climbed into the driver's seat as Captain Stone slid beside Emma-Lee, sandwiching her between the two men. Julius slapped the reins and clicked his tongue twice against his teeth, and the old brown and white mare moved forward with a jolt.

The summer sun was hot, but a steady cross breeze between the two rivers kept them comfortable as the wagon lumbered north along the sandy road. Emma-Lee tried to ask Captain Stone a question, but the rumble of the wagon smothered her voice, so she spent the twenty-five minute ride taking in the beauty of the island.

The island north of Tropic gently widened, and fruit trees grew in abundance. Orange, tangerine, grapefruit, avocado, and mango trees formed small groves fanning out to the banks of two rivers. The groves gradually thinned and made way for dense wooded areas, the green heart of the island, where enormous banyan trees spread their low branches like arms reaching out to protect the lush beds of sea grapes and spicy pennyroyal below. Tendrils of long winding roots grew from the banyan branches straight downward, like fingers grabbing the earth to steady the wide trees as they balanced limbs of twenty feet or more in length.

Gray scrub lizards with black, ridged backs that made them resemble miniature alligators crawled among the undergrowth and occasionally darted out into the road. Emma-Lee pointed to a ten-inch lizard that was sunning itself on a rock beside the road. The pouch under its pointed snout flared into a coral fan bordered in tan as it raised its head to watch the passing wagon. *Its pouch looks like a teeny slice of watermelon. Wonder if it's dangerous.*

As if reading her mind, the captain leaned toward her. "Scrub lizards are harmless." He spoke loudly over the din of the wagon wheels. "No teeth."

Huge Caribbean pines, many with trunks five feet in diameter, grew close together in hammocks. Clapboard shanties peeked through the dense vegetation along the river's edge. Filtered sunrays glittered off their corrugated tin roofs like lightning bugs at twilight. Occasionally, barefoot children could be seen outside playing in small clearings or fishing off the riverbank. Emma-Lee wondered if any of them were her new schoolmates.

The wagon pulled to a standstill at a clearing about a mile north of the school. Captain Stone hopped down and lifted his hand to help Emma-Lee off the wagon. "We'll be lookin' for ya' in round about two hours, eh, lad?"

Julius nodded, his usual sullen expression unchanged. As soon as Emma-Lee had cleared the wagon wheel, he clicked his teeth twice and with a swish of leather reins, the horse resumed plodding down the dusty road.

"It's this way, lassie," Captain Stone said, turning toward a stand of camphor trees on the west side of the road. "We'll take the short cut through the woods; quicker than the long way around by road. Watch for snakes; rattlers like to nest in the palmetto bushes between trees." He led the way down a narrow footpath through the brush. He picked up a sturdy stick as long as his leg and swept it through the bushes on either side of the path. "If ya' ever hear rattles, stop dead in your tracks. A diamondback can jump one-half its length forward and is sure enough poisonous. Snakes only bite if they feel threatened. Don't give 'em a reason to."

Poisonous rattlesnakes? Emma-Lee eyed the captain's towering form and wondered what he would do if she suddenly shimmied up his leg, climbed on his back, and latched her hands around his neck.

"Listen, lassie, pay no heed to Julius and his unfriendly ways," the captain said as he kept up a steady pace through the woods. "He means no harm. Had a hard time of it for such a young lad is all, and he needs to find a reason to be joyful. God's workin' on him. Just give him time, and he'll be comin' around."

He pulled back an enormous, green leaf shaped like an elephant's ear and moved aside to let Emma-Lee pass into a clearing. A small, faded red barn was nestled between the trees at the back of the property. A half-dozen chickens scratching in the dirt broke into raucous squawking as the two intruders stepped into the yard.

"Oh, don't mind the chickens. Ma leaves the door to the coop open during the day and lets them roam. She calls them her 'watch-birds', and you can see they do every bit as good a job as a dog."

The dense greenery gave way to a cleared, patchy lawn surrounding the most unusual house Emma-Lee had ever seen. It looked like a miniature fairytale castle that had magically been transported from the days of King Author to this remote island in Florida.

"How on earth were those walls made?" Emma-Lee asked, stepping slowly toward the house. "It looks like millions of tiny seashells glued together."

"Aye, lassie, that'd be as near an explanation as a body could concoct. It's called coquina rock, Florida's native stone. It's actually a kind of limestone formed by tightly compressed coquina shells binding together on the seashore for thousands of years. As it hardens, it becomes coquina rock and with a bit of work, can be quarried and cut into blocks for building. Pap and I hauled these down from my sister's place in St. Augustine where there're ample deposits. A stronger foundation you'll never find. 'Tis nearly unshakable."

"Why, it's beautiful!" Emma-Lee said as she ran her hand over the roughly hewn mauve and tan shell-speckled facade.

"That it is. A constant reminder that through the ages, God uses nature itself to take care of His children."

Emma-Lee smiled as her eyes swept the amazing structure. Something about it reminded her of her first impression of the captain. Strong, intimidating walls at first glance were mellowed by arched windows that smiled welcomingly all along the length of the house. The top floor was white frame, seated majestically atop its stalwart base, and was crowned by three shingled gables.

The house overlooked a small cove on the Indian River, and as Emma-Lee looked up at the rooster weather vane on the A-frame roof, she saw a crow's nest and widow's walk extending across the roof and out toward the water. A brightly painted rain barrel stood like a chubby scarecrow beside a vegetable garden, which occupied one of the few patches of sunshine filtering through the canopy of oak branches.

"My father's an old seaman, he is," Captain Stone said with a strange smile on his face. "When he was a young man, before he found the light, he served the darkness with the likes of Pegleg Pete."

"Your father was a pirate?" Emma-Lee's eyebrows arched nearly to her hairline. The captain took her hand and led her across the yard to the bank of the wide river.

"Well, lassie, I suppose some would say so. It was in a bloody battle on the high seas that he was wounded and floated off alone on a bit of lumber. He drifted for three days with nothin' to eat or drink except rainwater he squeezed out of his shirt. He did a lot of reckoning with the Almighty durin' those long nights when he was surrounded by shark fins and the sleepless days when the sun beat down on him like fire from heaven itself."

Captain Stone bent down and picked up a palm-sized rock and tossed it into the river with a splash. "He was rescued by a fishing boat when he was on the brink of death and swore that since God had shown mercy on him, he would never go back to his thievin' ways. And he never did. A more honest, God-fearin' man you'll not find."

They turned and walked toward the front porch steps. "My mother worked in the hospital and nursed him back to health. She served as God's hands to heal him, body and spirit. She introduced him to the Bible and led him into a relationship with the Lord. Although he was nine years older, they fell in love and married. Pap bought a freighter and started a cargo transport business out of Sebastian, where I was born. Then later, my little sister came along."

The captain and Emma-Lee mounted the steps and stood before the front door. "The sea's in his blood, as it was his father's before him in Ireland. As it is in mine."

A plump, ivory-haired woman in a white, bibbed apron flung the door open and rushed onto the porch, engulfing the man and the little girl in one giant hug. "Oh, you're here! I've been waiting for you." She stepped back and bent at the waist, eye-level with Emma-Lee, half-circle spectacles magnifying her warm, honey-hued eyes.

The captain beamed with pride. "Ma, this is my new friend, Emma-Lee Palmer from Miami. She'll be staying with her aunt in Tropic for a spell."

"I'm very pleased to make your acquaintance, dearie. Cornelius told me all about you. You just call me Ma Stone like my grandbabies do. What a lovely girl you are! Quite an abundance of striking copper hair, but I see we'll need to fatten you up a bit. Thin as a hickory switch, you are. Do you take after your mama?"

Emma-Lee was at first overwhelmed by the barrage of attention, but then she looked into the smiling woman's eyes and felt the radiating kindness there melt away her shyness.

"Yes ma'am, I'm fair skinned like her, but my mother is blonde. Most people say I have my grandmother's coloring. She had red hair like me, but I never met her. Mama calls them my 'bountiful crimson curls,' but my brothers call them my 'crown of carrots.'"

Taking the confession very seriously, Ma Stone replied, "My, my, doesn't that sound just like brothers. Does it upset you, dearie?"

"Oh, yes. I'd rather have bountiful crimson curls than carrots on my head, wouldn't you?"

"I definitely would. Yes, I see your point."

"Ahoy there, mates," a male voice sounded from somewhere above their heads.

"Are ye here to swab the decks?" Three sets of eyes turned upward to see a grinning, wrinkled old man poking his thin neck out a second story window. White, frizzy hair formed a cottony halo around his head.

"Patrick, it's Cornelius, your firstborn, and his young friend Emma-Lee," Ma Stone called back. "Come downstairs and greet them proper." She leaned toward Emma-Lee and whispered, "Pap has an odd sense of humor sometimes, but he's harmless as a lamb." She headed for the door. "You two come on in the house, and I'll finish the conch chowder and cornbread. And I made a lovely tapioca pudding for dessert."

Ma Stone refilled Emma-Lee's lemonade glass three times and added a fat gingerbread cookie to her dessert dish. Emma-Lee felt pampered and cared for as Ma Stone fussed over her during "dinner," as they called the noon meal. Afterwards, the seasoned grandmother even put aside her needlework, which she seldom sat without, to braid Emma-Lee's hair as they lounged on the porch swing. Pap sat in a rocking chair, holding an unlit pipe between his teeth as he carried on an animated conversation with his son about the recent route changes for the Verily.

"Why do you call your boat the Verily?" Emma-Lee asked. "Is that the name of someone in your family?"

The two men chuckled, and Ma Stone smiled as her hands deftly wove the strands of Emma-Lee's long red hair into two neat rows.

"No, wee 'un, it's from the Bible," Pap chewed the stem of his pipe. "*In truth* 'tis the meaning of the word, and there's nary a thing can withstand the strongest tempest on earth except the truth of God. What better name for a sea vessel could there be?"

"Actually, the name comes from Jesus' words in the third chapter of John, verse three," said Captain Stone. His face lifted toward the white, cotton candy clouds in the cobalt blue sky, and his eyes shone as he quoted, "Verily, verily, I say unto thee, except a man be born again, he cannot see the kingdom of God." He smiled at Emma-Lee.

A distinct whistle drifted through the woods from the direction of the road. Ma Stone had just finished tying the last braid off with a piece of yarn from her knitting box when they heard Julius' signal.

"Oh, do you have to go already?" protested Ma Stone, turning her disappointed face from the captain to Emma-Lee and back again. "At least tell me you'll be coming again soon. Now that you know where we live, dearie," she said addressing Emma-Lee, "you must come by for a visit whenever you can.

You don't have to wait for Cornelius to bring you. You're always welcome."

"Aye, lassie, we could do with a bit of cheerin' from yer wee face," added Pap with a grin.

Emma-Lee's heart swelled. She felt as if she'd found the grandparents she never knew.

"I'll come," she managed to squeeze out as Ma Stone hugged her tight. "School starts Monday, and I know I'll be busy, but I promise to come when I can."

Emma-Lee was lost in warm thoughts of grandmotherly hugs and delicious puddings as she and the captain hurried down the path through the underbrush. Suddenly, a harsh noise erupted at her feet that reminded her of the sound her brothers made when they ran by a wooden fence dragging a stick along the boards.

She stopped short and looked down. There, coiled like a thick rope with its triangular head poised to strike, was a huge snake covered with vivid diamond shaped markings. A column of ivory rattles on its tail was raised above its body, shaking with a deadly, heart-stopping rhythm.

Chapter Seven

"Don't move, lassie." The captain's voice had a hollow, far-away quality, like an echo from a tunnel. Emma-Lee felt as if she was standing still, but the forest was spinning around her.

The horrible rattling noise made her insides contract. She stared into the cold, black eyes of the snake, which grew large and seemed to open and shut like shutters. *Make it stop!* She wanted to put her hands over her ears to block the frightening sound, but she somehow knew her life depended on staying motionless.

Slowly and noiselessly, Captain Stone circled behind the reptile. He held the long stick he had dropped in his parents' backyard and picked up again before entering the woods. In one quick swoop, he thrust the stick through the center of the snake's coiled body, hoisted the thick circles of serpent above the layers of brush, and hurled it out of sight.

Emma-Lee felt her sweaty body sway, and suddenly the captain's big hands were supporting her shoulders. "There now, 'tis all over. And what a fine, brave lass ya' were, going head to head with a six-footer and keeping your wits about ya' all the while."

She blinked her eyes hard to hold back tears. "I don't know, Captain. I think my wits up and left right after the rattling started."

He chuckled heartily as he took her hand to lead her toward the road, brandishing the stick ahead of him like a sword. "Don't ya' know that's the very definition of bravery, little one? Facing something that frightens the wits right out of ya' and doing what needs to be done anyway!"

As they stepped onto the road, the captain tossed the stick into the shallow ditch bordering the woods. "For the next battle," he said with a wink. "You just never know when the devil is going to strike or in what form. It always pays to have a weapon handy."

Julius looked more than a mite irritated as he waited in the wagon, fanning himself with his dirty cap. "It's hot as a buck stove out here, Cap'n," he said in a monotone voice as the two wayfarers climbed onto the seat beside him.

"Aye, that it is." The captain took off his cap to run a hand through his damp hair. "And you've no idea how close we've come to jumpin' out of the fryin' pan into the fire."

Emma-Lee's jaw dropped at the captain's use of her father's favorite saying.

"Julius, I wish ya' could have seen the lassie here, facing down a diamondback rattler a far piece longer than she is tall, never wavering, never giving an inch. She was braver than many a grown warrior, she was." He put his cap on and saluted her. "I'd be proud to have her as my admiral, any day."

Casting a surly look at Emma-Lee, Julius wiped his face on his shirttail then clicked his tongue, and the horse trudged forward, leaving a cloud of dust hanging in the air.

* * * *

Aunt Augusta and Emma-Lee spent Sunday completing last minute preparations to make the schoolroom spotless for the first day of school. The building was deserted that day since the circuit-riding preacher wasn't due to hold church for another three weeks. The old school sexton, Amos, tottered up the walkway while they were busy washing windows.

"Hallo, ma'am. I come by to see if'n ya'll are needin' some help t' get the schoolhouse fit fer tomarree." The small, hunched man spit a stream of tobacco juice into the bushes then removed his battered hat and held it to his chest with both hands. He flashed an every-other-tooth-missing smile that reminded Emma-Lee of a jack-o-lantern.

"No, Amos. I believe we are precisely on schedule with the facilities. You just mind that those thorn bushes don't grow too close to the building and make sure there is a clear path to the outhouse."

"Wal, yes'um, I always do."

"And you know we don't want the children to injure themselves with that broken hand pump out back, so we expect the water bucket to be full each morning and a goodly supply of wood to be brought in for cold weather. We'll need a fire for the children after their walk to school if it's below sixty degrees."

Seizing the opportunity to impart knowledge, Aunt Augusta turned to Emma-Lee. "Autumn on the island isn't much different than summer, except that the sun is a bit less brazen, and a cool breeze often plays through in the mornings and evenings."

With cleaning rag in hand, Aunt Augusta swept her arm toward the two rivers to emphasize her point. "The great stretches of tropical waters surrounding the island make it ten degrees cooler in the summer and the same number of degrees warmer in the winter than the mainland. Frost is unheard of here, but lows of forty-five degrees can certainly chatter the children's teeth and make manipulating pencils difficult."

"Yes'um, that's so, it shorely is," Amos cut in, nodding profusely. Emma-Lee got the feeling he'd had a lot of practice learning to politely interrupt Aunt Augusta when she got going. It was like trying to stop a bull from charging.

"I done cleaned out that ole' pot-bellied stove and put a shine on 'er that'd right sure make a locomotive proud. It's all set t' go, but it be only the first of September; ain't gonna do much chillin' in the mornin's 'til nigh Christmas. Wal, if'n you won't be a'needin' me, I'll mosey on home." He nodded good-bye and turned down the earthen path toward the road, noticeably limping.

"Aunt Augusta," Emma-Lee said as she watched the uneven gait of the stooped man. "Why does Mr. Amos walk like that?"

"Child, it's not polite to discuss the infirmities of others." Aunt Augusta glanced at the back of the man disappearing through the trees. "But I'll tell you one thing. It would behoove a body not to wade into an ocean-fed river to fish. Sharks can slip up behind an unsuspecting person and rip the flesh from his leg before he knows it."

Emma-Lee's eyes widened, and she felt goose bumps creep down her legs. As much as she liked to swim in the shallows, she'd remember the beckoning blue water of the Indian River wasn't the place to play.

* * * *

That evening, after the dishes were washed and put away, Aunt Augusta announced that she would be taking her regular sunset walk—alone. Emma-Lee watched through the front window as her aunt strolled down the sandy road toward town. Emma-Lee didn't know she had a lower speed than "full ahead."

Before reaching the docks, she turned toward the Indian River and approached an outcropping of rock protruding over the water. Emma-Lee uttered a surprised gasp as the dignified schoolteacher kicked off her shoes and peeled down her stockings, hiked up her long skirt over white pantaloons, and climbed out onto the rocky ledge.

The glowing sun appeared to be on the verge of dropping into the river. It was an amazing sight. Moving to the front porch, Emma-Lee felt a shiver of delight as the sky was bathed with varying shades of pink. Streaks of fuchsia, peony, and rose stretched from the horizon toward the heavens. The reflection of the sunset on the water created a huge basin of shimmering pink jewels.

"God sure must like pink," Emma-Lee said aloud. "I guess Aunt Augusta does, too," she added, watching the straight-laced woman she thought she knew dangle one leg over the water like a carefree child reveling in the glorious sunset.

* * * *

The bright Monday morning sun rose in a cloudless blue sky. A warm breeze tripped over the island between the two rivers. After a hurried breakfast of oatmeal laced with corn syrup, Aunt Augusta packed two tin lard pails with salt pork, leftover soda biscuits, bananas, and small clusters of grapes. She handed one pail to Emma-Lee as she stood for inspection at the front door of the cabin.

Aunt Augusta regarded her niece from her brown, button-top school shoes to her green gingham dress covered with a crisp white apron. She had pressed it herself the night before with the sadiron she'd heated on the stove before the supper fire had burned out.

"Can't you do something to tame that wild mane of yours, child?" Aunt Augusta frowned at her niece's mass of flyaway red curls.

"Mama usually braids it."

"I see. A skill I've never mastered, to be sure."

"I 'spect you could learn."

"Ex-pect. I expect I could also if I had a mind to."

Aunt Augusta gathered her school books and papers into a wicker basket and followed Emma-Lee onto the front porch, pulling the door shut behind her. The folks on the island seldom locked their doors. There was no need.

"No doubt the children will have heard about your arrival by now. The island's mouth-to-mouth telegraph system is flawless in its efficiency. News spreads faster than butter on white bread." Aunt Augusta grimaced as she turned and caught another glimpse of her niece's hair. "Perhaps I *will* give braiding a try so you won't bear such a strong resemblance to an African lion tomorrow." She patted her own meticulous topknot from which no hair dared stray out of place.

Birdsong, waves gently swishing ashore, and the sound of cicadas chirping in the trees accompanied the two during their twenty-minute walk to school. Emma-Lee's trembling hands contrasted her peaceful surroundings as she wondered what surprises she would encounter in her brand new life.

* * * *

The children gathered in the schoolyard, chattering and giggling, as they arrived by groups of two or three. Aunt Augusta issued a curt, "Good morning, children" as she swept by them, mounted the three steps to the schoolroom, and closed the door soundly behind her.

Emma-Lee, who had been following her, was left standing outside on the middle step. She felt cold butterflies bounce off the lining of her stomach as she turned to find eleven pairs of eyes upon her. She hoped her oatmeal would stay down.

"Are you Teacher's niece we heared about?" asked a barefoot, freckled-faced boy with tight blond corkscrew curls hugging his scalp. His knee-length pants were ripped at the bottom, revealing a scab on his right knee resembling a black medallion.

Emma-Lee's face flamed as she nodded her head. She studied the toe of her left shoe.

"Wal, what's yer name then?" the ragged boy asked, taking a step toward her.

Emma-Lee swallowed hard. "Emma-Lee. What's yours?"

"Name's Thomas Albert Dinkleberry Junior, but folks call me Tom-Tom." He turned to point out the other children. "This here's my brother, Cleotis, and over yonder's my cousin, Sticks. They're both in the fourth grade, and I'm in second. Louis here, he's my best friend, and he's in second, too."

"I'm in third grade," Emma-Lee said, making eye contact with Tom-Tom for the first time. One of his front teeth was missing, and she saw a twinkle of mischief in his caramel-colored eyes.

"Then you'll be settin' by Myrtle the turtle," he said, grinning in impish delight at a group of girls standing nearby in a semi-circle. "She's my sis' and slow as a slug. That's her betwixt Ruthie Ann and Punkin. Punkin's real name's Lizardbreath, but ever'body 'cept Teacher calls her Punkin."

A round-faced girl with wispy hair the color of lemon taffy hair sneered at Tom-Tom, "Listen here, Tom Turkey. My name is *Elizabeth* McNamara."

She turned and addressed Emma-Lee much more civilly. "My daddy started calling me Punkin when I was a baby and now everybody does. I'm in grade four. Pleased to meet 'cha." She held out a chubby hand to shake Emma-Lee's.

"That's my brother, Elmer, over there throwing rocks in the river with Theo. They're both in grade seven. Mary

Margaret's sitting on the stump behind them. She's graduating the eighth grade this year. Thank the good Lord."

Punkin stepped toward Emma-Lee and leaned near her ear to whisper, "Mary Margaret's sweet on Elmer. How stupid can a girl be?"

At that moment, a clamor drew all eyes to the road to watch a black motor car with a canvas top, its four rubber wheels stirring up clouds of dust as it pulled to a clanking, shuddering stop. A sound like a gunshot erupted from its rear. The car jumped forward and then sputtered into silence as if it had been suddenly shot dead.

A round-bellied, well-dressed man in a bowler hat stepped down from the seat behind the long steering wheel that rose from the right side of the floorboard. He walked around the rectangular hood of the car where two headlights that looked like paint cans turned sideways protruded from the square metallic grate on the front of the car.

Two girls sat primly on the seat, waiting until the man helped them down one by one, handing each girl a shiny, store-bought lunch pail, He kissed their cheeks before climbing back into the car and noisily resurrecting it to life.

Punkin whispered, "That's the Snodgrass sisters. Their daddy's rich and doesn't want them to come to the Tropic school, but the school board made them." The girls crossed the dusty road, stepping gingerly so not to muss their shoes. "Elsie, the one in the pink pinafore, is in grade five, and Leona, in the lavender dress, is in grade six."

Emma-Lee watched in fascination as the most beautiful girls she'd ever seen pranced across the schoolyard, well aware of the attention they generated. They both wore stylish hats and pointed button shoes that matched their dresses and carried dainty little purses trimmed in lace. Leona flashed a coy smile as the two stopped in front of the group of gawking children.

"Why, Elsie, I do believe our schoolmates have noticed our new clothes Papa ordered from the Montgomery Ward catalog. They've probably never seen a mail order catalog before." The two girls giggled as their eyes swept the group and stopped abruptly on Emma-Lee. Apparently the Tropic mouth-to-mouth telegraph system stopped short of the Snodgrass home.

"My, my, what have we here? Who are you?" Elsie asked. She transferred her purse to the hand holding her handsome lunch pail and used her free hand to flip one thick braid the color of maple sugar over her shoulder.

Emma-Lee felt like her tongue had swollen to the size of a watermelon.

"Are you deaf or simply rude? I asked who you are," Elsie demanded, resting her hand on her hip and cocking her head to one side.

Emma-Lee was never so glad to hear Aunt Augusta's voice as the schoolhouse door suddenly opened and a shrill order rang out. "All right children, time to begin. Tardiness is inexcusable; an important lesson to learn while you're young." She stepped through the doorway and rang a small bell mounted on the wall as the children filed into the classroom.

Emma-Lee waited until the other children had placed their lunch pails or wicker baskets on one of two shelves inside the door, a high shelf for older, taller students and a lower shelf for the younger grades. She tentatively pushed two pails closer together to make room for hers on the bottom shelf.

The other students hung their hats on the row of nails along the wall and had begun taking their seats by the time Emma-Lee got her pail situated. She walked toward the open chair beside the girl Tom-Tom had introduced as Myrtle.

"Is this seat taken?" Emma-Lee asked in a tiny voice.

"I can't rightly hear ya' if ya' don't speak up," responded the freckled little girl with unkempt blond curls and a dirt smudge on her chin.

"Is anyone sitting here?"

"No. This is the third grade table, and there ain't any other third graders here. Reckon it's yours."

"Yes, Emma-Lee, that is your place," Aunt Augusta called from her desk at the front of the room. "A place for everyone and everyone in his place. Now, children, settle down for roll call."

After a brief introduction of the class to "Emma-Lee Palmer from Miami," (with no mention of their relationship), Aunt Augusta distributed books and assignments to the older children and began chart recitation with the second and third grades. A large chart on an easel was brought forward, and Aunt Augusta pointed to vocabulary words with a long, pointed stick while the children recited aloud. They soon progressed to grammar and a sentence structure chart, diagramming nouns, pronouns, verbs, and adjectives.

Emma-Lee felt comfortable with these exercises for she read every night with Sarah back home. Emma-Lee loved books better than anything, and Sarah and she alternated reading aloud Sarah's favorite classics, which enabled Emma-Lee to become fluent with difficult vocabulary words.

Myrtle, however, was struggling with the basics and seemed lost entirely when they sounded out words like *coincidence* and *laughter*. She pronounced "vegetable" like "veggie-table," to the snickers of Louis and her brother, Tom-Tom.

Aunt Augusta passed out workbooks and reading assignments to the two girls, and Myrtle was still on the first page when Emma-Lee had completed three. Emma-Lee glanced at her seatmate's worksheet with its large, crooked letters and covered her own neat work with her speller before cautiously raising her hand.

The older children had just begun their seatwork, and Aunt Augusta had returned to her desk. The classroom was filled with the scratching sound of pencils as thirteen students worked on their assignments. Aunt Augusta glanced up to see the arm of the fourteenth student suspended in mid-air.

"Yes, Emma-Lee, what is it?" She sounded annoyed.

"Umm. I finished my...I'm not sure what..."

"For heaven's sake child, speak up. I can't understand you when you mumble."

Emma-Lee spoke louder. So loud, in fact, her lone voice in the silent classroom sounded to her ears like the resounding call of a whippoorwill at midnight. "I'm finished. What should I do now?"

All eyes previously bent over their work looked up. Pencils paused in mid-sentence.

"Why, you couldn't be finished already. There are twenty minutes left before water break," Aunt Augusta said. She pushed back her chair with a sharp scraping noise and strode over to the first grade table. Picking up Emma-Lee's workbook, she quickly scanned each completed page.

"Hmmm. I see. Well, go ahead and do the next section if you understand the work. Otherwise, just sit quietly and wait for the rest of the class to finish."

Aunt Augusta's pace slowed considerably on her return trip to her desk, her brow knitted in thought. She glanced at the third grade table every few minutes until water break, a quizzical look on her face, as her niece breezed through the next two sections in her workbook.

Emma-Lee had always been mesmerized by the magic of words and was enjoying the stories when something popped her right ear. A paper spitball bounced onto her writing slate, and she looked over her shoulder to find Cleotis grinning at her. Just beyond his disheveled dark hair, the cold, violet eyes of Elsie Snodgrass glared menacingly.

* * * *

That evening, Julius Duckett sat in the back corner of the tavern, across the table from a short, stout man smoking a stogie. Julius felt camouflaged in the dark, smoky room, as if he could do just about anything and not be noticed. It was a good feeling.

He sat up straight and tried to look as grown-up as possible when the grisly-bearded bartender in a dirty white apron plunked a glass mug of beer on the table in front of him. The bartender turned and addressed the boy's table companion.

"Here you go, Mr. Snodgrass, a beer for your guest. Will there be anything else?"

"Thank you, Willie. I think we're fine for the moment."

"Yes sir." The bartender cut his eyes toward Julius as he turned to go. Julius thought he saw the man shake his head as he walked toward the bar.

The portly man placed his black bowler hat on the table, his eyes narrowing to slits. Shifting the stogie from one side of his mouth to the other, he leaned forward. "Now, Mr. Duckett, my man Lox here tells me you're willing to do a little work for me. Is that correct?"

Julius glanced at the tall, muscular man standing behind Mr. Snodgrass. His presence made Julius nervous—so nervous that his words tumbled out like rocks down a hill.

"Well, yeah—I mean, sir, yes, sir. Mr. Lox followed me in here yesterday and said he heard that I work on the Verily and asked me if I might like to make some money transporting a few items upriver, and I said, well, maybe I would if the deal was good, only..." Julius took a deep breath and tried to ignore the sick, twisty feeling in his stomach. Could he be making a big mistake? "Only, I was just wondering—sir—how much money we're talking about, and mightn't I get in trouble with the law?"

Mr. Snodgrass blew a puff of dark, foul-smelling cigar smoke in Julius' face and sat back in his chair, his ample belly straining the buttons on his starched white shirt.

"Suffice it to say, Mr. Duckett, that my clients will pay handsomely for these items to be discreetly procured in Sebastian and delivered to their agent in Oak Hill. Both locations are on the regular shipping route of the Verily. There will be three separate deliveries, each three months apart, and Lox will inform you of rendezvous arrangements, which will change with each assignment. You will make twice the monthly salary Captain Stone pays you at the completion of each delivery."

Julius eyes nearly popped out of his head. "For *each* delivery?"

"For each delivery. And no, you will not encounter police involvement because you will not be caught. The items are very small and easy to conceal, and these men are professionals. They will make sure the acquisitions are clean and unsuspicious. Your job is simply to secure the items on board the Verily—without the knowledge of the good captain, of course—make your drop-off, and collect your money."

Julius' left cheek twitched, and he shifted in his chair. "What if Cap'n Stone finds out? He's pretty savvy to everything that goes on and off his ship."

"It would not be to your benefit, or his, if you were to get sloppy and allow the captain to gain knowledge of this operation. His reputation is sterling, which is why we did not approach him in the first place. If he finds out, he will no doubt go directly to the authorities. And if that happens...well...very bad things happen to young men who don't keep their end of the bargain. Isn't that so, Lox?"

The big man folded his massive arms across his chest and leered at Julius.

Julius swallowed hard. Could he really go through with this? He stared at the bubbles sliding up the inside of the beer glass, becoming one with the head of foam on top. The captain had given him a job when he was down to his last nickel and had been good to him, better than any other man in his life had been. He'd hate to bring trouble on him.

Clang. A small sack of gold coins landed hard on the table, startling Julius and sloshing beer out of the glass. Mr. Snodgrass pushed back his chair and stood, bowler hat in hand. "Here's your down payment. Your acceptance means you're in, no backing out. If you prove yourself with this operation, there's plenty more where that came from. You could collect a nice little stash, Mr. Duckett. Be able to buy your own ship one day."

He held out his right hand. "Do we have a deal?"

Chapter Eight

The pale light of early morning peeked through the windowpane as Emma-Lee and Aunt Augusta stood before the oval mirror, solemnly taking in Aunt Augusta's first attempt at braiding her niece's immense head of hair. Lopsided and loose, sprigs of red hair stuck out everywhere. Aunt Augusta studied her ill-fated work of art from every angle. After a long moment of silence, she shook her head.

"Gracious, child, you look like a scarecrow in a hurricane."

Surprised by her aunt's attempt at humor, Emma-Lee began to giggle. Suddenly, an odd, snorting noise erupted from Aunt Augusta. A sound Emma-Lee had never heard before filled the room. Aunt Augusta was laughing—a raspy, breath-dragging sound that reminded Emma-Lee of a mule braying. That thought made her laugh even harder, until tears dripped down her cheeks.

With the help of a dab or six of corn oil, Aunt Augusta finally grasped the fine art of subduing her niece's mass of hair.

Later that day, when Aunt Augusta dismissed school for noon break, Emma-Lee waited until the other children had rushed to the shelves by the door for their lunch pails and dispersed into the yard. She picked up her pail and looked out at her classmates. Yesterday, she'd sat alone on the steps eating her lunch, wistfully watching the other children gather beneath the shade trees. But today would be different. Today she would dig deep beneath her natural shyness and reach out to make a friend.

Elsie and Leona Snodgrass sat together with Amy Freeman on a blanket Amy unfolded and spread on the smoothest patch of grass in the yard. They kept their distance from Myrtle, Punkin, and Ruthie Ann, the shy seventh grader with the round, wire-rimmed eyeglasses, who sat on stumps or exposed tree roots in the shade of the huge oak tree in back.

The older boys ate their lunches on the bank of the river, pole fishing or skimming stones afterward. Mary Margaret sat on an upturned bucket, staring moony-eyed at Elmer, who ignored her completely. The younger boys grabbed bites while they tended to the more important business of climbing trees and chasing each other around the schoolyard.

Emma-Lee took a deep breath and timidly approached Myrtle, Punkin, and Ruthie Ann. "Would it be all right if I ate here?" She tried to stop her knees from knocking together.

The girls, who were just opening their lard pails, looked up. A moment of silence followed that seemed to Emma-Lee like an eternity.

"Why, shore. Grab a stump. There's plenty around," Punkin said, diverting her attention back to her lunch. She dug her hand into the pail and brought up a piece of cold venison wrapped in a piece of greasy butcher paper. "I hate it when my ma reuses the paper so much it gets slimy." She unwrapped the paper, dangling it with her fingertips as she would a dead cockroach.

Emma-Lee sat down on an oak stump and breathed a sigh of relief.

"Yeah, me, too," Ruthie Ann said, wrinkling her nose so that her glasses slid sideways. "My ma says it saves money so I should just live with it and not be such a 'Miss Nice-Nasty.' I wish just one day I'd open up my pail and find my meat wrapped in wax paper all neat and nice-like."

The heads of the girls turned in unison as they gazed across the yard where Elsie and Leona were chattering happily as they unwrapped their wax-paper encased chicken breasts, daintily pinching the white meat into bite sized bits. Elsie noticed the girls watching and waved her white linen napkin with pinkie finger held high and a mocking smile on her face.

"Who does she think she is, the Queen of England?" Punkin muttered as she turned back to chow down on her deer meat.

"At least you have meat," Myrtle said quietly. "My ma says we can either have it for lunch or supper but not both." She bit into her hard tack biscuit smeared with lumpy blackberry jam.

"I have way more than I can eat here." Emma-Lee unwrapped her salt pork. She divided the meat in half and held one of the pieces out to Myrtle. "Won't you help me finish this so I don't get in trouble for wasting it?"

"Well," Myrtle eyed the pork hungrily, "if it'll keep you from getting a whippin', I reckon' I can help out." She eagerly took the offering and dug in.

Punkin watched Myrtle happily munching away and flashed a greasy smile at Emma-Lee. She wiped her mouth on the underside of the stained white apron covering her faded blue calico dress "Your hair looks a heap better today than it did yesterday. Did you braid it yourself?"

"No, my aunt did," Emma-Lee said, smiling back. "She had to use corn oil to keep me from looking like a scarecrow."

The girls laughed.

"I don't have as much hair as you do," Punkin said, still chuckling, "But Ma slicks mine down with spit and pulls the braids so tight that my eyes turn into slits and everything looks flat as a flapjack."

The girls laughed again, this time drawing the unwanted attention of the Snodgrass sisters and Amy.

"What's so funny?" Leona called across the yard.

"Yeah, did one of your mama's pack you boiled skunk for lunch?" Elsie asked and then convulsed into giggles with the other two girls.

"Why? Are you missing your sister, Elsie?" Punkin shot back, pinching her nose.

The two parties turned their backs to each other, leaving the feud for later while they attended to the task at hand—eating. The tree stump group chewed in amiable silence for a full minute.

"Why did you come to the island, Emma-Lee?" Punkin asked. The other two girls turned to Emma-Lee, curiosity brightening their eyes.

Emma-Lee swallowed hard. "I don't really know." She paused to wipe her hands on her apron. "There's something wrong at home, but I don't know what it is." She averted her eyes and began folding and refolding her meat wrapper into a tiny square.

"What do you mean?" Ruthie Ann asked.

Emma-Lee felt uncomfortable with this subject but didn't see how she could avoid the natural interest of her classmates. "I don't understand everything. All I know is that they don't want me there anymore. I don't even know what I did wrong." She bit her lip and blinked hard to keep the tears from flooding her eyes.

Punkin, Ruthie Ann, and Myrtle looked at each other, sympathy written on their faces.

"Maybe you didn't do anything wrong," Punkin said, a bit too loudly. "Maybe your pa robbed a bank and they don't want you to go to jail with the rest of the family so you can break them out before the trial."

Emma-Lee smiled despite the open wound in her heart.

"Or maybe they just found out you're a Russian princess, stolen at birth from the Russian royal family, and they're hiding you from the spies who are looking for you in Miami," Punkin offered, warming up to this exercise of imagination.

"Or maybe they don't like your carrot hair, and they're trying to get rid of you," Elsie's voice rolled across the yard, prompting Leona and Amy to burst into giggles.

"Hush up, Snobby-grass," Punkin retaliated. "It's none of your business."

"You think everybody's business is your business, Lizardbreath," Amy said, looking to her two cohorts for support. Elsie and Leona sniggered, and the three girls huddled together, giggling and gesturing toward Emma-Lee.

"Why does Amy turn so nasty when she's with Elsie and Leona?" Ruthie Ann asked. "She's not so bad by herself, but put them together, and she's plum full of the devilment."

"I've known Amy since both of us were in diapers, and she's really not nasty, at least not most of the time," Punkin said, noisily chewing a nectarine. "You know her father owns the Tropic Mercantile. I think the Snodgrass sisters are only friends with Amy so her daddy will do favors for their daddy. Plus," she rolled her eyes, "they need a servant when they're away from home."

As if to prove Punkin's point, Elsie and Leona wandered toward the stumps where the girls sat while Amy bustled about cleaning up three lunch pails and folding the blanket.

"So how do you like school, Little Red Mop Top?" Leona asked Emma-Lee, her delicate pink lips down turned in a sneer.

Emma-Lee found it hard to chew the grape she had just popped into her mouth.

"It's only the second day and already you're Teacher's pet, aren't you, Little Red Mop Top?" Elsie taunted.

"Yeah, watch out, Elsie," Leona said, "Mop Top thinks she's so smart, she'll probably try to catch up with you in fifth grade."

"And, of course, Auntie Teacher will do everything she can to get her there," Elsie said. Her violet eyes grew hard. "But it'll be a snowy day in June before you beat me in a spelling bee. I'm the best and don't you forget it."

"Who could forget it, Snobby-grass," Punkin chimed in, "when you tell us everyday?"

Ruthie Ann, Myrtle, and Punkin laughed, but Emma-Lee concentrated on swallowing her grape without choking.

* * * *

Throughout September and October, Emma-Lee received weekly letters from Sarah. They contained long, factual accounts of events in the city, the neighborhood, and the household. Sarah rarely shared her own thoughts or feelings but, instead, described life happening around her. She spoke as a spectator instead of a participant, as if she were seated in a chair in the middle of a ballroom dance. Her words seemed cold and forced somehow, devoid of emotion, leaving in their wake a sense of subtle discord.

Even Aunt Augusta noticed. After Emma-Lee read one of Sarah's letters aloud, her aunt remarked, "Something's not right with that girl. Where's her usual spunk? Why does she sound so dispirited?" Emma-Lee wondered, too.

Mama would often add notes to Sarah's letters, assuring Emma-Lee of her love and expressing how much she was missed. Papa never wrote. He was hardly ever mentioned in the letters. Emma-Lee knew he was busy at the newspaper office.

Every Thursday, Mr. Futch, the postman, ferried the mail across the Indian River to the island and delivered it to the general mercantile to be distributed by Sam Freeman, the proprietor, postmaster, and official Tropic town clerk. Emma-Lee faithfully had her own letter for home written and ready to drop off at the mercantile each Wednesday after school, so Mr. Futch could add it to his mail sack on Thursdays for delivery to the post office in Eau Gallie.

Emma-Lee's letters were full of blazing island sunsets, a family of lizards that lived beneath the back porch, tall egrets with great white plumes nesting on the riverbanks, and the horde of island mosquitoes that, according to Captain Stone, could stand flat footed and drink out of a pickle jar.

She told of fierce panthers the islanders called "pa'nters" that prowled the island at night, their eerie hunting cries echoing through the trees. She described the banyan trees that looked like a family of tangled octopuses with their long tentacles reaching every which way, flower-perfumed air that reminded her of Mama's garden, and the citrus trees that looked like round Christmas trees decorated with bright orange, grapefruit, and lemon bulbs.

She lamented to her family the vast amounts of schoolwork that took up most of her time, but because she was moving along so fast, Aunt Augusta said she might progress to fourth grade books by Christmas. Captain Stone was fond of saying, "Emma-Lee soaks up her lessons like a loaf of sourdough in a pot of gravy."

She told of helping Aunt Augusta clean chalkboards at the end of the day when quiet settled over the empty classroom. The island people, her friend the captain, and Amos, the school sexton who limped from a long-ago shark attack, all found their way into her long letters. Emma-Lee wrote that she missed her family but was careful not to beg to come home. She knew somehow that it would not be permitted and that her mother's sad face would only grow sadder if she knew of her daughter's homesickness.

* * * *

The third Saturday of October dawned mild and sun-kissed. Emma-Lee bounded out of bed as she had every Saturday morning for the past six weeks and dressed herself as quickly as possible. Pulling back the curtain to her room, she saw that the clock on Aunt Augusta's nightstand said it was nearly eight o'clock. She'd have to hurry!

She ran a brush through her hair and left the curls freely dancing around her head. No time for ribbons or braids today.

"I'm leaving now, Aunt Augusta!" she called as she hurried through her aunt's bedroom where a lump under the bed sheet jumped at the sound of her voice. She knew Aunt Augusta wouldn't be angry at the intrusion; she looked forward to their Saturday morning tradition as much as Emma-Lee.

Running down the sand road toward the docks, Emma-Lee wondered what wonderful surprise the captain would be bringing today. It had become the highlight of her week, when Captain Stone's regular Saturday shipping route brought him down the channel by Tropic at a quarter past eight. Although his tight schedule wouldn't permit a stop, come rain or shine, he'd steer the Verily close to the longest dock and toss out a brown paper bundle addressed to Emma-Lee.

She reached the dock and scampered past two fishing boats tied fast by ropes as thick as her fist. Reaching the far end, she leaned as far over the water as she dared, straining her eyes toward the southern horizon. Finally, the familiar white freighter cruised into view. White clouds of steam puffed into the air and melted into the early morning mist.

Emma-Lee quivered with excitement as the boat neared the dock. She could see Julius at the wooden ship's wheel and the captain at the deck rail, a brown, string-tied package in his hands.

"God bless ya' Admiral," he called as he tossed the parcel across the watery gap between the dock and boat. Emma-Lee liked the nickname he'd taken to calling her since their rattlesnake adventure.

The package landed with a *plop*, and she ran to pick it up. Waving wildly, she shouted her thanks until the boat was out of sight. She turned and skipped down the road toward the cabin, where she knew Aunt Augusta would be peeking out the window to watch the Verily glide by.

Racing through the door, Emma-Lee skidded to her knees on the floor and ripped into the brown paper. Aunt Augusta stood in her bedroom doorway with sleep-tousled hair, chenille robe hastily thrown over her nightgown, attempting to look disinterested as she stole glimpses at the parcel being gutted. Emma-Lee smiled up at her.

"I'm hurrying!"

"I didn't say anything."

"I know, but you're waiting."

"Nonsense. Your little gifts from Captain Stone have nothing to do with me." Aunt Augusta turned away and busied herself by flipping through a book on her nightstand. Every few seconds, she glanced over her shoulder at her niece's progress with the package. Out came three sticks of peppermint, a nickel bag of gumdrops, a little book about a puppy, and a pink hair bow.

"Pink! How can I ever wear a pink bow in my red hair?"

Oh well, she loved it anyway. She loved everything the captain gave her. Her most special treasure had been in his very first surprise package. It was a small brown corduroy bear with shiny, black button eyes. She'd named it "Cap," after the captain himself. The little stuffed animal was soft and squishy and just the right size to cuddle at night in the cot-like bed that had been delivered her second week on the island. Somehow, the tears flowed less often now that Cap was here to listen to her whispered secrets. The recurrent train nightmares had almost disappeared.

The captain always included a small item for Aunt Augusta in the packages, too. They were useful household items, not at all personal, but Emma-Lee liked to see the way Aunt Augusta's face colored when she was presented with a shoehorn or knife sharpener from the captain.

Today it was a seashell-encrusted pillbox. The corners of Aunt Augusta's mouth twitched as she tried to hide her pleasure when Emma-Lee handed the gift to her. Emma-Lee watched her aunt retreat into her room, fingering the delicate shells with a strange little smile on her face.

* * * *

Aunt Augusta taught piano lessons to Elmer, Punkin, and Ruthie Ann after school on Thursday afternoons at the cabin.

Emma-Lee, who would have preferred to play with her schoolmates as they waited for their lessons, spent the time on the back porch doing piles of schoolwork on a makeshift table of pine boards laid across two fruit crates.

The last Thursday of October was unusually hot and overcast. Some unseen force seemed to be stirring in the air, causing a peculiar restlessness in the children all day at school. Emma-Lee had a hard time concentrating on her homework during the afternoon piano lessons.

Punkin tiptoed around the house from the front porch where Aunt Augusta had instructed the children to wait their turns. The girls were careful not to speak until dissonant chords of the off-key melody from the living room masked their whispers.

"Hey there, Emma-Lee. What're you doing?"

"Hi, Punkin. I'm working on arithmetic figures. Aunt Augusta wants me to finish third grade by Christmas, and it's hard keeping up with all the homework."

"Yeah, but you're smart. You came in third in the spelling bee, and most of the kids are older than you. You even beat me, but I got one of those stupid words with all the silent letters."

"My words were pretty easy. I just forgot that rule about 'i before e except after c'. I went down on 'believe', and Elsie won."

"Well, I *believe* Elsie always wins, or she pouts like a baby." The girls started to giggle but stopped abruptly when Aunt Augusta's piercing voice broke into Elmer's butchered rendition of Beethoven's "Ode to Joy."

Punkin's eyes bulged like the jowls of a courting lizard. She clapped her hand over her mouth and crouched below the porch rail. But it was a false alarm. Aunt Augusta was only scolding Elmer for spending his time hunting rattlesnakes instead of practicing piano.

The awful song resumed, worse than before.

"He does, you know," Punkin whispered. "Hunt rattlesnakes, I mean. Ma says it's too dangerous and gets real mad at him, but he gets fifty cents a piece for diamondback hides. Pa taught him how to flush them out of saw-tooth palmettos and blow their heads off with his hunting rifle. Their bodies keep on wiggling for nigh on ten minutes after their heads go missing. Elmer skins 'em and stretches the hides out to dry on the south side of the barn, and we have rattlesnake stew for supper."

Emma-Lee shuddered at the memory of the black, soulless eyes of the last rattler she'd seen. "I don't think I'd ever try to find a rattlesnake on purpose," she said soberly.

"Aw, shucks, its fun! Elmer said he'll take me with him some day when Ma's gone visiting her sister on the mainland. Aunt Louisa works for a doctor over there."

The image of Dr. Hartman's kind housekeeper, Louisa, flashed into Emma-Lee's mind. "Does she work for Dr. Hartman in Eau Gallie?"

"Now how in thunder did you know that?" Punkin's voice rose in surprise.

"Shhhh," Emma-Lee cautioned as the piano suddenly stopped, and Aunt Augusta's chair scraped the floor. Emma-Lee motioned for Punkin to duck behind the side of the house, and the last strands of taffy-colored hair disappeared from view just as Aunt Augusta's frowning face appeared at the open window.

Emma-Lee scribbled some figures on her worksheet with her stubby pencil.

"How is the division coming?" Aunt Augusta asked, her keen eyes sweeping the porch and back yard.

"Very well, thank you," Emma-Lee answered. She glanced up at Aunt Augusta casually. "Was I too loud? It helps me remember my multiplication tables when I say them out loud."

"Oh, I see. Not a' tall. Carry on then," Aunt Augusta's chin dipped in a curt nod as she turned away. Soon the tortuous musical fiasco cranked back up.

Wisps of feathery hair appeared at the corner of the house, followed by Punkin's freckled nose and then her round, dimpled cheeks. "Whew! I thought we were done for. See, I knew you were smart. Reciting your times tables—Ha!" Her wide lips spread into a brand-new-front-teeth-too-big-for-her-mouth smile. Emma-Lee thought she looked like a plump rabbit.

"I'd better get back around front. Elmer's almost finished skinnin' that cat, and I'm next. I'll save you a stump tomorrow at lunchtime."

In the weeks to follow, Emma-Lee would remember those words and realize that Punkin had no way of knowing that tomorrow's lunchtime would never come.

Chapter Nine

The next morning, the previous day's overcast sky had darkened to charcoal gray. A stiff wind blew the leaves of the citrus trees lining the dirt road into a swirling mass of green as Aunt Augusta and Emma-Lee made their way to school through intermittent sheets of fine rain. Whitecaps dotted the normally calm Indian River as churning waters tossed breaking waves upon the sandy shoreline.

A knot of damp children huddled beneath the eves of the schoolhouse, awaiting the arrival of their teacher. They quickly followed Aunt Augusta and Emma-Lee inside, solemnly put their lunch pails away, and took their seats.

Roll call was brief. The three Dinkleberrys were present, as were Elmer, Punkin, Louis, Sticks, and of course, Emma-Lee. Heavy rain began to pelt the windows, competing with Aunt Augusta's voice for the children's attention.

"It's getting worse. Looks like we're in for a major storm," Aunt Augusta said as she made her way down the row of windows overlooking the agitated river, opening each in turn, and leaning outside to draw the shutters closed. The brisk wind blew sprigs of hair loose from her topknot before she could close the shutters.

The closed-up schoolroom was stifling and dark, the air still and heavy. The only breeze came from the high, breadbox-sized window protected from the rain by the porch overhang. A nameless ominous tension hung in the air. Something felt wrong. Very wrong. Emma-Lee felt hard seeds of fear begin to take root in her stomach.

Aunt Augusta lit two kerosene lanterns and turned to survey the children who had braved the weather.

"I've half a mind to cancel school today."

Obviously unmoved by the spontaneous cheers from her students, she continued, "But since your parents saw fit to send you, why don't we start our geography lesson and see how things are shaping up outside over the next half hour or so?" Groans rose from all around.

The wind only howled louder as it swelled beneath the eaves of the schoolhouse. To Emma-Lee, it sounded like an army of angry ghosts. The eyes of the children grew large with alarm as the eerie lament intensified. Myrtle scooted her chair closer to Emma-Lee's. Her quivering legs rattled their table. Bursts of heavy rain pummeled the metal roof, drowning out Aunt Augusta's voice as she described the ivory coast of Africa.

"Teacher, we can't hear what you're sayin'," Tom-Tom shouted above the din.

Suddenly, the shutters on the middle window facing the river burst open, and hail pellets the size of marbles popped the glass with a sound like Independence Day firecrackers. Emma-Lee could see the slender pine sapling outside the window, arching like a rainbow as the fierce wind buffeted the island. Silver lightning split the ebony sky.

"Miss Lemstarch, I'm scared!" Punkin cried, springing from her seat. Myrtle squealed and leapt up to follow Punkin toward Aunt Augusta's large desk. The sound of the storm was nearly deafening.

"What's happening?" shouted Cleotis, jumping to his feet. "Is it a twister, Miss Lemstarch?"

Bits of glass and hail blew in through the broken window. Elmer, the oldest student present, shielded his face with his history book and tried to lean out through the shattered window to close the shutters which were flapping crazily in the wind.

"No, Elmer, you'll get hurt," called Aunt Augusta. "Children, get as far away from the window as you can. Let's move the lanterns and our chairs to the other side of the room—"

Before she could finish her sentence, a huge crash shook the wooden building. The enormous oak tree under which they had so often eaten their lunches upended by the roots and slammed into the ground, its thick branches scraping the north wall on the way down, splintering timbers and chalkboards.

Screams filled the air. Books flew, loose papers scattered, and pencils rolled across the plank floor as the children charged toward Aunt Augusta's desk, upsetting tables and knocking over chairs in their haste. Emma-Lee felt herself being carried forward in the rush by Tom-Tom, Sticks, and Cleotis, who had been sitting behind her. They all huddled together beside the teacher's desk, panic growing like mounting steam inside a boiling tea kettle.

"Now, now children!" Aunt Augusta's voice faltered. "We must maintain control. I'm sure the worst is over, but we'll gather together in the corner to wait it out."

At that moment, the corrugated tin roof squealed in ear-piercing protest as gale force winds roared down and ripped rusty nails from the wooden frame, peeling back metal strips like the skin of a banana. The storm blasted into the room through the widening gaps in the roof as sheets of tin were blown away as easily as leaves in the autumn breeze. The shutters burst open on the rest of the windows with explosive *bangs*, and the thick glass panes shattered, showering shards of glass upon the tables nearest the windows.

Amid the chaos of drenching rain, wailing voices, and wind-whipped papers plastering themselves everywhere, Emma-Lee was squeezed breathless by Punkin, who had wrapped both meaty arms around her chest from behind and was hysterically shrieking into her right ear.

A deep, thundering bellow, much like the sound of the locomotive that carried Emma-Lee away from home, grew louder and resonated throughout the schoolroom. The horrible noise seemed to have a life of its own, like a vicious monster completely out of control. It reached inside Emma-Lee and filled her insides with its dark, ominous discord. The bucking floorboards vibrated right through her shoes. Fear in its truest form gripped her. Would she ever see Mama or Sarah again? Was she going to die?

Aunt Augusta's voice entered her consciousness, screaming, "Get down! Everyone get down on the floor!" Emma-Lee looked up just in time to see a limb the size of a small tree fly in through the open roof, striking her aunt's left arm as she used her body to shield the group of children from the flying debris. Pain distorted Aunt Augusta's face, but she pulled her students tighter together and threw her body across them.

Emma-Lee's knees gave way from the weight of the descending huddle, and she was forced to the floor. She landed face down on top of a trembling Tom-Tom with Punkin blanketing her back. Myrtle's arm lay pinned across her throat, making it difficult to breathe. No longer screaming, Punkin whimpered like a whipped puppy, still clutching Emma-Lee's slender torso with all her might.

Emma-Lee lay motionless in the pile of writhing, sobbing bodies for long minutes that seemed like hours as the bedlam of the storm wrecked havoc around the terrified children. Chairs flew through the air like matchsticks. Rolled maps and textbooks became missiles, attacking the students as if seeking revenge for unlearned lessons. The unseen beast attacked mercilessly, beating them relentlessly with stinging rain, hail, and tree branches. Elmer and Aunt Augusta, on the outside layer of the huddle, bore the brunt of the trauma.

Finally, the sound of the invisible train subsided. It grew fainter and fainter, as if moving farther down the tracks into the distance. A strange silence descended, broken only by the stifled sobs of the children. Emma-Lee wondered if she was still breathing. She couldn't move at all and was painfully aware of Punkin's knee jabbing her side.

Voices could be heard in the distance, calling, shouting, and clamoring. "Twister...wiped out my barn...Matheson's roof...gone...children...oh, no...school...hurry!"

The voices became clearer as the classroom door scraped open. From deep within her classmate cocoon, Emma-Lee recognized the distinctive Irish-laced tone of Captain Stone and the gravelly voice of Amos, the sexton.

The voices of the fathers of the other children filled the air, shouting reassurance to mothers and other family members anxiously waiting outside the destroyed structure. Emma-Lee, wedged fast between Tom-Tom and Punkin, could only listen and wait until a path through tree branches, broken chairs, overturned tables, and waterlogged books was cleared to the huddle of humanity in the corner of the ruined classroom.

"Miss Lemstarch, are you hurt, ma'am?" the captain asked, deep concern in his voice. "I see you've thrown yourself atop the children to protect them when the twister hit. An admirable piece of bravery, that—sacrificing yourself for them. You're bleeding a bit. Here, let me help you up, ma'am." A pathetic feminine groan could be heard above the steady pattering of rain falling through the broken roof onto the debris surrounding them.

"Her arm's broke, it is," interjected Amos' grating voice, "maybe more'n one place. And she's cut up right bad. Here—" the sound of ripping cloth could be heard—"this undershirt was clean this mornin'; let me wipe up some of that blood fer ya', ma'am."

"The children—are they all right?" Aunt Augusta's hoarse voice asked.

"Shaken up, to be sure, but they look to be fine," Captain Stone said, "thanks to your quick thinking. Only the biggest lad here on top seems to have a few scrapes like yourself. Let's get you to your feet now."

Emma-Lee heard scuffling noises and Aunt Augusta moaning in pain. Then the captain's soothing voice again, "Sit down here, ma'am, and Amos will support your arm and look after your injuries while we get these children sorted out. As soon as the weather clears a bit more, the Verily will be at your service. We'll get you right over to Dr. Hartman on the mainland."

Anxious fathers reached for the hands and feet of their offspring protruding from all sides of the tangle of children. Captain Stone's voice sounded strained. "Emma-Lee, are you all right in there? I see your foot, lassie. At least I think it's yours. We'll get you out in short order now. Thank the good Lord I was close enough to port at Tropic when I saw the storm blowin' up."

The men gently lifted the children off the pile one by one, checking each for injuries before proceeding to the next. Elmer suffered a dozen shallow cuts from flying glass and debris and complained of a sore leg from getting walloped by a chair in flight. The other children were all drenched and shaken, but bruises and sore muscles were the only souvenirs of the schoolhouse twister none would ever forget.

* * * *

Emma-Lee slowly awakened from her turbulent sleep on the cot in Dr. Hartman's sun-drenched guestroom. A whirling kaleidoscope of images of the events of the last twenty-four hours had caused her to toss and turn all night.

Flying chairs and airborne books; the horror of struggling to breathe while trapped in a smothering pile of trembling bodies; the destroyed classroom with its tin roof peeled like a sardine can; the ancient oak that had seemed so strong, so permanent, toppled across the schoolyard like a giant's carcass; twisted roots towering over her head, ripped from the earth and pointing skyward like accusing clawed fingers.

The most troubling memory of all returned again and again during her tortured sleep: the whimpering, terrified children—her friends—being comforted after the harrowing ordeal by their fathers, their champions, while Emma-Lee sat alone.

"It's all right, my little Punkin. I'm here. The storm is over. You're safe here with me," Mr. McNamara had crooned to his daughter as he hugged her tight. Punkin wrapped her arms around his neck and sobbed into his shirtfront, "Pa, take me home. Please, I want to go home."

I want to go home, too, Emma-Lee thought, *but I don't have one anymore. My father is hundreds of miles away and wouldn't come even if he knew about the storm. He's always too busy working.* A new question rolled through her brain as raw pain stabbed her heart. *Why doesn't he do what fathers are supposed to do... take care of his children?*

Then, like a healing balm, another memory, sweet and tender, was superimposed over that unsettling scene. Suddenly, Captain Stone was sweeping her into his arms and carrying her away—away from fear and destruction—away to safety aboard the Verily.

The longer of the two docks had collapsed, destroyed by the twister. But as the captain carried her past the twisted lumber trailing in the water, she felt secure and warm in his arms. She was feeling much better when he finally placed her in a chair in the bridge and tucked a soft blanket around her before returning to help Amos escort Aunt Augusta on board.

Emma-Lee didn't remember much about the voyage across the churning river. She vaguely recalled Aunt Augusta being whisked away to the mainland hospital when the Verily docked. Her next recollection was Louisa helping her out of a coach and leading her by the hand to the kitchen table in the doctor's house. She could recall few words but felt comforted by Louisa's calming voice and gentle hands that bathed her, fed her hot pea soup, and carried her to the soft sheets of the familiar little cot.

It was Louisa's smiling face that peeked into the bedroom now as Emma-Lee tried to sit up amid the jumbled nest of bedclothes.

"Good morning, little lady. Had a restless night, did you?" She entered the room, wiping damp hands on her apron. "I declare, I've never seen a soul churn a bed like that. Could 'a made a turn of butter if I'd thrown some cream in there with you." Louisa crossed the floor and began to extricate the child from the tightly wound sheets.

"They kept your aunt at the hospital overnight and set her arm. It was a bad break, but thanks be to the Almighty, only one bone. She'll be arriving here this afternoon." Louisa stripped the sheets and shook them out with a crisp *wap* before smoothing them again over the mattress.

"I'm sure Dr. Hartman will want to keep an eye on your aunt one more night. Captain Stone said he could ferry you two to the island on Sunday. What a friend you have in that man. He stayed at the hospital until they shooed him away last night." Louisa patted the neatly made cot.

"Here, let me help you change into your clothes." She pulled the silk camisole that had served as a nightgown over Emma-Lee's head. Looking at the shimmery fabric in her hand, she frowned and shook her head.

"I surely hope the doctor won't be upset about me taking this from the forbidden room. You had no nightgown, and it's the closest thing I could come by." She caressed the soft folds of material. "It's not like the missus will be using it again, God rest her soul."

"She died, didn't she?" Emma-Lee asked in a subdued voice.

"Yes she did. And when her heart stopped beating, his stopped right along with it. He won't allow any of her things to be removed from this house. Keeps them all closed up in that room like a shrine. Not healthy, if you ask me."

Louisa reached for a short stack of folded clothes on the dresser. "Here, gal, I washed and ironed your clothes from yesterday. It's a fresh start for you today."

As Louisa's deft fingers fastened the row of buttons on the green and tan calico school dress, Emma-Lee thought about the doctor and his strange behavior toward her the day she'd arrived on the train. He wasn't being mean. He was sad. That was all. How would she feel if she'd lost Mama or Sarah? It would be like her heart had stopped beating, too.

"Was she a nice lady, the doctor's wife?" Emma-Lee asked, holding her arms out for Louisa to slip on her newly starched white bib apron.

"Oh, yes, Mrs. Hartman was the nicest of ladies—thoughtful, generous, always laughing, and pleasant to be around. A joy to work for, she was. This house feels empty without her." Louisa spun Emma-Lee around and began tying her apron strings into a bow at her back.

"Would she be mad that I wore her slip as a nightgown?" Emma-Lee asked, twisting her body to see the housekeeper's face.

"Heavens, no, child," Louisa grasped Emma-Lee's narrow shoulders and repositioned her to finish the bow at her waist. "I'm sure she would be right proud. Mrs. Hartman always wanted children but it wasn't to be."

Louisa turned Emma-Lee around to face her. "You look mighty respectable, I'd say. But what on earth will we do with this hair of yours?" She took handfuls of unruly red curls and began smoothing and shaping the mass into one thick braid, which she coiled around the child's head like a crown. "We'll need some hairpins. Hold the end of this braid and come downstairs with me. I have some extras in my handbag."

Emma-Lee followed the housekeeper down the stairs and noticed she'd made an effort to knot her own thin, lemon taffy-colored hair into a stylish chignon, but countless strands had escaped to form a wispy halo around her face. It made Emma-Lee think of a familiar head of hair.

"Louisa, do you know Punkin McNamara?"

"I most certainly do. She's my niece. And how do you know Punkin?"

"She's my friend at school."

"Well, mark my words. That's one gal you'd do well to keep clear of!"

"Keep clear of—why?"

"I love that child dearly, but she's chock full of the mischief. Both of my sister's young 'uns are good kids, but they've got nary a lick of sense. Punkins gets herself in trouble all the time, and mark my words, she'll get you in a peck of it, too!

Chapter Ten

Dr. Hartman arrived from the hospital with Aunt Augusta in the late afternoon. Bandages swathed her left arm encased in a white fabric sling that hung around her neck. Her pale face distorted by pain, she was ushered straight to bed in the guest room.

The doctor soon returned downstairs and gave Louisa instructions for Aunt Augusta's medication before climbing into his buggy and departing down the road in a rumble of horse's hooves.

Louisa took a tray up to Aunt Augusta before joining Emma-Lee at the kitchen table for a supper of broiled beef and fried potatoes. They had just taken their first bites when Captain Stone rang the door chimes. Louisa scurried around, fixing him a plate despite his insistence that she finish her own meal first.

"I'd no notion of interrupting your meal, miss," the captain said when they were finally seated at the kitchen table. "It took a wee bit longer for Julius and myself to load a cargo of timber than I'd figured."

"Give it not a second thought, Captain," said Louisa with a smile. "It's a pleasure to have you here. What time will the Verily be casting off in the morning?"

"Tis early, I'm afraid. Eight o'clock at the latest." Captain Stone turned to Emma-Lee. "Do ya' think your aunt would be willing to convalesce at the cove for a few weeks? My parents have invited the two of ya' to stay with them until Miss Lemstarch is back on her feet, so to speak. It'll take at least that long for the school house to be repaired, so she wouldn't be missin' anything."

"That's a terrific idea!" Louisa exclaimed. "I was wondering how the two of them would get along with Miss Lemstarch limited to the use of one hand. Assuming, that is, that Miss Emma-Lee here hasn't perfected her cooking and cleaning skills yet."

"Speaking of cookin' skills, Miss Louisa, I surely am appreciating yours." The hungry seaman took a deep whiff of crispy potatoes pan-fried in bacon grease. "I wonder if you'd allow me the honor of askin' the Lord to bless this wonderful food?"

"Of course, Captain."

Three heads bowed. "Thank you, Heavenly Father, for this bountiful meal that has been so kindly provided by the hands of your daughter, Louisa. We ask your blessings on her life and this food to the nourishment of our bodies. Oh, and please comfort and heal Miss Lemstarch who's ailing mightily above our heads as we speak. Amen."

* * * *

Captain Stone underestimated the stubbornness of Augusta Lemstarch. He had run out of good reasons in his effort to convince her of the sensibility of recovering at the cove by the time Dr. Hartman arrived and entered the discussion in the guest room.

"Don't be stubborn, Augusta," the doctor said with calm authority. "It's the perfect solution. These people have graciously offered to take you in, and there is no one else. I've been taking care of your medical needs for ten years. Listen to me. You will go."

"But, Doctor, I barely know these people, and I certainly can't impose on their hospitality by inflicting a handicapped woman and a helpless child on them for heaven knows how long."

"You most certainly can," Dr. Hartman said.

"Emma-Lee is hardly helpless," interjected the captain. "Ma and Pap are more than eager to spend time with her again. And ya' won't be handicapped for long, Miss Lemstarch. Please allow them to help."

"It's out of the question," Aunt Augusta stated with finality.

"It's doctor's orders," Dr. Hartman said. "Make the arrangements please, Captain. Case closed."

* * * *

Adjustments filled the first week at the cove. The biggest was getting to know the God-focused ways of Ma Stone and Pap, which included prayer at mealtimes and before bed, and Bible-reading together every morning after breakfast. Emma-Lee and Aunt Augusta naturally were included, but having never been exposed to such practices, sat quietly and listened.

Captain Stone joined them for a late breakfast the first Sunday. Ma Stone asked him to read from the Bible after the table was cleared. He chose the story of Jonah, a man who tried to run away from God but found that there was nowhere he could go that God was not. Even the dark, smelly belly of a great fish in the depths of the sea. Emma-Lee had never heard the story before and was quite intrigued, as was Aunt Augusta, whose gaze was riveted upon the captain as he read, her expression one of deep thought.

Emma-Lee noticed the captain glancing at Aunt Augusta several times during the reading, and she hoped he noticed the silk stockings and floral scarf Aunt Augusta had gone to great pains to don (with her niece's assistance) in anticipation of his arrival.

On weekdays, the inquisitive girl enjoyed roaming the big house with its two round porthole windows facing the river and second floor catwalk leading to a brass ship's bell mounted on the roof. Pap allowed her to ring the bell at noon every day, its beautiful peals as pleasantly refreshing to her ears as summer jasmine was to her nose.

Pap took her exploring in his "treasure trove," an attic full of old nautical equipment. He proudly demonstrated his cutlass—a seaman's sword that pirates used in the old days. The two adventurers unearthed a battered seaman's chest and enjoyed digging through the "loot" and dressing up in the old pirate's clothes within.

Pap perched a moth-riddled British admiral's hat called a *tricorn* atop Emma-Lee's head as she steered the wooden ship's wheel mounted on a post, pretending to hunt for Jonah's whale. Two harpoons with rusted metal arrowheads on long wooden shafts formed an "X" on the wall behind her.

She learned to pull a palm-sized brass telescope into full three-foot extension to search for shark fins cutting the water. The wizened seaman showed her how to wick a kerosene starboard light and to read a boat compass, its black face floating inside a water-filled dome so that no matter how rough the seas, the dial would remain horizontal. The eager sailor-in-training was often interrupted by the piercing voice of Aunt Augusta, calling her downstairs to assist with one task or another.

Aunt Augusta, of course, needed much help at first in caring for herself with one arm. Unaccustomed as she was to depending on anyone for help, she was often grumpy when tasks were not accomplished to her precise and timely expectations. Unable to dress or bathe herself without assistance, she depended on Emma-Lee or Ma Stone and constantly complained of the lack of privacy.

She could do nothing in the kitchen but set the table, which took an inordinate amount of time. She had difficulty even holding a book to read and had to lay it in her lap to turn the pages. This often produced the unfortunate result of the book fluttering closed, losing her place and eliciting a muffled screech of frustration from the avid reader.

Ma Stone exhibited immense patience with Aunt Augusta, assisting without being asked and speaking soft words of encouragement as she encountered difficulties in functioning one-handed.

The older woman's habit of humming hymns as she worked in the kitchen or on her needlework had a calming effect on the entire household. Ma Stone's peaceful countenance soothed Aunt Augusta as she gently brushed the teacher's hair into a chignon in expectation of the captain's regular Sunday visits.

Pap, too, was helpful when he wasn't exploring with Emma-Lee or up in his crows nest on the roof looking out over the teeming Indian River. He meticulously performed the odd jobs Ma Stone gave him—shelling peas from the garden, bringing in firewood for the stove, even hanging wet laundry on the clothesline strung across the side yard in the tropical sunshine, still bright and hot in October.

After dinner each evening, Pap sat in the old porch rocker, telling Emma-Lee mystical tales of the sea and his own adventures as a young sailor on Pegleg Pete's infamous schooner, the Sea Raven. He spared the dark details of his marauding days as a pirate but told and retold the story of his miraculous rescue at sea with such passion Emma-Lee could almost feel the relentless scorching sun on her skin and smell the salty sea air.

"Aye, girl, I was a goner but for the Almighty hearing me cries and sendin' that fishing boat far out of its normal route to find me. The captain said he'd no idea how they'd drifted so far south of the channel, but I know; 'twas a bonified miracle, nothin' less. The good Lord arranged it to save me life, He did. So I asked forgiveness for having been such a black-hearted fool and gave the rest of me meager life to Him."

On Emma-Lee's second Wednesday evening at the cove, she sat in the creaking porch rocker and listened to Pap complete his rescue story for the third time that week. The child's short legs hung high above the floorboards as she shifted her weight forward and back to rock rhythmically over the uneven planks—*ther-thump, ther-thump*. She thought about the old man's words and the events that brought her to this place.

"Pap, I hear you and Ma Stone and the captain talk about God like He's right beside you. Sometimes I feel like He's far, far away and doesn't know what's happening. Or maybe He just doesn't care about a little girl like me."

"No, lassie, He always cares." Pap said. He chuckled softly under his breath. "But sometimes He has to take drastic measures to get our attention."

"Like taking children away from their family when they don't even know what they did wrong?" Emma-Lee lowered her eyelids and stared at the worn floorboards.

Understanding dawned in Pap's clear blue eyes. He rubbed his bristly chin in thought. "Did ye consider that yer not really separated from yer family? Not if God's yer Heavenly Father, that is. The Bible says in the eighth chapter of the book of Romans, 'Neither death, nor life, nor angels...nor height, nor depth, nor any other creature, shall be able to separate us from the love of God, which is in Christ Jesus our Lord.'

"Why, He's right here protecting ye all this time, and seeing to it that ye have yer aunt to take care of yer needs." Pap looked toward the screen door where Aunt Augusta's high-pitched voice carried from the kitchen as she complained to Ma Stone about not being able to peel a carrot with one hand. One of his bushy eyebrows rose. "Or maybe fer ye to take care of her needs as the case may be.

"Regardless, when the Lord sees fit to call us unto Himself, we best pay attention, whether we be six or sixty. 'Tis the most important decision of our whole lives."

"Pap, I want to know God like you do, but I don't know how."

Pap's whiskered face broke into a smile.

"Lassie, it'd be me privilege to show ye the way."

The old man and the young girl knelt on rough porch timbers as the sun set in a blaze of glory on the horizon above the distant banks of the Indian River.

"Address Him as your Heavenly Father, which He is. Are ye ready to do that, lassie?" Pap's gnarled fingers gently curled around Emma-Lee's delicate hand.

"Oh, yes." Emma-Lee closed her eyes tight, creating a deep furrow in her brow. "Papa God," she paused, opened her eyes, and smiled up at Pap. "I'm so glad He's my Heavenly Papa."

"Now what would ye like to say to Him, child?"

Scrunching her eyes shut again, she continued her prayer. "I'm sorry I got so upset at Mama and Papa for sending me away. Please forgive me for anything I did to make them stop wanting me. Oh, and I'm sorry I don't like Aunt Augusta sometimes. But that's getting better.

"Papa God, thank you for loving me. Please take my life and watch over me as my Heavenly Father. I'm much obliged. Amen."

"Amen," Pap said. He smiled warmly at the earnest child before him.

Pap tilted Emma-Lee's chin up with his crooked finger and looked straight into her eyes. "Just remember ye aren't alone, lassie. Not on the long train ride away from your family. Not in the darkest of nights. Not through the most terrible of storms. Remember that *nothin'* can separate us from the love of God."

"Yes, sir." Emma-Lee nodded solemnly. "He's a father who'll take care of me all the time, no matter where I am or what I do."

A minute later the screen door opened, and the two ladies stepped outside to see the sunset. Although Aunt Augusta looked a bit puzzled as to why her niece and the grizzled old man were joyfully embracing as they knelt on the crude porch floor, a warm knowing smile spread across Ma Stone's face.

Chapter Eleven

Emma-Lee felt a strange mixture of happy and sad as she stood at the Stone's front door saying good-bye. The three weeks at the cove had been like a salve to her wounded spirit. Her feelings of upheaval and fear had gradually been replaced by peace. She had a new father now. A Heavenly Father.

"We'll be prayin' for ye, lassie, 'tis somethin' ye can count on," Pap said with a wink.

Ma Stone tenderly patted her hand. "Come see us any time, and we'd love to welcome you and your aunt to church when the circuit riding preacher comes back through next month. The school house should be repaired in no time with the island men working on it so hard, and you know the church meets there the third Sunday of each month."

Aunt Augusta and the captain busily sorted out mounds of luggage on the porch.

Ma Stone reached for something on the small table just inside the door. "Here dearie, this is for you. Pap and I talked it over, and we want you to have it. It belonged to Cornelius when he was about your age. It's a children's Bible with lots of wonderful pictures. Don't rightly know if your aunt has a Bible at her house, but you'll need God's word close to your heart now that you've become a child of His."

Emma-Lee's bright smile fairly sparkled.

"Thanksgiving is in a few weeks. I'll be inviting you and your aunt to come spend the day with us." Ma Stone glanced at Aunt Augusta, who was instructing the captain in the proper way to carry a hatbox. "I truly think God's working in her heart. We'll just have to give it more time and prayer."

* * * *

At the same time in a harbor far downriver, a man with a hard body and shifty eyes glanced down both sides of the street before melting into the deep shadows of the alley behind the Sebastian Tavern.

"Julius Duckett?" the tall man asked, standing so close that the bulging muscles of his right arm brushed Julius' left shoulder.

"Don't you recognize me, Mr. Lox? It's only been three months since the last hand-off."

"You will identify yourself at each and every rendezvous."

"Oh. Yes, sir. It's me, sir. Julius Duckett."

The man cast the boy a look of disdain. "I hate working with amateurs. Do you still have the chest I gave you?"

"Of course, sir. It's still hidden on the ship, just like you told me. I'm supposed to leave it there until after the last delivery and then weight it down and sink it in the river."

"Good. The clients were pleased with the last shipment. Here's the second. Never slack off guard for one moment—remember your life depends on the absolute secrecy of this operation."

Julius shuddered involuntary as the small brown bundle passed from Lox's oversized hand to his inside jacket pocket. Lox must have noticed, for he locked eyes with the boy for a full five seconds.

"You're not going yellow on us, are you, boy?"

"No sir. No. I wouldn't...I'm not...no."

"Then get going."

Julius breathed a shallow sigh of relief and turned to leave. Fingers like steel spikes gripped his arm. "Oh, Mr. Snodgrass said to tell you there might be a bonus in it for you if this delivery goes as smoothly as the last one."

"Yes, sir. Thank you, sir. I'll do my best."

"Just make sure your best is good enough."

* * * *

Emma-Lee smiled and stroked the worn Bible in her lap as she bounced along in the wagon bed on the return ride to Aunt Augusta's cabin. The wagon wheel bumped over a stone in the road and bucked Emma-Lee off the fruit crate on which she was sitting, nearly jostling the Bible out of her hands.

"You all right back there, Admiral?" Captain Stone's voice called from his post beside Aunt Augusta on the driver's seat. "Not too bumpy for ya, is it now?"

"No, sir," Emma-Lee yelled above the din of the rumbling wagon wheels. "I like it. It feels like when my brother Michael used to pull me in my wagon down the rock trail at home."

The captain smiled at her over his shoulder before addressing Aunt Augusta quietly. "Miss Lemstarch, if ya don't mind my asking, will Emma-Lee be goin' home for a holiday visit? It's been nigh on three months now—a mighty long time for a wee lass to be away from her family."

Aunt Augusta watched her niece scramble to regain her seat in the rollicking wagon bed and then leaned toward the captain to speak in a low voice meant for his ears only. "Well, you see, Captain..." The wagon rolled over a raised tree root and rocked decidedly to the left, throwing Aunt Augusta's shoulder into the captain's and causing her lips to brush his ear.

"Oh, my, I'm terribly sorry," she said, her voice breaking in mid-sentence. "It was the wagon and the boots...I mean roots, and I couldn't hop, that is, help..."

"No, no, it's quite all right." He cleared his throat. "I'd be honored if you'd call me Cornelius, ma'am."

Aunt Augusta blushed and stared at the backside of the horse in front of her. "Certainly, Cornelius, if you wish." She straightened her sensible hat and smoothed her dark skirt with her good hand. "You may call me Augusta."

"Very well, Augusta." For the next thirty seconds, two tongue-tied adults found the swishing tail of the mare intensely interesting.

The captain coughed and shifted in his seat. Twice. "So, Augusta, you were about to tell me the plans for Emma-Lee."

"Yes, well, those are a bit uncertain at this point...Cor...Cornelius," she nearly choked on his name. As he studied the road ahead, she studied him through the corner of her eye.

His dark brown mustache and beard flicked with gray had been neatly trimmed since she saw him last week. *All the better to see his full lips and fine teeth when he smiles. Impressive. He must be very conscientious about cleaning his teeth. Nice and white. Dental hygiene is important. Says a lot about a man.* She nodded with approval.

The fishy odor that usually clung to his sun-browned skin was replaced with the faint spicy scent of men's aftershave. *He must have taken his Saturday night bath early this week. My, my—such a gentleman!*

Her eyes discreetly swept down his torso. A clean, blue cotton shirt outlined his broad shoulders and chest, the sleeves rolled just below the elbows. The sun-bleached hairs of his forearms glistened atop well defined muscles as a testimony of an honest life of hard labor. And then there were his hands holding the reins. Ah, such wondrous hands, rough and calloused but somehow still intensely sensitive.

Drawn by a force foreign to her and sensing no resistance from him, she scooted ever so minutely in his direction, closing the distance between them to a scant four inches. Taking a deep breath to steady her tingling nerves, she leaned toward the captain and spoke directly into his ear.

"You see, Cornelius, there is some degree of trouble within the family which my sister has not fully disclosed to me. I am only telling you this because I know you care for Emma-Lee and will be prudent in your knowledge of the situation."

He answered with a look of concern. "Of that you can be sure."

The two were now face to face, their noses only inches apart. Aunt Augusta swallowed hard but did not allow herself to back away. Self-discipline was, above all, her strong suit. After a long moment, the captain reluctantly returned his eyes to the road. The wagon lumbered on.

An uncomfortable silence followed, during which Aunt Augusta struggled within herself as to the proper discourse of a lady during such circumstances. Should she resume a respectable distance from the captain, or would it be scandalous if she moved a bit closer so that Emma-Lee would not overhear their conversation? She'd never been this drawn to a man before and had never considered the possibility that she might be. To her surprise, she was finding it quite enjoyable.

He doesn't seem adverse to my proximity.. Is he merely being polite? He's such a fine, upstanding man; he may be trying to spare my feelings. I don't want to appear too forward, but an opportunity like this may never come again.

In the end, his alluring masculine scent overrode her sense of propriety, and she slid another inch closer to him.

"Cornelius, you've been very kind to Emma-Lee since her arrival here, and your family has shown immense charity toward me during my convalescence. I want you to know I am most grateful. I've no idea why you reach out to strangers in need like you have to us. I don't know how I can ever repay you."

"There's no need for repayment. We do it because we love the Lord and He wants to show his love for others through us."

"Yes, your mother said as much to me at the cove. She spoke of giving my heart to God as well, but there are some painful personal things in my past I haven't yet been able to reconcile. I truly hope that I will one day. The love and joy your family shares have been an inspiration to me and certainly to Emma-Lee. She looks happier than I've ever seen her."

"It's nothin' short of a wonder, it is, the peace He'll bring to your heart when you turn over your life to Him."

"Peace is something the child has had little of in her home, I'm afraid. Fenton, that hothead of a man my sister married, keeps all their lives in turmoil, although I must admit my suspicions are not based on eyewitness accounts. But I've read between the lines of Ellie's letters and seen the way she cowers when he's angry. He has a frightful temper. Ellie discloses very little, but I can tell she's desperately unhappy. Now I'm seeing signs of the same quiet misery in Sarah, her eldest daughter."

"I'm awful sorry to hear that. Do ya' fathom what the problem may be?"

"I've no proof of anything. He behaves quite respectably when I visit at Christmastime, although he seldom engages in conversation with me. If some sort of abuse is going on, no one discusses it. It's a well-guarded secret."

They both glanced back at Emma-Lee, who had opened the captain's old picture Bible to a cramped-looking Jonah inside the belly of a huge fish.

"That's the worst kind of secret," the captain said, shaking his head, "the kind that ruins lives. Do ya' think he's harmed Emma-Lee?"

Aunt Augusta sighed. "I don't know. But I do know Ellie was determined to get her out of that house. That's why she wrote and begged me to take her in. I think she fears for the child's safety if she stays there. So you can see why our holiday plans are unsure."

"Aye, I see."

"Another complication is that Emma-Lee's birthday is December twenty-third, and I'm sure she harbors a secret desire to be home on the day she turns ten. Ellie has yet to address it, and I'm just not sure what is best for the child."

They rode along, each deep in thought.

"I want ya' to know, Augusta," the captain said finally, "that if I can be of any service a' tall, I'd be pleased to have ya' call on me. I always thought I'd have my own little girl to look after one day, but the Lord hasn't seen fit to bring it to pass." He leaned ever so gently to his right so that his shoulder lightly touched hers and looked squarely into her eyes. "I've grown right fond of Emma-Lee. I'd do most anything for that child."

Aunt Augusta shivered as she saw in his eyes—eyes the hue of the sea after a storm—the unspoken message that his words of devotion were meant for her, too.

Chapter Twelve

Emma-Lee smiled as she looked at the unlikely group of people gathered around the Thanksgiving table. Ma Stone placed a roasted wild turkey at the head of the table, and Pap sharpened a long carving knife against a stone, a sparkle in his eye and grin on his wrinkled face.

Captain Stone and Aunt Augusta sat on the left side of the table, carefully avoiding eye contact with each other by staring at Emma-Lee on the opposite side of the table. Julius hunched on Emma-Lee's right, the boredom on his face making it clear he had accepted the dinner invitation only to appease his employer.

Truth be known, he had nowhere else to go.

It's Thanksgiving, and I do feel like giving thanks, Emma-Lee thought. *Papa God, even though I miss my family, I'm thankful you brought me to this table with these people. Even Julius. Maybe he's nasty because he's lonely. You can fix that, Papa God, like you fixed the hurt in my heart.*

Emma-Lee flashed a bright smile at Julius, who frowned in return and fixed his attention on Ma Stone's fine china plate before him.

Pap raised his hands and prayed for God's blessings on the food and souls present. A heartfelt "amen" resounded from the captain. Ma Stone began passing bowls of steaming green beans, buttery creamed potatoes piled high in a deep bowl, spicy stewed tomatoes, and Aunt Augusta's contribution, soda biscuits with orange blossom honey.

"Why, Miss Lemstarch, how on earth did you make such fluffy biscuits with only one hand?" Ma Stone asked. "You've managed well on your own, I'm pleased to see."

"All I can say is that necessity certainly is the mother of invention," Aunt Augusta responded in her no-nonsense, schoolteacher voice. "Creativity with body parts is essential. A rolling pin can be manipulated with one hand and an elbow if one is motivated enough. I've learned how useful knees can be to hold a mixing bowl for stirring. Teeth are for carrying small objects, and feet can be quite helpful in folding laundry."

Hearty chuckles rolled from the captain and Pap and even Julius raised an eyebrow at the mental picture of the proper schoolteacher manipulating petticoats with her toes.

"The mothers of my students and many of the townsfolk have graciously brought over meals, so I haven't had to do much cooking. Many of them had more damage from the tornado than we had, but they've insisted on helping us clear the yard, cut up fallen tree limbs, and repair the portion of the porch that blew off."

"Aye, I heard they worked every spare minute on the school house, too, 'til it was useable again. How are yer classes comin'?" Pap asked, spearing a bite of turkey with his fork.

"As well as can be expected under somewhat crude circumstances," Aunt Augusta said. "The broken windows and chairs have been removed, but the replacements have not yet arrived. We are enjoying the fresh breeze, and the smaller children sit on upturned buckets. Many books were damaged beyond repair or lost in the storm, but the children are sharing the few we have left until new ones can be ordered. I've tried to do more combination-grade oral lessons in the week since school resumed, and that method seems to be working reasonably well. We're getting by."

She picked up her fork and continued talking, but in a gentler tone, a tinge of amazement coloring her voice.

"The children have really come together in unity since the storm. It's inspiring to watch. Even the ones who weren't there at the time have been caught up in the tight bond they've formed. The older children help the younger ones with schoolwork, and they all share, well, everything. The boys have even cut back on the shenanigans they pull on the girls. The children seem kinder, more appreciative of each other." A troubled look came over her face. "Only the Snodgrass girls haven't returned."

"They weren't there the day of the storm, either," Emma-Lee said. "Tom-Tom said Amy Freeman's father told his mama they may not come back. They were talking at the mercantile the other day."

"Not come back?" Ma stone asked. "Why not?"

Aunt Augusta breathed a soft sigh. "Apparently Mr. Snodgrass is trying to convince the school board the Tropic school was so damaged by the storm that a proper education is no longer possible and his children should be transferred to Lotus Landing." She looked pained, as if the words had jagged edges. "The storm was just an excuse; he's been looking for one for a long time. He doesn't think much of my teaching skills." She listlessly stirred her potatoes.

"That's absurd!" the captain exclaimed, slamming his fist on the table. Plates jumped, water danced in glasses, and forks were suspended in mid-air as five surprised faces turned toward Cornelius Stone.

"What in thunder does that man know about teaching? You're the best teacher this island's ever had—everyone says so! All Randolph Snodgrass knows about is runnin' his shippin' business which, I might add, has gained him a reputation among the freight haulers as an unreasonable, tight-fisted, slave driver who doesn't hesitate to alter the truth to his own advantage."

Everyone froze in shocked silence.

"Cornelius! What an uncharitable thing to say!" cried Ma Stone.

Aunt Augusta gazed at the captain wide-eyed, her sharp features softening. A scoop of creamed potatoes fell off her forgotten fork onto the table with a *plop*.

Why, she's almost glowing, Emma-Lee thought, staring with amazement at her aunt's countenance.

"I'm sorry." The captain looked down at his plate. "You're right, Ma. I shouldn't have said that, especially at the Thanksgiving table."

"Though there's ne're been a truer word spoken," muttered Pap.

Julius choked back a laugh.

The rest of the dinner passed in conversation about world news in the newspaper the captain brought from the mainland. Amazing things like the sensational new book by the Englishman Barrie, called *Peter Pan*, and the first Olympic Games just held in St. Louis where the United States won no less than twenty-one events!

No further mention was made of the captain's unusual outburst.

* * * *

After dropping off Emma-Lee and Aunt Augusta at their cabin in the late afternoon, Julius scrambled from the wagon bed into the front seat vacated by the schoolteacher. As the captain turned the old mare toward the docks, Julius said, with a cocky grin, "Cap'n, in the six months I've worked for you, I ain't ever seen you blow your top like you did at the dinner table today."

"Aye, lad, 'twas a shameful display."

"Not compared to the displays my Pa used to put on. I just never seen you talk bad about anybody before. Couldn't figure it out. Ain't natural not to badmouth folks that do you wrong."

"Not natural, maybe, for our sinful natures, but surely not Christian-like. I let my anger get the best of me."

"What made you so angry?"

The captain shifted in his seat and pulled his cap brim down low over his eyes. "I suppose I didn't cotton to Rudolf Snodgrass making Miss Lemstarch feel bad about her teachin'."

A sly smile exposed the boy's crooked teeth. "So you're sweet on her, are you, Cap'n?"

Captain Stone winced. "I don't know as I'd put it just like that. I've a lot of respect for the wonderful job she does with those children. Did ya' know she sacrificed herself for them when the twister hit the school? That's how she injured her arm, protecting other people's children. There's so much caring and compassion in her that she keeps hidden—I don't think people take the time to understand her. She's a remarkable woman."

"Yeah, she's remarkable all right." Julius snorted. "But she's no spring duckling, and you're past forty. Why haven't you ever married, Cap'n?"

"Don't rightly know, lad. I've followed the Lord's leading all my life, and He just hasn't led me down the aisle."

Julius shook his head. "I'll never understand how you can talk about God like He actually tells you what to do. He ain't ever told me what to do. Except maybe to run when my pa was drunk and dead set on beating me to a pulp. I figure God's so mad at me for all the bad things I've done, He's got no use for telling me anything anyway. Mama was the only one that could tell me anything worth listening to, and since she died, I've been figuring things out on my own."

Captain Stone took his time in replying. It was rare that Julius opened the door to personal conversation, and the captain didn't want to hasten the slamming of the door too quickly.

"So ya' never yearn for anythin' more, lad? A real relationship with a Heavenly Father who made ya' and loves ya' more than any earthly father ever could?"

The color drained from Julius' pockmarked face, and his thin shoulders sagged. He may have been sixteen and on the brink of manhood, but at the moment, he looked like a defeated little boy. He looked out toward the Indian River where the waning sun was dropping toward the horizon.

His voice was low and serious. "Maybe. But that kind of father is only real to people like you who had decent pa's. Mine wasn't worth an iron slug and never will be. I can't imagine anybody caring about me like the God you're always talking about."

Captain Stone considered his words before speaking. "You're becoming a good ship's mate, Julius, and you've learned a lot over the past months. But there's something very important ya' need to know. Are ya' savvy about pearls?" The captain, with his Irish lilt, pronounced them "piels."

A look of alarm suddenly flashed in the boy's eyes. "Pearls? What about them?"

"Do ya' know that pearls are formed inside oysters only through years of hardship? The pearl is formed layer by layer as the oyster tries to protect itself from constant irritation and friction from a grain of sand or tiny bit of plankton. The result of all that turmoil is a beautiful pearl, perfect and immeasurable in value. Nothin' compares to it. But the *only* way the pearl can form is by hardship."

"What do pearls have to do with me, Cap'n?" Julius seemed to be having trouble keeping his voice steady. He looked everywhere but at his employer, fidgeting uncomfortably as the wagon approached the storage shed at the docks.

"Don't ya' see it, lad? You're the pearl. Matthew chapter thirteen, verses forty-five and forty-six say, "The kingdom of heaven is like unto a merchant man, seeking goodly pearls; who, when he had found one pearl of great price, went and sold all that he had, and bought it."

"I don't understand, Cap'n. I'm ugly as raw sin, inside and out. My pa said so. Everybody says so. Even I know it." He cut a side glance at the kind seaman sitting beside him. "I deceive good people. How could even God see me as a pearl?"

"You're not finished yet. You're still being formed, Julius, but you've the makings of the pearl of great price that God purchased. He bought your soul and paid for your sins, every last one of them. He'll truly love ya' and lead ya' through this life as your Heavenly Father, just like He does me."

The wagon pulled to a stop, but the two sailors stayed on the wagon seat.

"I wish I could believe that."

"Ya' can, lad. All ya' have to do is ask Him to help ya'. He'll do the rest." The captain gathered the reins in his left hand and encircled the shoulders of the boy-man with his right.

Julius' restlessness was palpable. He sweated profusely and was obviously struggling mightily with some inner foe. His shoulder muscles contracted and relaxed then contracted again. His pale face looked troubled, more troubled than the captain had ever seen him.

Suddenly, he changed perceptibly. His face hardened, and his back stiffened. The small window of transparency into his soul was shuttered into darkness. The inner battle had been forfeited.

"I need to start loading the Verily for tomorrow's run," Julius said as he squirmed out of the captain's embrace and climbed down from the wagon seat. He took three steps and then paused, turned and looked meaningfully at his employer.

"Pearls..." he muttered under his breath. "How could...?" He shook his head and turned to leave.

Cornelius Stone felt the lead weight of disappointment drop into his belly as he watched the boy walk away.

Chapter Thirteen

By the first week of December, Aunt Augusta began to use her injured arm again. On a warm, sunny Wednesday three weeks before Christmas, she was exercising her weak hand by picking up stray pencils and washing chalkboards after school when Punkin rushed in the classroom.

"There you are. I thought you'd still be here!" Punkin skipped up behind her best friend and tugged playfully on one of her red braids. Emma-Lee diligently worked on homework while she waited for Aunt Augusta to finish her after school chores.

"I just got home when Ma said we're gonna walk to the docks after supper to pick up a special delivery package from Aunt Louisa. Since that's not far from your cabin, I thought it would be the perfect time for you to come over and visit a spell. Ma said you were invited for supper, and we can walk you home after."

Emma-Lee squealed and clapped her hands with glee. She and Punkin had been wishing for this opportunity for weeks. Both girls looked expectantly at Aunt Augusta.

The tired schoolmarm dropped her washrag into the bucket of soapy water and rubbed her swollen left wrist. "I don't know, Emma-Lee. You have to finish conjugating your verbs in chapter seven, and it may take you all evening to complete your mathematic equations."

"No, ma'am, it won't take that long. I've already done half the arithmetic, and I'm really good at conjugating verbs so chapter seven won't be hard." She jumped to her feet, anticipation dancing in her blue eyes. "Please, Aunt Augusta!

It's the first time I've been invited to play after school, and I'd really like to go! Please, oh, please!"

"Well..." As Aunt Augusta studied her excited niece, the furrowed lines around her pursed lips eased into a whisper of a smile. "I suppose you *have* been working hard on your lessons. You're very close to beginning grade four. And you've been doing a lot of extra chores at home with my arm out of commission." She dropped both hands by her side and sighed. "All right, you can go. Just remember your manners, Emma-Lee."

"Oh, thank you, thank you, Aunt Augusta!" Lost in a moment of joy, Emma-Lee threw her arms around her aunt's waist, inadvertently pinning her tender left arm to her side. The howl that resounded from the open windows set to flight the flock of mallard ducks floating on the river just outside the schoolhouse.

The girls chattered like courting crows as they walked the dusty half-mile to the McNamara cabin on the banks of the Banana River. The house was small but clean. Mrs. McNamara sliced potatoes into a pot of water at the kitchen table while Elmer and his best friend, Theo, hovered over a checkerboard set up on a woven throw rug near the vacant fireplace.

After Emma-Lee greeted Punkin's mother, she was served a glass of fresh-squeezed lemonade by Punkin, and formally escorted to the tweed settee in the living room. In the corner, a longhaired, black and white cat draped itself across a rung of the ladder ascending to the loft where the family slept. The cat lifted one sleepy eyelid at the intrusion and uttered a faint, "mew" before resuming its nap.

"Pretty cat," Emma-Lee said as she sat beside Punkin on the couch.

"Didja' know that there's a talking cat?" Elmer asked in a bored tone, lifting his shaggy, blond head from the checkerboard to glance at Emma-Lee for the first time since her arrival.

"What?" Emma-lee looked from Elmer to the cat and then to Punkin.

"Yep, that cat shorely can talk," Punkin said, nodding seriously.

"Cats can't talk," Emma-Lee said.

"This 'un can," Elmer said, his voice pepping up a decibel. "I ain't funnin' ya'! Tell her, Punkin."

Punkin walked over to the cat and scratched the top of its silky head. A purr filled the air so loud and thick Emma-Lee thought she could feel the couch cushions vibrating.

"About a year ago, Lady here took up company with a huge tomcat that started hanging around our property. Tom grew up with a pack of young pa'nters, and by the looks of him, I 'spect he was part pa'nter himself. Picked up a few of their habits, I reckon'; he was as rough and wild as they come."

"The cat was raised by panthers? Why didn't they eat him?" Emma-Lee asked.

"What are ya', stupid or somethin'?" Theo piped up.

"Stop it, Theo. She's not from around here," Punkin said. "They're not cannibals, Emma-Lee. After all, lions and tigers and pa'nters are just big cats."

"Oh," Emma-Lee said in a small voice.

"Anyways, Tom didn't take to people much, but he and Lady got along real fine. One day, four of the cutest, tiniest kittens you ever did see appeared on our back porch, and Ma spread a clean gunny sack in a box and put Lady and her young'uns in it. When he wasn't off hunting, Tom stayed out back in a clump of palmetto and watched them." She paused and smiled to herself, as if she was enjoying the story as much as Emma-Lee.

"Sometimes he'd bring a dead field rat or a lizard up and lay it on the porch. When it was quiet, and he thought we weren't here, he'd sneak up to play with the kittens. He and Lady would make this strange crooning noise to each other, like human babies bawling. It was a sound they never made at any other time...just like they were talking. But if Tom saw one of us, he'd light out of there. Right skittish, he was, never let nobody come near him.

"One morning, the kittens were playing on the porch, and the neighbor's Siamese cat ran out of the brush and grabbed the head of one of the babies in its mouth. Ma saw it and threw Elmer's boot through the open door and whacked that Siamese upside the head. Durn cat dropped the kitten and took off through the woods toward the neighbor's house."

Elmer jumped to his feet, launching into the tale as if he'd been telling it all along. "When that ole' tomcat showed up an hour later, Ma was still trying to set the kitten's broken jaw. You never heard such carrying on as when Lady told Tom all about the attack out back. Tom was mad as a swatted hornet, and they talked back and forth for a good ten minutes before Tom disappeared into the woods.

"Later that afternoon, Mrs. Doogan came over to see Ma and wanted to know what in tarnation was wrong with that ole' tomcat. She said he'd marched right up on their porch and without any reason, jumped their Siamese and broke its neck with one bite of his big jaws."

"Naw, he didn't!" Theo said.

Debora M. Coty

"He surefire did!" Elmer replied, punching Theo in the arm. "Ask Ma!"

"Yes, Theodore, that's a true story," Mrs. McNamara said from the stove where she was lighting a fire under the pot of potatoes. "Goes to show you can't be too careful when you treat animals unkindly; you never know when one of their friends might be a revengeful alligator or an irritated pa'nter inclined to pay you a visit one dark night." A mischievous smile creased her flushed face as she opened the oven door and bent to take out two crusty loaves of bread.

The warm, yeasty smell of fresh bread wafted into the living room, and four young stomachs took to growling.

"Oh, Ma, can't we have just one Johnny cake? We're gonna starve to death before supper's ready," Elmer whined.

"What's a Johnny cake?" Emma-Lee whispered to Punkin.

"You don't have Johnny cakes in Miami?" Punkin shook her head in amazement. "It's a slice of rat cheese on a hunk of shortbread."

"Rat cheese?"

"Yeah—you know, the kind with holes all through it. You never tasted anything so good when you're hungry! Ma gives us Johnny cakes sometimes when Pa is late getting home for dinner."

Mrs. McNamara placed the bread on the table and turned to the children with her hands on her hips. "I told you, supper will be ready within the hour. Why don't you kids go outside and give a poor woman a little peace? Stay in the yard, you hear? I'll holler when it's time."

The girls went out first and sat on the steps of the back porch. Elmer and Theo loped outside a few minutes later. Elmer was trying to hide something under his shirt—a long, thin object wrapped in a croaker sack. Theo ran interference between Elmer and the house, blocking the view of anyone who happened to be observing from the kitchen window. The boys made for the woods, looking over their shoulders every few steps until they cleared the yard.

"I know where they're going," Punkin whispered, jumping to her feet. "Come on, Emma-Lee. We're going, too!"

Emma-Lee hesitated, remembering Mrs. McNamara's instructions to stay in the yard. She watched Punkin race after the boys and quickly dismissed her reservations. Soon she was enjoying the excitement of ducking behind trees with Punkin as they secretly followed the boys.

The chase took them down a faint trail into the thickest part of the woods where sunlight was muted by a heavy canopy of tree branches. It was like a jungle, where tendrils of winding dense vines and palmetto roots had never been cleared.

"Are we allowed out here?" Emma-Lee whispered as she and Punkin crouched behind the wide trunk of a Caribbean Pine, taking turns peeking at the boys as they huddled together in a Ficus hammock. A shotgun muzzle glinted in a filtered sunbeam.

"Not really. But the boys would never let us go hunting with them if we didn't sneak along. Ma would skin all of us if she knew we were this far off the road."

"Hunting?" Emma-Lee's voice squeaked. "What are they hunting?"

At that moment, a fierce rattling noise erupted from the scrub palmetto at Punkin's feet. Chills shot up Emma-Lee's spine as horror seized her. That same terrible sound had invaded her dreams and turned them into sweat-soaked nightmares since her rattlesnake encounter in the woods with the captain.

"Don't move, Punkin. It's a rattler!" Emma-Lee's voice sounded strangled.

The girls froze and slowly looked down. The coiled snake lay half hidden by Palmetto fronds, its triangular head covered with diamond shapes rising high above the foliage at one end of a large green leaf and bone-colored rattles visible at the other end.

It's not nearly as big as the one that almost bit me at the cove, Emma-Lee thought as she stared at the two-foot snake. *Must be a baby.* Punkin paled to a deathly white, and Emma-Lee felt sweat break out on her forehead. Her clipped words came in short spurts, edged with fear.

"Stay put, Punkin. The boys are near. Elmer's got a rifle. Don't—"

Suddenly, from the same clump of bushes, another set of rattles and then another joined the horrific chorus, the three dissonant pitches creating a terrifying, heart-stopping disharmony. Emma-Lee's sweat turned cold as her voice rose with each syllable, "Oh, no, we've stumbled into a rattler nest..."

Punkin screamed and started to run. In a flash of movement, the first snake struck like a bolt of colored lightning, sinking its razor-sharp, venomous fangs into the soft flesh just behind her ankle. Punkin crashed into her friend, knocking Emma-Lee to the ground in her furious effort to escape.

Both girls shrieked hysterically as they crawled and clawed to their feet, fighting clinging vines and thorny branches that ripped at their skin and threatened to hold them captive. Grasping each other for support, they fled until collapsing in a small clearing twenty yards away.

Elmer and Theo heard the commotion and flew through the dense foliage to find Emma-Lee curled in a tight ball beside her friend. Punkin was writhing on the ground, clutching her right ankle and half moaning, half whimpering, "Ooh, my foot is burning. It's on fire! Somebody help me, please!"

Theo's adolescent voice cracked in the quiet of the forest, "Lord 'a mercy, she's snake bit!"

Chapter Fourteen

"What do we do?" Emma-Lee heard Theo's voice as if from a great distance. She breathed hard as she hid her face in her hands.

"My pa said the first thing is to stop the poison from spreading." Elmer dropped his rifle and pulled up his shirt. "Dang, I forgot my belt this morning. Give me yours, Theo, and be quick about it!"

Emma-Lee slowly sat up, watching as Elmer clinched Theo's belt six inches above his sister's ankle, her foot already swollen to the size of a mango. Emma-Lee and Theo gawked at the drops of crimson blood oozing from the two fang holes in Punkin's ankle.

Elmer looked around frantically. "I wish we had a knife. I could cut open the bite and try to suck out the poison."

"What? Then *you'd* die!" Theo said, slapping his hands to both sides of his dirt-streaked face.

"You don't swallow it, knot head; you spit it out," Elmer said, kneeling beside his sister.

"Elmer, maybe you should try to suck it out even though you don't have a knife," Emma-Lee said. "If you don't, she could die, right?"

They all stared at Punkin, who was hugging her knees to her chest and rocking back and forth on the ground, her face wet with tears. Elmer blinked, thinking hard.

"Okay, I'll try. But then we've got to get her back to the house as fast as we can to get whisky and some onion poultices to draw out the poison. Ain't no doctor on the island, and if we wait for one to get here from the mainland, it'll be too late." He looked from Theo to Emma-Lee. "Theo and I can carry her back but you've gotta run ahead and tell Ma to get a flask of whisky from the Doogan's and start slicing up that bag of onions in the barn."

"Me? I can't go back by myself—I don't know the way!"

"Well, there ain't nobody else. I need Theo to help me carry Punkin. You're too little."

Punkin's breathing was growing shallower by the minute. Her rocking was slowing. Her eyelids fluttered shut.

She'll die if I don't warn her mother to get everything ready, Emma-Lee thought, swiping at the warm tears dropping off her chin. *But I'm scared. What if a snake bites me on the way? What if panthers—pa'nters—jump out of the bushes and tear me to pieces?*

"I can't!" Emma-Lee cried.

"Yes, you can! Now stop bawling and start running. Don't think about anything else but saving Punkin. Head east, away from the setting sun and don't stop till you've reached our yard." Elmer's voice wavered and tears flooded his eyes. "You've gotta be brave. We all do, or she won't make it. Now *git*!"

Emma-Lee ran until her lungs felt as if they'd explode. She broke through the jungle of twisted roots and tangled vines, sobbing and praying aloud in short, scattered bursts. "I've got to be brave...but I'm not...Papa God, you are...can you make me brave, too?"

Emma-Lee's foot caught on a raised oak root, and she sprawled head first into the dirt. She lay there winded, but her mind raced on. *Captain Stone said being brave is facing something scary and doing what needs to be done anyway.* She struggled to her feet. *Okay, Papa God, I know you're here with me. Make me brave for Punkin and show me the way.*

Debora M. Coty

Caked dirt and decaying leaves covered her dress and clumped on her dirty, tear-streaked face. Emma-Lee wiped the mud from her stinging eyes. She blinked at the orange sun peeking through tree trunks as it hung low in the western sky. It would be dark soon. Elmer's words came back to her: "Head east, away from the setting sun."

She took a deep breath and bolted in the opposite direction of the sunset.

Flying past a stand of coconut palms, she leaped over dozens of brown coconuts littering the ground. Nothing looked familiar here. She sprinted in spurts, looking in vain for the trail they'd taken into the woods.

I'm lost, Papa God—please, please help me! She plowed through a thicket into a small clearing and hunched over, the stitch in her side stabbing with pain and her body bruised and aching. Leaning on the trunk of an oak tree to catch her breath, she felt...something strange. Like—she was not alone.

Don't be silly. You're all by yourself in the middle of the forest. Her chest heaved great, drawing breaths. Try as she might, she could not shake the feeling someone was watching her. She slowly straightened, muddy sweat dripping off her filthy clothes. Looking around, her breath froze in her throat. What she saw made her heart jump like a bullfrog.

Shining like tiny lanterns from the shadowy underbrush, two unblinking yellow-green eyes stared at her.

Oh, no, whatever it is, it's big. Is it a pa'nter? I can't run away from a pa'nter! I've got to get help for Punkin. What do I do now, Papa God?

As if in answer to her question, the bushes rustled and parted. A large, furry creature emerged. Four tawny paws tread lightly, almost delicately on the dirt in the direction of the helpless girl.

What is it? Emma-Lee wondered. *It's either a young pa'nter or the biggest cat I've ever seen. Is it coming after me?*

The tawny feline glided over the terrain as if on a mission, its taut muscles rippling beneath golden fur, ears erect. The little girl nearly fell as the enormous cat rubbed against her legs, knocking her off balance. A strange, mournful sound emanated from the fanged mouth as the animal boldly looked up into her eyes.

Suddenly, Emma-Lee realized who it was. "Tom, is that you? I thought you didn't like people." The cat circled Emma-Lee once, then twice, all the time crooning his odd, melodic cry. After the third time around, he veered off into the woods to the east, casting his slanted eyes back over his shoulder at the confused girl. The volume of his eerie yowl rose until it echoed through the trees.

"Are you trying to tell me something?" Emma-Lee shook her head. The sinewy cat darted ahead three yards before turning back to watch her response. "You want me to follow you? But where are you taking me? I need to go to the McNamara's cabin, and there's no time to waste."

Emma-Lee considered her choices. She could either wander around in the woods, lost, while her friend was dying, or believe that God sent this unlikely messenger to lead her to help.

She didn't hesitate another moment. "Okay Tom, I'm coming."

Emma-Lee followed the cat as he wound through the forest, his strong legs pumping as fast as the child behind him could run. Suddenly, the woods thinned out, and they were on the grassy, western bank of the Banana River. Tom began sprinting north, gaining a large lead on Emma-Lee, but she

Debora M. Coty

could see where he was heading. The McNamara cabin was visible in the distance now, beyond Tom's golden streak of fur in the tall, waving grass. And then he disappeared into the woods.

The spent girl stumbled up the cabin steps to the back door, too winded to shout. Even as she collapsed on the porch, she dug deep inside for the last bit of strength she had to pound on the door with her small fists. Mrs. McNamara was there in an instant, concern lining her face.

"Gracious, child, whatever is wrong? I've been calling you children for fifteen minutes. Where are the others?"

"Snake bite...rattler," Emma-Lee croaked. "...Punkin..." She gasped for air. "...Boys carry her...get onions, whisky...ready."

"Merciful heavens—Wilber!" Mrs. McNamara yelled into the house through the open back door. "Come quick! Punkin's been rattler bit."

Mr. McNamara ran onto the porch, one shoe in his hand and brown suspenders hanging loosely at his sides.

"Wilber, run to the Doogan's for a bottle of whisky! I'll start chopping up onions. They have to be beaten up real fine to make a poultice for snake poison. The boys are bringing her home. We need to be ready when they get here."

Mr. McNamara nodded and rushed back into the house. Emma-Lee was still sitting beside the door trying to catch her breath when he flew out again, heading for the neighbor's a quarter mile away.

Mrs. McNamara was already lugging a big burlap sack of onions down the path from the barn. She dragged it up the steps, propped it beside the door, loaded her arms with onions and began peeling, dicing, and pulverizing them with a wooden mallet at the kitchen table.

Five minutes later, Elmer and Theo staggered into the yard, carrying an unconscious Punkin between them.

Under Mrs. McNamara's direction, the boys laid Punkin on the settee, which she'd covered with a cotton sheet. Punkin's foot was now grotesquely swollen, nearly the size of a saucepan, and had turned a dark, dusky color. Red streaks were beginning to creep from Theo's clinched belt up her leg. Punkin's mother packed the wound with the onion poultice, tears streaming from her eyes. Emma-Lee couldn't tell if she was crying because of the strong, stinging onions or because her only daughter straddled the thin line between life and death.

"Emma-Lee, can you please bring as many onions as you can carry into the kitchen? The bag is on the porch. We'll have to change this poultice every half hour." Mrs. McNamara wiped her daughter's ashen face with a damp cloth. Punkin stirred and cried out, "No, Elmer, don't spill the orange juice! Don't you know how long it took to squeeze all those oranges?"

Emma-Lee's mouth dropped open in surprise.

"She's delirious, out of her head," Mrs. McNamara said, more to herself than to Emma-Lee. "She doesn't know what she's saying. Probably won't get better until Wilber gets back and can get that poison out of there." She leaned down and kissed Punkin's clammy forehead. "You'll be fine, my baby. Everything's going to be all right." The words, meant to comfort and encourage, instead rang of doubt and anguish.

As Emma-Lee turned to leave the room, she saw fresh tears that had nothing to do with raw onions spring to Mrs. McNamara's eyes.

Chapter Fifteen

Emma-Lee lay in bed that night, shaking in spite of the warmth of her blanket. She relived the disturbing events of the afternoon over and over in her mind. Punkin had remained delirious, crying out nonsensical words as her unseeing eyes stared into space and her arms flailed against invisible foes. Her leg continued to swell and distort to incredible proportions although her parents worked feverishly on the snakebite. Supper sat cold and forgotten on the table.

Mr. Doogan had brought over another jug of homemade whisky and a sack of onions. Without a word, he began peeling and chopping onions in the kitchen. The pungent odor permeated the house, but no one noticed.

The children stood against the back wall watching helplessly. Fear and uncertainty hung in the air like mist after a hot summer rain shower. Just before nightfall, Theo had walked her home. Aunt Augusta insisted on sending Albert, the dockhand, for Dr. Hartman in Eau Gallie, regardless of the hour.

Unanswerable questions paraded through the mind of the tortured girl tossing in her bed. *What if Punkin dies? Could I have done something to keep it from happening? Why did I go along when I knew it was wrong to leave the yard? Punkin would've stayed if I'd stayed. It could have been me standing by that rattler nest instead of her. Why, Papa God, why?*

Emma-Lee squeezed Cap until her knuckles were white and hid her face in the stuffed bear's soft belly as she sobbed. Aunt Augusta heard her niece crying from her own tousled bed in the next room and padded in to stand beside Emma-Lee's bed, unsure of how to comfort her. In the end, she did what she knew best—she counseled with the objective logic of the schoolteacher.

"We've done all we can, child. Crying about it will not help. Dr. Hartman will come as soon as he can and Elizabeth—Punkin—is in good hands. Her father is an experienced woodsman, and her mother is quite capable of handling emergencies."

Emma-Lee looked up at her aunt with red, swollen eyes. The damp curls around her face stuck to her flushed cheeks. "I know, Aunt Augusta, but my insides still hurt. Punkin's the special friend that Papa God sent me when I prayed for one. Why would He let something terrible like this happen to her?"

Aunt Augusta adjusted and readjusted her robe. She shifted her weight from one foot to the other while concentrating on the shaft of moonlight angling through the tiny window above Emma-Lee's bed. She began to speak, but the first word trailed off before its completion. It was difficult for Augusta Lemstarch to admit she did not know the answer.

"Do you believe God hears us when we pray, Aunt Augusta?"

"Well, I used to." Aunt Augusta stepped toward the foot of the bed, her face obscured by the darkness. "After my parents—your grandparents—died in the fire, I stopped having much to do with God because it seemed evident He had nothing to do with me."

Her angular shoulders slumped, and the authoritative edge in her voice faded. She suddenly seemed so soft, so vulnerable.

"But since meeting Captain Stone, I've not been so sure of that. At the cove, when the captain was reading about Jonah running away from God, I couldn't help but consider myself. I think that's exactly what I've been doing. Just as Jonah couldn't escape God, even in the bottom of the ocean, I haven't escaped Him by hiding on a remote island all these years."

She seemed to have forgotten Emma-Lee was in the room. Her voice was wistful, full of longing. "I'm just afraid He hasn't heard my voice in so long that if I call out, He won't hear me now."

Emma-Lee pulled her blanket aside and sat on the edge of the bed. "I know Papa God heard me when I was lost and scared in the woods today. I prayed for help, and all of a sudden, Tomcat came out of the bushes and led me straight to Punkin's mother. Afterwards, I told Elmer about it, and he said there was no way that wild cat would ever come near a human like that. But he did, Aunt Augusta. He did because Papa God sent him to help me."

"Why do you insist on calling Him 'Papa God,' Emma-Lee?"

"Because Pap said he's my father in heaven—like my father in Miami, only better because Papa God is with me all the time and is taking care of me everywhere I go."

Aunt Augusta sank down on the bed beside her niece. "Sometimes, people misinterpret coincidences as God's handiwork—"

"No, ma'am," Emma-Lee interrupted. "I *know* it was Papa God's doing. He was answering my prayer."

Aunt Augusta sighed. "I'm not foolish enough to argue about matters of which I know nothing. I can't say whether God does or does not answer prayer. But I do know He seems to be extraordinarily real to some people. It's like they have a relationship with Him the rest of us don't. Cornelius calls it

God's grace." She shook her head thoughtfully, an element of awe coloring her tone. "Grace is not a concept with which I have been personally familiar. Then I broke my arm and the Stones—perfect strangers—took us in."

"What is *grace*, Aunt Augusta?"

"Grace is unmerited favor, or in terms you'd understand, getting better than you deserve. It's a step beyond justice, which is getting exactly what you deserve, good or bad."

"I don't understand."

"Well, say a child steals a peppermint stick from the mercantile. Justice dictates that the child be punished for her sin with a sound spanking; she must make a public apology to the merchant and pay for the candy. I understand that way of thinking. It's the way I've always lived my life—a fair and equitable system. No surprises. Good behavior brings favor; bad behavior brings punishment."

"So where does grace come in?"

"Say the merchant realizes the child was hungry because her parents could not afford to feed her. Acting in grace, he not only forgives the child for taking the candy but gives her bread and milk as well. She should rightfully be punished for her actions, but instead he gives her better than she deserves."

The two sat side by side in the small moonlit room, each deep in her own thoughts.

"What I don't see, though," said Emma-Lee in the quiet moment "is why Papa God answers some prayers, and others He doesn't. He heard me today, but I've been praying for my family to be together again for months now and..." Her words drifted off as she realized her confession might hurt Aunt Augusta's feelings.

Emma-Lee reached out soft fingers and lightly stroked her aunt's careworn hand. "I'm sorry. I know how much you've done for me, and I love this island, really I do. It's just that I never stop wanting to be with my own family."

"I know." Aunt Augusta's voice was barely above a whisper. "It's been nineteen years since the fire, and I've never stopped wanting to be with my family, either." Their eyes, both brimming with tears, met in mutual understanding through the caress of the night's gentle darkness.

* * * *

The next week seemed to move in slow motion for Emma-Lee. Reports of Punkin's progress varied from day to day. On Tuesday morning, Elmer announced to the class that Punkin's swelling was down, and she'd recognized her mother, but by Wednesday, she was rolling in feverish delirium again, her foot as purple and round as a ripe egg plant.

Dr. Hartman tried unsuccessfully to convince Punkin's parents to admit her to the hospital in Eau Gallie. When they insisted on keeping her home where they tirelessly cared for their daughter, he and Louisa made daily house calls to the island, the doctor bringing medicine and Louisa providing nutritious meals to accompany the piles of cornbread, cakes, and pies provided by caring neighbors.

Emma-Lee went through the motions of school like she was living in a dream. Nothing felt *real*; she worked her arithmetic figures, answered geography questions, ate lunch with Ruthie Ann and Myrtle, and even competed in a spelling bee, but her heart wasn't in it.

Her heart hovered prayerfully beside the sweaty, thrashing figure of her best friend.

Word spread quickly of Punkin's plight, and the atmosphere of the island became one of solemn waiting. Afternoons at the Town Square market were as busy as ever but a muted aura hung over the inhabitants. Voices were lowered, children were hushed, barking dogs quickly silenced. Even the symphony of squirrel chatter and birdcalls that provided the ever present background music for island life seemed strangely stifled—as if the island itself was offering respect for one of its own, battling for her life.

Even Elsie and Leona, who had reluctantly returned to the Tropic school after Thanksgiving at the insistence of the school board, seemed different. Their attitudes had become subdued toward Emma-Lee. Instead of their usual snide remarks and malicious pokes about "Little Red Mop Top," they ignored her altogether, spending their noon and water breaks giggling with Amy Freeman about their new target for ridicule, poor Myrtle Dinkleberry.

"Myrtle the turtle finds schoolwork a hurdle," they chanted in singsong verse when the teacher was out of earshot.

"What's the matter, Muddle, left your brains in a puddle?"

It was common knowledge that Myrtle struggled to keep up with even the most elementary lessons and was constantly behind in her seatwork. Emma-Lee felt sorry for Myrtle but was afraid to speak up on her behalf for fear of drawing the scathing attention of the three girls back to herself. Deep down inside, Emma-Lee knew Punkin wouldn't have kept her tongue if she were there. Punkin stood up for her friends.

Emma-Lee's cowardice made her hang her head in shame. Why couldn't she be brave now like she'd been in the woods? In some ways, bullies were scarier than rattlesnakes. *Some lessons just don't stick, Papa God.*

The days dragged by with the entire village of Tropic seeming to hold its breath.

Friday morning, Aunt Augusta rang the school bell, and the children took their seats, more solemn than usual. All eyes turned to look at the empty chairs of Punkin and Elmer. It had been nine long days since the attack.

Aunt Augusta had just called the first name for roll call when Elmer burst in, panting and sweaty. He leaned on the door, gasping for breath.

"It...it finally...happened."

Emma-Lee's breath caught in her throat.

"What happened, Elmer?" Aunt Augusta asked, rising from her chair.

"Punkin...her fever broke. She...she just woke up this morning...all regular like...'cept her eyes were bloodshot and all...redder than fresh-killed coon guts."

"She woke up?" Emma-Lee cried. "She's going to be all right?"

"Yup—she just sat up like nothing...like nothing happened." Elmer took two quick breaths. "Ma and her watched the sunrise through the kitchen window...Pa fed her bread sopped in beef broth. First thing she's 'et in three days."

The classroom erupted into cheers. Emma-Lee felt Aunt Augusta's gray eyes upon her as relief and thankfulness washed over her. It was as if a fallen tree had been lifted off her chest and she could breathe again.

"Thank you, Papa God. Thank you," Emma-Lee whispered.

At the noon hour, Aunt Augusta approached Emma-Lee, Myrtle, and Ruthie Ann as they opened their lunch pails in the shade of the banyan tree bordering the schoolyard. Tom-Tom,

Louis, Cleotis, and Sticks shimmied up the thick roots hanging like ropes from the enormous spreading branches. Swinging on the vine-like roots and playing "Monkeys in the Jungle" was their favorite game. The girls paid the noisy chimps overhead little attention as they ate.

"Emma-Lee, may I have a word with you, please?" Aunt Augusta asked in her authoritative voice. She led her niece away from the other children to a quiet corner beneath the eaves of the schoolhouse.

"First, I wanted to tell you how happy I was to hear about Elizabeth's—Punkin's—recovery. I know you've been continuously praying for her. In fact, I've been praying too, for the first time in years." A hint of a smile tugged at the corners of her thin lips. Emma-Lee was surprised. Aunt Augusta rarely smiled at school.

"Anyway, I'm very pleased she's taken a turn for the better, and I know how much it means to you."

"Thank you, Aunt Augusta."

"And I do have some other news to share with you. I've actually known for several days but didn't think it was the appropriate time to tell you. But now, with Elizabeth's turnaround this morning, perhaps the time has arrived."

Emma-Lee stood still, her breath barely moving in and out. Dared she hope?

"We will be traveling to Miami for your birthday and the Christmas holiday. Your mother is quite anxious to see you, and I think it is important for you to be reunited."

As her words sank in, Emma-Lee gasped with delight and flung her arms around the startled woman's waist. "Oh, thank you, Aunt Augusta. This is the best day ever! Two of my prayers have been answered."

"I thought that would make you happy." Aunt Augusta spoke quietly as she awkwardly patted Emma-Lee's head. "You've been through quite a lot for a little girl. Everyone needs a mother, regardless of age or circumstance."

Emma-Lee stepped back, smiling broadly at her aunt, cheeks rosy with color and a fresh lightness in her spirit. The plaintive cry of seagulls flying overhead pierced the humid island stillness, bringing back a feeling of normalcy like a familiar, gentle breeze.

Aunt Augusta's voice resumed its no-nonsense quality. "You do understand our time in Miami is limited, don't you? We will depart from the Eau Gallie station on the twentieth and must return by the twenty-seventh to prepare for the beginning of the new school term on January second."

"Yes ma'am, I understand." Emma-Lee nodded, her eyes twinkling and a radiant smile lighting up the shadows of the darkest corner of the schoolyard. "But those seven days will be the happiest week of my life. I just know it!"

Chapter Sixteen

Papa and Sarah met them at the train station in Miami five days before Christmas. The late afternoon sun backlit Papa's tall hat and pin-striped suit as he approached, casting a long shadow and making him appear even more formidable than usual.

He politely shook Aunt Augusta's hand and stiffly returned Emma-Lee's hug, then busied himself seeing that the luggage was loaded and strapped down on the rack of his gleaming carriage, a stunning burgundy barouche with black trim. He paused only to rub a speck of dust off the shiny door with his white handkerchief. Emma-Lee knew appearances were of utmost importance to him.

Sarah threw her arms around Emma-Lee and hugged her so hard, the little girl felt as if her lungs had been flattened like pancakes and would never refill with air again. The feathery plumes on Sarah's pink hat tickled Emma-Lee's nose. For a moment, Emma-Lee wished she could wear pink but knew her red hair prohibited it. Pink always looked so pretty with Sarah's blond hair and fair complexion.

"Oh, my darling Emmie, I'm so happy to see you. I've missed you more than I could ever tell you."

"I was so full of missing you, Sarah, some nights I thought I'd explode."

"I helped Mama make all your favorite foods for supper."

"Chicken and dumplings?"

"Yes, and sourdough pecan rolls and butterscotch pudding."

"Really? Butterscotch pudding? Ooh, I haven't had any in so long!"

"I can make butterscotch pudding," Aunt Augusta addressed Emma-Lee in a tone of mild annoyance. "You never told me you liked butterscotch pudding."

"All right, enough chit-chat," Papa broke in. "Get in the carriage now, girls. Your mother will have supper waiting." Papa climbed up on the driver's seat and took the reins.

Sam, the family's faithful gelding, snorted and shook his chestnut head as Emma-Lee passed by. She stopped to stroke his long, silky jaw. "I missed you too, Sam."

"Emma-Lee," her father's stern voice commanded. "I told you to get in the carriage. You've only been home two minutes and already you are disobeying."

"I'm sorry, Papa. It won't happen again, I promise." She climbed wordlessly into the barouche and settled herself snugly beside Sarah.

Aunt Augusta sat on the seat facing them and removed her sensible black hat adorned with its pointy black feather. She placed it carefully on the seat beside her and withdrew a book from the traveling basket at her feet. "I'd just like to finish this chapter on the migration patterns of dolphins while there's still light," she told the girls as she perched her reading glasses atop her nose and leaned her book toward the window to catch the last rays of sunshine.

The familiar smell of leather polish and the jostling of the carriage as Sam's hooves clip-clopped on the cobblestone road made Emma-Lee feel warm inside. She smiled up at Sarah. Her sister took her hand and gently squeezed it. Emma-Lee noticed Sarah's mouth was smiling but her eyes were not.

"There's something I need to tell you," Sarah whispered, casting a furtive look at Aunt Augusta, who appeared to be engrossed in migrating dolphins. "It's about Mama."

"Mama?" Emma-Lee whispered back. "What about Mama?"

"She...she broke her toe," Sarah's liquid aqua eyes slid down to her little sister's hand clasped in her own. "She tripped over a chair last week and fell." He gaze moved up to Emma-Lee's shining blue eyes. "She's quite bruised—from the fall—but she gets around all right and doesn't like to talk about it. That's why I wanted to tell you now, before you see her and start asking questions."

"Does it hurt?" Emma-Lee asked, concern etched in the furrow on her forehead.

"Not so much. At least not as much as it did. Broken things have a way of healing with time."

Sarah looked over Emma-Lee's shoulder out the window at the passing townscape, as if considering her own words. Barely discernibly, she shuddered. "Anyway, dearest, I think it would be best if you don't say anything about it."

"Did she see a doctor?" Aunt Augusta's harsh voice startled the sisters.

"Oh, I'm sorry if we disturbed you, Aunt Augusta," Sarah said, a blush creeping from the ruffle of her high collared peony blouse to her fashionable, wide-brimmed hat. "We were speaking quietly, so you could read without interruption."

"Yes, that was thoughtful of you," Aunt Augusta said as she removed her glasses, the creases around her mouth deepening as her lips tightened into a thin line. "But my hearing is quite astute, and I did overhear your whispered conversation. Did Fenton call the doctor to see to Ellie's wounds after the accident?"

Sarah drew in a deep breath and sat up straight, her face tensing into a hard look Emma-Lee had not seen before. It almost looked like a mask. "I...I'm not sure."

"What do you mean you're not sure?" Aunt Augusta leaned forward, her eyes now slits of dark light. "Did the doctor come, or did he not?"

Sarah stared at her shoes. She shifted in her seat. Tiny beads of sweat broke out on the bridge of her nose. She remained silent despite Aunt Augusta's obvious expectation of an answer.

Emma-Lee stared at her sister, confused by the transformation that had occurred in the months since she had seen her last. Sarah would have never before defied Aunt Augusta or any adult who had asked her a direct question. *Sarah has better manners than anyone*, Emma-Lee thought. *Why won't she answer? And why does she look like she's about to cry?*

"It's because he didn't want the doctor to figure it out, isn't it?" Aunt Augusta spoke low and fast. Her fingers tugged a page of her book so severely, it ripped from the binding.

"No...no." Sarah shook her head, her voice small and shaky. She glanced over her shoulder at the thin wall of wood separating the carriage passengers from the driver. "I'm sure he wanted to call the doctor. There must have been some reason why the doctor couldn't come. Papa loves Mama. He loves all of..."

She stopped abruptly. Her glistening eyes silently appealed to Aunt Augusta and then shifted to Emma-Lee beside her, whose puzzled, innocent gaze was trained on the sister she adored.

Aunt Augusta slammed her book closed, the sudden noise causing the sisters to jump in their seats. She thrust the book back into her bag and glared out the window, anger radiating from her like heat from a furnace.

What's wrong? Emma-Lee wondered. *Why is Sarah acting strangely? And why is Aunt Augusta so mad?*

They rode on in uncomfortable silence for the last ten minutes of the journey to Flagler Street. Just before dusk, the carriage pulled up to the low iron gate in front of the three story Victorian house Emma-Lee had always called home. Although it was December, Mama's bougainvilleas were still blooming in the mild Miami winter, their bright pink flowers intertwined through the black metal fence posts lining the well-kept yard. Mama had always loved her flowers. As long as she could remember, Emma-Lee had enjoyed working with Mama in the yard as she devotedly tended her garden.

Emma-Lee climbed down quickly and waited on the manicured lawn as Sarah and Aunt Augusta descended the carriage steps. The front door burst open, and Mama, holding tightly to the wooden stair railing, hobbled down the three granite steps to the pebble walkway, walking gingerly on her bandaged left foot.

"Mama!" Emma-Lee ran into her mother's arms. "Oh Mama, I've missed you so! I have so much to tell you."

"Oh, my sweet girl, you can't imagine how much I've missed you!" Mama held her close, so close Emma-Lee could feel Mama's ribs through her dress. *I don't remember Mama being this skinny before I left for the island. Why, her arms are as thin as river reeds.*

"Haven't you been well, Mama?" Emma-Lee asked, backing away from her mother's embrace to look into her face.

She was shocked to see a large purple bruise covering most of her left cheek, jaw, and neck. The puckered skin surrounding an inch-long scab above her left eyebrow looked angry and swollen.

"Why, of course I'm well." Mama's eyes flickered toward the carriage where Papa was removing the luggage. "I've just been a little under the weather since I fell and hurt myself, that's all. I can be frightfully clumsy sometimes. It's nothing to bother about, darling." She turned to her older sister as she approached.

"Augusta, how wonderful to see you! I'm so glad you could make it this year."

The women embraced, displeasure evident on the elder sister's face. "You're hurt badly, Ellie," Aunt Augusta whispered into her sister's ear. "This has gone on long enough."

The hug was cut short by Mama's nervous, clipped laugh, strangely devoid of humor. "Now, Augusta, this isn't the time to discuss such things. A lovely supper is waiting." She called toward the open front door. "Dexter, Archibald—come help carry in the luggage. Michael, I'm sure your father would like you to take care of Sam."

Turning back to Emma-Lee, she knelt and cradled her daughter's face in her hands. "Just wait until you see how much Nannie Mae has grown. She's sitting up now all by herself, and she's looking more like her big sister Emma-Lee every day."

* * * *

Augusta Lemstarch frowned as she stood back and watched her beloved sister struggle up the steps to her home. The boys ran around their mother and down the walkway toward the carriage, barely acknowledging their aunt as they rushed past. Sarah and Emma-Lee, hand in hand, followed their mother, step for step, carefully slowing their pace to match hers.

This is just not right, Augusta thought. *Something must be done before*—

Fenton brushed by her from behind, lightly jostling her with the valise he was carrying. Bounding up the steps, he paused at the threshold and turned, the light from the parlor silhouetting his inflexible form in the gathering darkness. His dark eyes met those of his sister-in-law. Something unspoken passed between them in the twilight, something foreboding and subtle.

"I'll put your things in the guest room, Augusta, so that no one meddles with them. Meddling with one's personal belongings can be a very unpleasant and costly venture, don't you agree? And I know you value your privacy...as we do ours."

He tipped his hat and pivoted, disappearing through the doorway. Fine hairs prickled the back of Aunt Augusta's neck, sending a cold chill down her spine.

* * * *

Emma-Lee spent the first four days at home basking in the warmth of her family's attention. Mama hugged her at least ten times a day, smiling more than Emma-Lee remembered for a long time past. Sarah read her favorite books aloud every night and spent long, delightful hours with her each day.

During the mild, sunny days, the two sisters walked hand in hand down the plank sidewalks of Avenue D and daydreamed in front of the glittering, Christmassy shop windows lining the bustling street. Together they skipped to the corner soda fountain to share a strawberry cream or to Salem's bakery just to smell the hot cross buns as they came from the oven. One afternoon, they even took a steamboat across the Miami River to the Miccosuki Indian village to watch the painted Indians wrestle live alligators.

Two days before Christmas, Mama baked a lemon spice cake with fluffy white icing for Emma-Lee's tenth birthday, and the family sang best wishes to her after supper. Mama presented Emma-Lee with a beautiful new collectors' doll from the family (the kind you look at but don't play with), and Aunt Augusta produced a small cache of gifts from the islanders.

There was a handmade cat finger puppet with tiny wire whiskers from Punkin, a shiny model schooner from Captain Stone, a packet of new pencils from Aunt Augusta, a Jonah picture book from Ma Stone, and Emma-Lee's favorite, a slingshot from Pap, fashioned from a Y-shaped stick and a strip of rubber from an old bicycle tire.

Emma-Lee was surprised and pleased that her brothers didn't pick a single fight with her the entire week. They seemed, in fact, to be making an extra effort toward civility. Michael, the eldest, actually initiated a few conversations about life on Merritt Island when he wasn't busy racing the new red bicycle he'd just received for his thirteenth birthday.

Archibald wasn't home much, preferring to play baseball with other fifth grade boys in the vacant sand lot at the end of the block. But the evening of Emma-Lee's birthday, Archie admired her slingshot and allowed her to take his chair next to the fireplace as he and the other boys listened, mesmerized, at her recount of Punkin's rattlesnake attack and Tomcat, who came to the rescue.

Dexter, two years younger than Emma-Lee but only half a head shorter, gallantly offered to let her fire his popgun during a rousing game of "Soldiers" in the back yard. He even shared his stash of peppermint candies with her.

Only Papa seemed unaware his missing daughter was home at last. On the night of her birthday, he worked late as usual, arriving home just as supper was served. He was quiet throughout the meal and retired to his study immediately after the birthday presents were opened. Emma-Lee knew he would remain there until the rest of the household had gone to bed, as he had every night since her arrival.

As her siblings scattered and Mama and Aunt Augusta cleared the table and washed the dishes, Emma-Lee tiptoed in front of Papa's locked study door. She couldn't walk away. She stood biting her lip, wishing hard it would magically open and Papa would welcome her in to sit on his knee and tell her how much he'd missed her and never wanted her to go away again.

She took a step closer, imagining the feel of Papa's scratchy tweed jacket as she leaned against his chest. She could almost feel his arms around her, the way Punkin's daddy held her, the two of them laughing together over a joke or singing silly, off-key songs at the top of their lungs. She kept wishing so hard that she got on her hands and knees and stretched her fingers as far as she could under the door.

Silence was the haunting reply.

Just after dawn on Christmas Eve, Mama and Aunt Augusta were already in the kitchen kneading bread dough and preparing pecan stuffing for the Christmas goose. As Papa left for the newspaper office at his customary seven o'clock, Sam's protesting whinny awakened Emma-Lee. She hopped out of bed, too excited for sleep to rob her of another precious moment.

Padding downstairs, she heard the comforting sounds of her mother and aunt moving about behind the kitchen door, which was slightly ajar. It hadn't closed since Archibald rammed it with a stalk of sugar cane last summer when he was pretending to joust with Sir Lancelot. Papa hadn't yet found time to repair the splintered door jam.

Emma-Lee reached for the heavy wooden door and found it unyielding to her small hand. As she braced her night-gowned body against the door to push, she was stopped cold by Aunt Augusta's strange words, slightly muffled but quite recognizable through the crack in the door.

"Come now, Ellie, you're thirty-three years old. How long do you think your body can take this abuse?"

"Please, Augusta, I don't want to talk about it."

"Why not? The children haven't risen yet, and *he* isn't here. I'm not your enemy. I'm your sister. And I appear to be the only one who cares enough to figure it out."

"There's nothing to figure out. You're letting your imagination run away with you. It was a clumsy accident, that's all."

"A clumsy accident? Like the one last spring when your shoulder was so bruised you could scarcely raise your arm or the previous fall when you didn't leave the house for two weeks because of your blackened eye?"

"How did you know about that?"

"Emma-Lee saw it all, although she's too young to put two and two together. I've questioned her—discreetly, mind you—during our walks to and from school, and she has related those and other incidents that suggest to me you are in danger."

"Don't be ridiculous. The only danger I'm in is self-imposed by my two left feet."

"Stop it, Ellie, stop it right now! I was five years old when you were born, and I looked out for you throughout your entire childhood. You were so naively trusting and feather-headed, you were never one to heed warning signs. Mother depended on me to keep an eye on you every day of your life...until the fire..." Aunt Augusta's voice broke.

Not a single familiar cooking sound emitted from the kitchen. The impending silence was full of tension, like a pacing dog with hackles raised in anticipation of a fight. Emma-Lee felt her jaws clench and stomach tighten.

Mama's voice was beseeching, almost pleading. "Please don't fret, Augusta—"

"Of course, I'll fret. I'll fret because you're my only sister, and I love you." Aunt Augusta's voice was thick with emotion. "I'll fret because I see the danger—for you and for Sarah! Yes, I've seen the bruises no matter how well she tries to hide them. It's that monstrous rage inside him, Ellie. He lashes out against helpless women under his control. The boys are safe enough because...well, because they're boys. He spanks them when they're disobedient and then is done with it. But not you. And not Sarah. She's a woman now, too. His anger at the rest of the world is transferred to you and runs rampant."

"Oh, Augusta, I don't know what to do." Mama's voice sounded broken and desperate. "He never touched Sarah until this spring. I can't stop him"—she nearly choked on the words that tumbled out like a flood—"and he won't agree to send her away because she helps with the other children and housework so we can get along without a maid and a cook. He says he doesn't want any outsiders poking their noses in our business."

"For obvious reasons. He would be reported to the police. You were right to insist that Emma-Lee leave the house. It's only a matter of time before—"

At that moment, the stairs creaked behind Emma-Lee, and Dexter's sleepy voice filled the hallway, "Is breakfast ready yet?"

A pregnant silence followed. Soon Emma-Lee heard the thudding of dough against a breadboard and scraping sounds of a spoon against the side of a metal pot.

"Come on in, dear. The oatmeal is nearly finished." Mama's voice sounded a little too cheerful.

Emma-Lee stepped aside as Dexter shoved the sticking door and entered the warm kitchen. The yeasty smell of bread dough, mingled with the pungent odor of garlic and cloves laid out on the table, created a potent aroma. The little girl shrank against the immovable wall of wood at her back and suddenly felt queasy. As she gazed at the beloved bowed form of her mother and contrasting erect figure of her aunt through the opened door, her stomach turned a somersault.

"Good morning, darling," Mama called, catching a glimpse of Emma-Lee over Dexter's shoulder as the hungry boy ambled to the table. She smiled at her middle daughter. "It's a little cool this morning, isn't it? All the better for Christmas, I suppose. Let me pour you a glass of milk. Are you feeling well? You look a bit pale."

"No, ma'am, I mean, yes, ma'am, I'm just...my stomach's upset."

Little puffs of white powder hung in the air, encircling Aunt Augusta like clouds around a volcano as her clenched fists relentlessly pummeled the flour-dusted mound of bread dough on the table in front of her. She looked more like she was beating it up than kneading it.

Abruptly ceasing her pounding, she turned to study Emma-Lee. Her eyebrows formed a straight, dark line like the edge of an approaching thunderstorm on the horizon. Emma-Lee could tell her aunt's shrewd eyes had taken in every detail of her distressed expression.

"Oh, my, are you coming down with something?" Mama asked, limping across the floor to place soft hands on her daughter's forehead and cheek. "There's no fever, thank goodness. Did you eat something contrary to your constitution?"

Emma-Lee squirmed under the scrutiny of the two women.

"Perhaps you should go back to bed for a spell," Aunt Augusta said with a discerning gleam in her eye. "Sometimes the disagreeable becomes more tolerable with time." Emma-Lee had a feeling she wasn't talking about nausea.

"Yes, dear, maybe you should go back to bed," Mama said, obviously missing the hidden meaning of her sister's words. "The other children won't be up for another hour yet. I expect you'll feel much better by then."

But she didn't. Distraught, Emma-Lee returned to her bed only to toss and turn for the next half hour, fluctuating between confusion and heartsickness. Thoughts tumbled inside her head like dice inside a cup.

What did that conversation in the kitchen mean? Could there be more to Mama's accidents than she had let on? Why did Aunt Augusta think Mama and Sarah were in danger? Would Sarah be upset if I try to talk to her about it?

Although she couldn't understand the implications of her aunt's words, Emma-Lee knew the conversation was a closed subject between two adults, and she dare not bring it up or they would know she had been eavesdropping. The consequences would be severe.

Emma-Lee slipped to her knees beside the bed and folded her hands.

"Papa God, Captain Stone says we should turn our burdens over to you. He says your shoulders are a lot stronger than ours and that we should let you carry our burdens for us. So I'm giving this one to you. It's a big one. It's so heavy it crushes my heart. Amen." She curled into a ball on the woven rug beside the bed and slept, exhausted.

Twenty minutes later, Sarah tiptoed in and gently shook her shoulder. "Come to breakfast, dearest."

Emma-Lee awoke with a start, thinking she was in her little closet room on the island. She stretched and watched as Sarah picked up a book from the floor. As she bent over, her skirt slid up the back of her legs, and Emma-Lee glimpsed the greenish-gray of a healing bruise discoloring her calf.

A sudden burning sensation stabbed her chest. "Papa God," she whispered, "this burden won't stay given away; it's already jumped right back into my heart."

Chapter Seventeen

There was no time to speak to Sarah privately during the next twenty-four hours. On Christmas morning, the family gathered around the garlanded cut pine in the parlor that Mama and Aunt Augusta had brought inside and decorated with colorful glass balls while the children slept. A shiny silver star perched slightly askew on top.

Mama and Sarah voiced their pleasure with the cigar boxes-turned-jewelry chests Emma-Lee had pasted with sea shells and colorful rocks she'd picked up on the island, and the boys looked happy enough with the rubber balls Emma-Lee had purchased from the Five and Dime with Sarah's help.

Papa nodded and nearly smiled when he unwrapped the pipe holder his daughter had fashioned from a cypress knot she'd found at the cove. Pap had cut a notch for Papa's pipe and shown her how to sand the edges smooth and polish the wood's rich grain until it shone.

Aunt Augusta seemed surprised when she opened the exquisite, lace-edged bookmark Emma-Lee had picked out especially for her from William Burdine's Mercantile, the best dry goods store in town. Sarah had suggested that a plain, sensible bookmark might suit their aunt better, but Emma-Lee insisted on the prettiest one in stock. Aunt Augusta blinked misty eyes as her young niece placed a soft kiss on her lean cheek. She awkwardly fingered the dainty tatting on the finest bookmark she'd ever owned.

She looked even more surprised, and uncharacteristically at a loss for words, when she unwrapped a small ivory-colored Bible with a note tucked inside, "With highest regards, from

Cornelius." Emma-Lee had smuggled the captain's secret gift from the island by bundling it in her nightgown at the bottom of her valise.

Aunt Augusta stared, at first uncomprehendingly, at the beautiful leather-bound book nestled in folds of tissue paper and long, curled ribbons of green and gold. Suddenly, her face colored an undistinguishable shade of maroon. She quickly rose and left the room, excusing herself with a string of incoherent words.

"Who, may I ask, is Cornelius?" Papa asked when Aunt Augusta had hastily retreated. He removed his round eyeglasses and polished them with his starched handkerchief. The thick black eyebrows that always reminded Emma-Lee of caterpillars arched like hairy fermatas over his dark eyes.

"I've no idea," Mama said incredulously. "I'm quite sure she hasn't mentioned a Cornelius to me."

"Cornelius is Captain Stone," Emma-Lee volunteered cheerfully. "He's the captain of the Verily and takes us back and forth from Eau Gallie to Merritt Island. He's my best grown-up friend. Aunt Augusta likes him, too, I think, but doesn't say so. We spent Thanksgiving with him and Ma Stone and Pap at the cove." Emma-Lee broke into a huge smile. "He's the most beautiful man I've ever met."

Archibald barely stifled a giggle at this astounding news. Papa's pipe fell out of his opened mouth on to his lap. Sarah and Mama looked at each other in amazement.

"Aunt Augusta has a beau?" Michael asked, looking like he'd just swallowed the stovepipe. Archibald and Dexter burst into hoots and peals of laughter.

"Now, boys, don't be impolite. There's nothing wrong with Augusta having a man friend." Mama paused as if trying to digest this tough piece of gristle. "It's just that the idea is a little new and strange to us. I don't think we should bring it up again—unless she does, of course."

"The chances of that are slim to none. My horse is more communicative than that woman," Papa said in a bored tone as he pushed Emma-Lee's pipe holder aside with the discarded gift-wrappings and rose to exit as well.

"Wait, Papa!" Emma-Lee ran to extract her gift from the debris. "Don't forget your pipe holder!" She placed into his big hand the special gift she'd spent hours painstakingly polishing then wrapped her arms around his left leg and hugged with all her might. "Won't you please stay with us a little while longer?"

Papa shifted his weight onto his right leg as the members of his family waited uncomfortably for his answer. It was a well known but never discussed fact that Papa's temper was triggered quickly and was a terrible thing to behold. They all tread lightly to avoid evoking the blast. But it was too late. The atmosphere in the room had gone from warm to frosty in a matter of seconds.

"Certainly not. I have more work to do than a child like you could possibly imagine. Newspapers don't stop running just because it's a holiday, you know." He scowled at the disappointed faces of those who loved him. Instead of encouraging him to reconsider, their crestfallen expressions seemed to provoke him to anger.

"You simply cannot understand, can you? I'm under constant pressure in my job and absolutely cannot fall behind. Old Man Stewart would like nothing better than to dismiss me, and here you're asking me to give him good excuse to do that very thing." His voice heightened, as if each word was a stick of wood stoking a smoldering fire into a blazing inferno.

"I've been here with you two hours already. What more could you ask of me? You're greedy! That's it, the whole lot of you—you're greedy and ungrateful. You wouldn't even have presents if it weren't for me and the endless work I do." His voice was very loud now, and his wife and children were attempting to shrink as small as possible to avoid the poisonous arrows of his words.

Suddenly, without warning, Papa kicked the upholstered ottoman into the end table beside the settee, sending the lamp and crystal flower vase thereupon crashing to the floor. Michael and Dexter, who were sitting on the settee nearest the end table, leapt to their feet. Baby Nannie Mae, who had been sleeping soundly in her pram in the corner, began screaming at the frightening sound of shattering glass.

Papa's voice escalated above the baby's high-pitched shriek. "Keep that child quiet, Elnora! How am I to get any work done with that confounded wailing?"

Mama rushed over to pick up Nannie Mae, but the baby wouldn't be soothed. Papa gripped his new cypress knot pipe holder and threw it like a baseball into the stone fireplace, which fortunately was not lit, but was full of cold ash from the previous day's fire. As the gray ash poofed into the air, he stormed off to his study and slammed the door.

A collective exhale, soft as a sigh, was left in his wake. The release of tension in the body language of everyone in the room clearly reflected relief that the ordeal was over. It could have been much worse.

"Why don't you boys go outside and play and I'll feed the baby in the kitchen so we won't disturb Papa," Mama's voice sounded bone tired although it was only mid-morning. "Sarah and Emma-Lee, would you please clean up in here as best you can?" She looked with a troubled expression at the ruined lamp and half dozen red roses lying in a pool of water atop the shards of shattered vase that had been a treasured wedding gift.

Emma-Lee followed Sarah to the broom closet where they collected the broom, dustpan, and cleaning cloths. They carried them silently into the parlor. Emma-Lee held the dustpan steady while Sarah swept into it tiny slivers of glass.

"Sarah," Emma-Lee began hesitantly, not knowing the best way to bring this up. "Do you think...doesn't Papa break things an awful lot when he gets angry?"

"Yes, I suppose. He's always on edge, and we try very hard not to set him off. But when he does..." She held up a once beautiful rosebud just beginning to open into full bloom. The stem was broken just below the bud, leaving it dangling pathetically by one strand.

"It reminds me of the chickens at the market hanging there with their necks wrung," Emma-Lee said. "I hate to see them; they always make me feel sad."

"Yes, me too. But it's the way of life. There's nothing to be done about it."

"What about Papa? Is there anything to be done about him? I heard Aunt Augusta tell Mama she was in danger. What do you think she meant?"

Sarah stopped sweeping and looked disturbed. She sat on the arm of the settee, holding the broom handle to her chest. "Mama has no choice, Emmie. She can't leave; she has all these children and the house to look after. She has no income except what Papa gives her. Besides, where would she go that he wouldn't find her and drag her back?"

Sarah looked out the window at the cool December breeze rustling the Sago palm fronds. "Then things would be even worse than before. Papa is a highly respected man in this community. Mama can't tell anyone about his violence. No one would believe her anyway; he never indulges his temper except at home."

"What about you, Sarah? Are you in danger, too?"

Sarah stood upright and took a deep breath. A resolute look washed over her delicate features, erasing the fear and doubt reflecting from her eyes and replacing them with a strength born of the will to survive.

"No, dearest. I'll be leaving as soon as I turn fifteen in May and complete the school term the following week. My friend, Eula Montgomery, moved to Jacksonville in July and has written that there are positions for young receptionists in her uncle's manufacturing plant. I can stay with her family at first and work my way up to secretary and eventually earn a suitable wage to lease a room at a boarding house."

"You're leaving home?" Emma-Lee couldn't have been more surprised. "What did Mama and Papa say?"

"Well, I haven't exactly told them yet." She knelt down and clasped her little sister's hands in her own. "You're the only one who knows, Emmie, and you mustn't tell anyone. Do you promise?"

The fact that Sarah would trust her with this most important secret made Emma-Lee feel quite grown up. Her eyes grew large and round as she nodded solemnly, "I promise. I'll not tell a soul."

Sarah gave her a warm hug and a big smile. "I knew I could depend on you. Now let's get this mess cleaned up and go play with our Christmas gifts."

Chapter Eighteen

"Won't you take a break and watch the sunset with me, Emma-Lee?" Aunt Augusta asked, her shawl already wrapped around her shoulders.

"I'd like to," replied the girl bent over her schoolbook, reading by the last rays of sunlight, "but I don't know if I'll be able to finish this chapter and write my Roman history report by bedtime."

"I realize I've set lofty goals for your academic accomplishments," Aunt Augusta said, concern edging her voice, "but you need to take a break now and then. You've been frightfully busy in the two weeks since we returned from Miami and you started fourth grade work."

Emma-Lee stared at her aunt in surprise. She'd never heard her urge anyone to quit studying for *any* reason.

"Come now, the sun is about to go down, and it will be over within fifteen minutes. Surely you can spare that much. I'll extend your bedtime to eight thirty tonight, how about that? Don't forget your wrap; the January night air is quite brisk."

The two climbed onto the rock outcropping just in time for the brilliant sunset over the Indian River. Emma-Lee loved to watch gleaming mullet jump in the briny river, inadvertently attracting the attention of hungry brown pelicans, which would swoop down and plunge into the indigo water headfirst in pursuit of their fish suppers.

Gazing at the last rays of sunlight casting hues of gold, russet, and rose over the shimmering waters always made Emma-Lee feel thankful for this special gift from God. He felt so near during these quiet times of reflection. Her heart felt full to overflowing with God's presence.

"Sometimes I think this island is a little bit of heaven that fell from the sky and landed between two rivers," Emma-Lee mused. "When the angels found it, they said, 'Suppose we leave it that way, for it looks so beautiful there'. So they decorated it all up with palm trees and orange trees and birds and sunshine and heavenly sunsets. I think Papa God comes here at the end of each day to smile."

Aunt Augusta considered her words seriously. "Yes, I believe God *is* near during His resplendent sunsets, enjoying them as much as we do. Perhaps that's why you and I find them wholly awe-inspiring."

They returned to the cabin, fully refreshed. Emma-Lee returned to her studies.

Aunt Augusta peeked over Emma-Lee's shoulder as she worked at the kitchen table by lamplight. "You're already making excellent progress through your grade four books. If you can remain diligent and maintain this pace, you could progress to grade five by May, or possibly even April," she said with a barely discernable smile.

"We've never before had a scholar advance so quickly in the history of the Tropic school." She always stopped short of actually *saying* she was proud of her niece, but Emma-Lee knew she wrote Mama of her scholastic accomplishments, for Mama lavishly praised her progress in her weekly notes on the back of Sarah's letters.

There was a decided difference in Sarah's letters in the new year. It was as if the virgin winds of 1905 blew a renewed freshness of spirit into her, with lovely bits of the old, optimistic, full-of-life Sarah shining through the veneer of her

Debora M. Coty

factual writing. Aunt Augusta commented that Sarah's tone certainly seemed more hopeful and wondered why.

Emma-Lee felt sure that she knew why but honored her promise to keep her sister's secret.

* * * *

The third Wednesday of January, Aunt Augusta escorted Emma-Lee to the McNamara cabin for a brief visit after school, just as she had the previous three Wednesdays of the winter term. Mrs. McNamara graciously served herself and Aunt Augusta tea in her only two delicate china cups in the parlor while Emma-Lee sat with Punkin on the porch, filling her in on all the school scuttlebutt.

"Ruthie Ann is pining away with a secret crush on Theo, who treats her (and all the other girls) like they're lower than cabbage roots. I'm getting pretty tired of hearing how *handsome* Theo is and how *clever* he is, when I've got eyes in my head that tell me the truth. Love must make you blind and stupid."

Punkin nodded and rolled her eyes.

"Cleotis, who Tom-Tom says has always been the fastest in the school, lost an after-school race to Sticks, who struts around like that peacock of Toothless Jack, showing off his tail feathers."

"Shoot fire, I could 'a probably whipped 'em both before my foot got bit."

"Elsie, Leona, and Amy are always teasing poor Myrtle, who's taken to eating her lunch on the front steps within Aunt Augusta's hearing, to escape their nastiness in the school yard. One day she burst into tears when she opened her lunch pail to find a live snail with a tiny slip of paper pasted to its shell labeled, "Myrtle.""

"They didn't!"

"They did! They were watching from behind a tree trunk and laughed like those ugly hyenas in Africa we read about in geography."

"That's plum awful. They've stooped to a new low, even for them."

"Wait, it gets better. In revenge of his sister, Tom-Tom snuck a scrub lizard into the classroom after recess and dropped it down the back of Amy's new Montgomery Ward catalog dress."

Punkin burst into giggles.

"Tom-Tom was so full of the devilment, he whispered to Amy, 'I heared ya' wanted t' meet my new baby gator. Name's Shredder.'"

Punkin laughed so hard her face turned a peculiar shade of purple.

"Amy screamed and jumped all around, knocking over desks and chairs, with pencils and books flying everywhere. It was terrific. She clawed at her dress until the poor tail-less lizard dropped to the floor and ran away. His tail, which had broken off during Amy's craziness, kept squirming and squiggling inside her dress lining long after the lizard was gone. No one would volunteer to stick their hand down there to grab the wiggling thing, so Aunt Augusta finally took Amy to the outhouse, where she peeled off her sweaty dress to get it out."

Punkin had laughed herself onto the floorboards by now, where she finally paused to take a breath. "Good thing those tails grow back, or that poor lizard would curse Amy every time it caught a glimpse of its little round butt!"

The girls erupted in fresh gales of belly laughs until a frowning Mrs. McNamara appeared at the door.

"Punkin, what on earth are you doing on the floor? And what is so funny that I can't hear my guest speaking in the other room? Please get up before you re-injure your foot and try acting like a lady, will you?"

The girls reseated themselves as ladylike as they could under the circumstances, still shaking with suppressed mirth and ever so happy to be together.

* * * *

Punkin returned to school the first week of February, limping on her still-swollen foot and considerably thinner. Elmer pushed her to school every day and to piano lessons on Thursday's in a little cart fashioned from an old wheelbarrow outfitted with a fluffy goose-down comforter and a pillow. Punkin was quite comfortable in her little chariot, holding her head high and smiling to passers-by like a benevolent queen, as her brother toiled away, voluntarily performing penance for his willful disobedience that resulted in her catastrophic meeting with the rattler.

Captain Stone continued to make his Saturday morning package drops at the docks, faithful as the tides. On brisk February mornings, the rising sun in rich, warm tones of ripe papayas would no sooner peek above the tree tops in the east than the Verily would appear as a dot in the distant southern channel of the Indian River.

Emma-Lee would be waiting, quivering in anticipation.

Since Christmas, his surprise packages had expanded in size and composition. Each carefully wrapped package not only contained candies and trinkets for Emma-Lee, but there were also an equal number of gifts and a folded note in a sealed envelope for Aunt Augusta.

As was their new custom, after the dock drop-off, Emma-Lee would skip down the dirt road to the cabin with the mysterious parcel, while Aunt Augusta put the finishing touches on a special breakfast of sorghum waffles and sliced mangoes, the table sparkling with her best china.

The "Captain's Treasure," as Emma-Lee called the surprise package, was placed in the honored spot at the center of the table, where it was eagerly eyed by the two as they ate. After the table was hastily cleared, Aunt Augusta would feign calmness, although her clattering teacup gave away her trembling hands as she watched Emma-Lee cut the knotted twine and tear through the brown paper.

There were always gumdrops or peppermint sticks, and since the captain had learned of Aunt Augusta's fondness for raspberry licorice, he often included a long strand. One Saturday, Emma-Lee laughed merrily as she held one end of the ropy candy over her head and found it was as long as she was tall.

Each week there were thrilling new surprises for Emma-Lee—clay marbles or sometimes real glass cat's-eye marbles; a set of jacks with a bouncy rubber ball; colorful hair ribbons or a tiny carved wooden flute. Once there was even a red toy harmonica.

For Aunt Augusta, there were little books of poetry, a lovely silk handkerchief, a glittery pin with pretty, colorful paste gemstones, or a decorated hair comb. Emma-Lee noticed how much more personal her aunt's gifts from the captain had become since the early days of household items.

Aunt Augusta would admire her gifts with a silent smile, gather them into her arms, and then disappear into her room, the door softly clicking shut behind her. Emma-Lee was more than happy to take her new toys outside to play while her aunt spent the following hour alone with her thoughts—and the captain's letter.

* * * *

On the third Friday of February, Cornelius Stone stood on the deck of the Verily under the churning, overcast skies of the Sebastian harbor. He double-checked the inventory of his new cargo of russet potatoes. Burlap sacks were piled knee-high on the rain-drenched deck of the Verily. High winds gusted around him, billowing his rain slicker into a mushroom and threatening to rip the sheaf of soggy papers out of his hands. Pea-sized bits of hail scattered on the deck like glass pellets spilling from a shattered sky.

"We'd better get these potatoes down into the cargo hold before they get ruined," the captain called. "That'd be a fine kettle of fish if I delivered damaged goods to the likes of Randolph Snodgrass! Julius, where are ya' lad?"

No answer. His mind snapped to attention. *Ah, I forgot—I sent him with the produce merchant to pick up that shipment receipt, and Franklin's on shore leave.* He folded the sodden papers into his pocket. *I'll take as many sacks as I can below deck; Julius should be back soon enough to help me finish.*

Hoisting a bag of potatoes onto each broad shoulder, the burly seaman descended the steps into the musty cargo hold. The hold was narrow and long, extending the full length of the Verily, from bow to stern. The corners of the dank room were cloaked in darkness and smelled of brine and kerosene. An opening in the port side of the stern led to the boiler room where Franklin kept a stock of wood for stoking the fire.

The captain deposited the bulky bags near a half dozen empty wooden barrels lining the stern wall and lit a kerosene lamp hanging from the low ceiling. The barrels weighed a good fifty pounds each, even without the tar or turpentine they usually transported.

He hurried up the slippery steps into the stinging downpour and was soon back with another load of potatoes. Up and down the steps he trudged with the heavy bags until he was exhausted. Collapsing on a large coil of thick rope to catch his breath, the captain wiped a mixture of sweat and rain out of his eyes and leaned on a stout barrel as his chest heaved.

Reckon I'm not as young as I used to be, he thought, willing his lungs to fill with air. *'Tis a good thing we have plenty of room on deck, and we don't have to use the hold much.* The precipitation above deck ebbed to a light trickle of rain as his breathing began to return to normal.

Guess there's no rush to get those last few sacks down now with the hail over and done with. Methinks Julius can haul them down when he gets back. He stood and began peeling his dripping rain slicker. *The foul weather's held him up in town, I'll wager.*

He tugged on the clinging sleeve of his raincoat, and his left arm suddenly swung free, upsetting a stack of empty fruit crates. As the captain knelt on one knee to gather the scattered crates, his eyes lit on a dark object wedged into the shadowy space between two barrels, barely visible in the dim light of the hanging lamp.

"Now, what could that be?" he muttered. "Don't recollect any unaccounted cargo."

Removing the lamp from its hook and angling the light toward the barrels, he leaned in for a closer look. It was a small chest, not quite the size of a breadbox, purposely placed in this obscure recess of the murky room where it couldn't be seen without bending low to the floor.

"What on earth...?"

The captain tugged at the wooden box, but it wouldn't budge. He rested the lamp on the rough floor planks and using his shoulder, shoved one of the unwieldy barrels aside. He lifted the worn ebony box and tested the rusty metal lock. It was old but secure enough to keep him out.

"I don't understand. Why would someone hide a locked box in the hold of my ship?" His bewildered voice reflected the curiosity and anger battling within his chest cavity, scoring equally stinging punches on his heart.

Feeling violated that someone had secretly invaded his ship, the captain placed the box on the floor within the lamp's circle of amber light and bounded up the stairs to the deck. He where he snatched the emergency ax from its resting place on the wall of the bridge.

He marched back down the steps, determined to get to the bottom of this. *Whack...whack...thud.* On the third blow from the blunt edge of the ax head, the lock detached and fell to the floor. Captain Stone knelt beside the chest and lifted the lid. Inside were layers of yellowed newspapers. He removed handfuls in fervent passion, discarding crumpled wads on the floor around him like crispy snowballs.

Suddenly, his seeking fingers made contact with a hard object at the bottom of the chest. He pulled out a rectangular, black velvet case.

"What in blue blazes is this?" He could remember no such shipment aboard the Verily. Opening the lid, he stared in dumbfounded amazement at the contents of the case.

"Yep, it's exactly what you think it is, Cap'n," a familiar voice spoke from the darkness of the stairwell. "Now back off and leave it be. Got nothing to do with you." The Verily's scowling second mate stepped into the pool of lamplight.

"Julius!" The captain held out the case, exhibiting a red silk-lined bed containing five exquisite black spheres. The golden light from the lamp cast a shimmering glow that reflected in the luster of the marble-sized globes.

"These are black pearls, lad, the rarest of treasures."

"I know. They're Tahitian black pearls and worth a fortune."

"But what are they doing on my ship? And how do you know about them?"

"I told you, Cap'n, it's got nothing to do with you. I don't know how you found 'em, but you'd best forget you ever laid eyes on 'em. The less you know, the better—for your own good."

Captain Stone felt a deep sadness erupt in his belly as he eyed the boy he had mentored, trusted, and yes, even loved. It wasn't hard to size up the situation.

"Ya' sold out, didn't ya' lad? Someone's paying ya' a lot of money to smuggle these pearls to some harbor on our shipping route." He looked down at the lustrous treasure in his hand. "These wouldn't be part of the Windhorst pearls that were stolen in Miami last May, would they? I read all about it in the papers. Mrs. Windhorst was distraught. Nearly had a stroke over it."

Julius cast his eyes at the floor.

"Oh, lad, tell me it isn't so."

The boy removed his wet cap, squinted his eyes, and rubbed the bridge of his nose.

"I just can't believe it, Julius. How could ya' get tangled up in smuggling stolen goods? And using *my* ship to do the dirty work! I'm so disappointed in ya', son."

Julius' head snapped erect, and his jaw tightened. His hands began to quiver. He looked the captain dead in the eyes. "I'm *not* your son. My pa was a lousy drunk who couldn't pull himself out of the gutter. You may think you can save the world with your God-talk and trying to help every loser that's dug their own pit, but not me. Not me, Cap'n. I figured out a way to save myself, and it's called money."

Julius slapped his cap back on his head and took a step toward his employer. He held out a skinny, shaking palm. "Now give me the pearls and go tend to your cargo."

The two locked eyes for what seemed an eternity.

"Ya' know I can't do that."

"Yes, you can, and you will if you know what's good for you. These men, they ain't like you, Cap'n'. Lox will *kill* me, and you too if those pearls don't get delivered. Now give 'em up."

"No, Julius. It wouldn't be right. These pearls were stolen."

"Maybe it ain't right, but it's the only way to stay alive." Julius dropped his hand to his side. Desperation filled his eyes. "Please, if you care anything about me, you'll give me those pearls."

"It's because I care about you that I won't."

The boy visibly shook from head to toe. His face twisted into an evil grimace. "You will give me those pearls, Captain!" he shouted, whipping a six-inch knife from its hidden sheath beneath his shirt. The steel blade glinted ominously in the lamplight.

Cornelius Stone had never felt so torn. He had grown to care about this boy—he'd loved him, prayed for him, and garnered high hopes for his future. And now everything had turned so ugly. The boy he'd rescued off the mean streets and invested almost a year in now stood threatening him with a knife. He felt angry, deceived, and hurt.

But even more, he felt overwhelming compassion.

"Put it away, Julius. There's no good in such as that. We'll figure a way out of this together."

"No! I'll figure my own way out. I don't need you or your God. I don't need anybody. Just give me the pearls, and you'll be rid of me for good."

"But I don't want to be rid of ya'. When I took ya' in to learn the shipping trade, 'twas because I wanted to spend time with ya'. I *wanted* to. I still do. No matter what you've done, I'll stick with ya', and we'll work it out together."

The hand holding the knife wavered discernibly.

"How can I believe that, Cap'n? Nobody's ever wanted to stay with me, even my own pa."

"Julius, I can't answer for your father. I don't know what demons he wrestled with. But as for me, I can do nothing on my own, but everything through my Heavenly Father who gives me strength. I've committed to Him that I would see ya' through to knowin' Him as your Heavenly Father, too."

The captain snapped the lid shut on the jewel case. "And I intend to keep my word. Now put the knife away, lad."

Julius lowered the knife to his side in defeat then slipped it back into its sheath. His eyes locked on the black case in the captain's hand. As quick as a hunted hare, he darted forward and snatched the case from the older man's hands, and before the captain could react, bounded up the steps two at a time.

He hesitated with one foot on the top step and one on the deck and looked back at his former employer—and friend. Sorrow filled his eyes.

"I'm sorry, Cap'n. I wish it hadn't ended this way." And he was gone.

Chapter Nineteen

Captain Stone had no choice but to cast off with his first mate, Franklin, the next morning. As much as he hated to leave Sebastian with Julius getting himself into heaven only knows how much trouble, people depended on him; he'd given his word. There were deadlines to meet and promises to fulfill. Business demanded his immediate attention.

But not his heart. The captain prayed constantly for his young friend and included a note in the gift bundle he dropped at the Tropic dock for Emma-Lee and Aunt Augusta on Saturday morning, explaining the situation and requesting prayer for Julius' safety.

Sunday, his day off, would be the day he could devote to finding the wayward boy. In the meantime, there were men of questionable reputation he would look up at his Saturday ports of call. Julius had mentioned the name Lox. For the right price, surely someone could tell him something about this fellow, Lox...

* * * *

Emma-Lee and Aunt Augusta tore into the surprise package at the Saturday morning breakfast table, unaware that anything was wrong. The captain had seemed his normal, cheerful self as Franklin steered the Verily close to the docks, and he'd tossed the bundle on the dock, calling out "Ahoy, Admiral, God bless ya' now, lass, and your aunt, too!"

But as Aunt Augusta emerged from her room white-faced and read his letter aloud, a shiver shot up Emma-Lee's spine, and a score of questions sizzled in her head. Where had Julius gone? Would he try to deliver the black pearls himself, or would he have a change of heart and turn them over to the police? What if the real smugglers got angry that the treasure was discovered? Would they hurt Julius?

Emma-Lee wanted to stop and pray that very minute for Julius. In fact, she asked Aunt Augusta if they could pray together three more times that day. Aunt Augusta, who was not accustomed to praying aloud, listened to her niece's heartfelt petitions and added her own "amen" at the end.

Sunday morning, Captain Stone didn't show up for the circuit-riding preacher's monthly service in the Tropic schoolhouse. That was strange. He'd *always* showed up for church, every one since Aunt Augusta and Emma-Lee had started attending after Thanksgiving. Emma-Lee, who sat with Aunt Augusta in the back, waved at Ma Stone as she turned clear around in her customary seat in the front row to gaze at the door, a puzzled look on her face and her son's chair beside her empty.

After the service, Aunt Augusta and Emma-Lee stood outside in the shade of the banyan tree, saying good-bye to the McNamaras when Ma and Pap Stone approached them.

"Augusta, do you know where Cornelius is this morning? It's not like him to miss church," Ma Stone said, worry lines creasing her face.

"No, ma'am, I don't know precisely, but I've an idea what he might be doing, based on a letter he sent me yesterday." She told Ma and Pap about the dreadful situation with Julius.

"It's my guess that Cornelius is probably searching for the boy. I haven't the foggiest idea how he'll find him and if he does, what condition he might be in after the smugglers get through with him." Aunt Augusta's eyes welled with tears, and her trembling hand flew to her cheek. "And I fear..." She took a deep breath. "I fear for Cornelius' safety as well."

"Prayer we'll be needing then. 'Tis the least and the most we can do fer 'im," Pap said as his gnarled fingers enveloped Emma-Lee's small hand. Ma Stone wrapped her arm around Aunt Augusta's waist, and the four of them stood there in a circle for the better part of an hour, earnestly pouring out their concerns to the only one who could help.

* * * *

Cornelius Stone was no stranger to the rough streets, the seamy areas where men hid dark business they preferred to shield from the light of day. He'd spent his share of time in these netherworld places, which tended to amass around the wharves and ports.

"I'm in this world, but I'm not of this world," he'd always said with a prayer for protection as he passed through vile places where men's lives were often valued at less than a few silver coins.

It was one of these mean streets he traversed at daybreak on Sunday morning, searching for an abandoned fish packing plant two blocks from the Fort Pierce wharf. He'd steamed the Verily south down the Indian River all night after spending a week's wage in the taverns of Oak Hill, chasing down information about a man called Lox.

Just before midnight, he'd finally been led to a half drunk, black-bearded seaman who claimed to know where Lox and his thugs based their covert operations and would be more than happy to share the information for a stout pint and a healthy wad of bills.

Dawn was breaking as the captain tread the quiet street. The rising sun sent tentative fingers of fresh light into dark, foul-smelling alleys where drunks lay curled around their empty bottles. Trash and broken glass littered the gutters, and an unconscious, bleeding man listed in a sitting position against the side of a building. The cloaked activities of night were now becoming visible in the stark light of day.

"It's got to be around here somewhere," the captain muttered, looking left and right. "He said it was just past the Seven Mile Tavern. There's the tavern, so where's...?"

His eyes locked on a ramshackle frame building and its weathered sign hanging askew atop a sagging threshold. The faded words on the sign read, "Kaden's Seafood." The front door and all first floor windows visible from the street were boarded shut. A cracked and dangling ramp led from a boarded side door to a loading dock. A row of broken windows on the second floor bore evidence of the rock-throwing boredom of men in various stages of inebriation in this lawless section of town.

Captain Stone surveyed the street and saw no signs of life. He crossed the cobblestone road and edged along the side of the building, looking for a way in. Rounding the corner to the alley behind the decrepit structure, he saw that the boards had been pried loose over a back window and were swinging freely. He cautiously pushed the splintered boards aside and peered into the dark warehouse.

Slivers of light from the boarded windows illuminated the room just enough so the captain could see it was bare, save broken-down tables and a stack of packing crates in one corner. He threw one leg over the windowsill and hoisted himself through the window, taking care to make as little noise as possible. He crept through the long, dim, packing room, listening, always listening, for any sound of movement. The odor of rancid fish and stale brine lingered in the air.

Making his way to the end of the room, he stopped in front of a rickety stairway descending into utter blackness.

Wait—was that a sound? He froze and listened hard. It could be, yes, surely it was—a muted raspy noise drifting from the floor below.

Feeling his way along the wall with one hand, the other reaching into the black emptiness before him, the captain descended the narrow stairs. The strange noise grew louder as he reached the basement, still indistinct but coming in regular intervals. He could see a faint, flickering light through a doorway at the far end of a large room.

The air was musty and dank. Rats scurried away from the tread of his boots. Breathing a prayer for help, the captain crossed the rotting floorboards, wincing each time a plank creaked its protest at his intrusion.

The noise became more distinct as he neared the doorway; he could now recognize the sound he'd heard many times before—the rhythmic, guttural breathing of a man snoring. He peeked around the threshold to see a man seated in a crude pine chair in the center of an inner room, his head tilted back, mouth wide open, hat brim pulled down over his eyes and feet propped up on the small table in front of him,

The stump of a burning candle was mounted on a jar lid with melted wax heaped onto the table at its base. An empty whisky bottle was lying on its side, resting beside the barrel of a black revolver.

The captain's gaze was drawn to the far side of the room where an obscure form was curled in a fetal position on the filthy floor. Could it be Julius? In the feeble candlelight, it was impossible to tell.

Captain Stone slid noiselessly into the room and inched along the wall toward the motionless body. *If it is Julius, is he unconscious, sleeping, or...dead?*

The captain paced his footsteps by the snoring pattern of the man in the chair. When the man exhaled, he took a step. When the man inhaled, he paused. He finally reached the unmoving body and immediately recognized the greasy, stringy brown hair. It was Julius. But was he alive?

Kneeling to swipe the unkempt mop of hair out of the boy's face, the captain flinched at the terrible image before him. The left side of Julius' face was severely bruised and grotesquely swollen; his distorted left eyelid was sealed shut with dried blood, his broken nose arched at a nauseating, unnatural angle. A sudden, gut-wrenching horror seized the captain as he realized he might be too late. *Oh, no Lord, he isn't ready for eternity yet. Please give him—and me— another chance.*

He frantically felt for the carotid pulse in the boy's neck.

A soft moan vibrated Julius' throat, and he stirred, his right eyelid cracking open enough for his dilated pupil to focus on his rescuer in the dusky light. "Cap'n Stone," his lips formed the soundless words as he tried in vain to sit up. A pain-induced groan escaped before the captain could cover the boy's mouth and shake his head vigorously in silent warning.

The snoring abruptly ceased, and the man in the chair smacked his lips together.

Cornelius Stone felt his innards turn cold, and his hand tightened on the handle of the knife in its sheath at his side. His heart pounded in his ears as he waited, still as a statue. He would fight for his young friend if he had to, but he prayed there would be another way.

The man shifted his boots on the table and re-crossed his arms. In due course, his jaw dropped, and the snoring picked up where it had left off.

The captain and Julius breathed deep sighs of relief. They looked at each other for a long moment. An unspoken message passed between them, a wordless declaration of trust. The boy's right eye began to drip tears. The captain extended his hand. Julius took it and gave it a meaningful squeeze.

Captain Stone cocked his head in mute warning toward the man noisily sleeping, and Julius nodded his understanding. The captain slowly helped Julius to his feet, the injured boy grinding his teeth in silent agony. Julius leaned heavily on the captain and pointed to his bare left foot, which was swollen and mangled. Several dark-hued toes jutting out at odd angles were obviously broken.

The captain pointed to the boy and then to his own shoulder. Julius grimaced but nodded his head. There was no other way. Captain Stone lifted him as gently as he could and draped him across his broad right shoulder as he had the sacks of potatoes on the Verily. Julius emitted an involuntary, "Oof" as the captain's sharp collarbone pitted his belly.

The snorer skipped a beat. The captain held his breath. The snoring resumed with vigor. *I never thought I'd be thanking God for whiskey*, thought Cornelius Stone.

He skirted the man in the chair and stole across the outer room, carrying his heavy burden. As he trudged to the top of the dark stairwell struggling with the additional weight on his shoulders, he miscalculated the last step and pitched forward into the wall. The resulting *thud*, although not loud by normal, light-of-day standards, seemed to the captain like a cannon-blast in the cavernous building.

The aging seaman, nearly exhausted from exertion, was electrified with a sudden burst of energy. On the wings of a second wind, he tore across the room's expanse to the open window, heaved the gangly boy through, and scrambled into the alley himself.

Hauling Julius onto his shoulder again, he felt a supernatural strength flow into his limbs and calm his heart as he dashed down the street, now awash in the light of a glorious Sunday morning. He headed toward the wharf, where Franklin was keeping the Verily ready to cast off on a moment's notice.

In the recesses of the alley, a pair of contemptuous, bloodshot eyes followed the captain's escape.

Chapter Twenty

The sun sank low in the western sky as four troubled islanders sat in porch chairs watching dark clouds gather over the Indian River. Aunt Augusta and Emma-Lee had accepted Ma and Pap's invitation to spend the afternoon at the cove following their hour of prayer in the schoolyard. A mid-afternoon lunch of fried trout and corn pone had done much to bolster their spirits, and they'd retired to the porch to spend their last few minutes together before Pap was to hitch the horses, Cain and Mabel, to the wagon to drive them home.

"Do you think he found Julius?" Emma-Lee voiced the question that was on everyone's mind.

"I don't know, dearie. We'll just have to keep praying and trust that God is in control," Ma Stone returned to her needlework, her agile fingers pushing the needle through the tapestry pulled taut by her embroidery hoop. "You know He always answers our prayers, although the answer's not always 'yes.' Sometimes it's 'no', and sometimes it's 'wait a while.'"

"Even if 'no' hurts something dreadful?"

Ma Stone thought about Emma-Lee's question before answering. "It's hard to believe that God is in control when things don't seem fair or right to us." She held up the intricate needlepoint image of a springtime garden she'd been working on for months. "What do you see, dearie, when you look at this side of the fabric?"

"I see pink, purple, and yellow flowers and a white trellis in a beautiful garden."

"That's right. From this side, the finished side, every stitch works together to create a tapestry—a blend of color by design so that the finished product is perfect." She flipped the material over to the backside.

"Now, what do you see on this side?"

"I don't know—knotted thread and little dabs of color here and there, pieces of flowers but not the whole thing. It's kind of a mess. You can't even tell what the picture is supposed to be."

"Exactly. And that's the way our lives are. God sees the finished picture, the completed person he plans for us to be, made up of the stitches of our experiences here on earth. But as humans, we only see the backside of the tapestry—messy bits and pieces of color and ugly knots that don't make any sense to us. From our limited perspective, we'll never see the whole picture until we're in heaven with Him. In the meantime, as believers, we trust that each stitch in the fabric of our lives is planned by the hands of the Master Creator."

Emma-Lee pondered that thought. "So Julius is an ugly knot in the tapestry of our lives?"

Pap chuckled. "Aye, lassie, methinks that'd be a good way to put it."

"Now, Pap," scolded Ma Stone, "you know that's not what I meant—"

At that moment, the chickens in the side yard began squawking as if a wolf had crept in among them.

"Not expectin' any company, are we, Ma? Yer watch-birds are goin' bonkers," Pap said as he pushed himself out of his chair and headed toward the ruckus. He'd just rounded the corner of the house when the ladies heard him exclaim, "Well, fer heaven's sake! Ye truly are an answer to prayer!"

They rushed around the side of the house to find Captain Stone trudging through the yard with a limp Julius slung over his shoulder.

"No time to talk now. Need to get Julius looked after so I can ride on to Lotus Landing for the sheriff." He staggered up the porch steps with his burden. "What about setting up the cot in that little room beside the kitchen, Ma? He's going to need a lot of medical attention, and it may be days before he sees a doctor."

"Yes, of course, that would the best place for me to tend to him. I'll get sheets and a blanket ready." Ma dashed ahead of him into the house. Pap hastily unfolded the cot in the small room that served as a walk-in pantry. Ma spread a clean white sheet on the dark green canvas.

The captain laid the unconscious boy on the cot and tenderly pushed the blood-matted hair out of his face. A collective gasp from the four people surrounding the bed summarized the shock of seeing his pathetic condition.

"He'll need lots of compresses, Ma. I'm not sure what all's damaged, but his nose and some bones in his foot are broken and likely some ribs, too. I think he's runnin' a fever as well. He was unconscious most of the voyage from Fort Pierce, and there wasn't much I could do for him."

"I dinna know how ye found him son, but are ye a'right yerself?"

"I'm fine, Pap. God was with me. I'll tell ya' all about it later, but I must make haste right now. Once they figure out 'twas me that took him, it won't be long before they come lookin' for him. With my head start and the eight hours it takes to sail here from Fort Pierce, they won't make it here before mid-day tomorrow. If I can turn Julius over to the sheriff's custody tonight, he'll be safe."

"Did he say who did this to him, son?" Ma Stone moved the cast iron skillet to the back of the stove to put a kettle and a pot of water on to boil.

"He did." The captain looked gravely at his mother and then at each beloved face in the room. "'Twas a thug named Lox and his henchmen. I don't know who they work for, but these are dangerous men. One of them, a foul fellow called Mack Leffers I had the misfortune of knowing a few years back, was left to guard Julius but drank himself into a stupor, which gave me opportunity to get the boy out. These men are armed and will do anything to keep Julius from spillin' the beans on their smuggling operation. I don't like leavin' you here alone with him, but they don't yet know 'twas me that took him. I don't see how they could possibly find him before I get back with the sheriff."

"No, you're absolutely right," Aunt Augusta interjected. "You're the only one of us who could cover the distance to Lotus Landing quickly enough. Go. We'll be fine. Emma-Lee and I will stay the night, so I can help your mother take care of Julius."

The captain looked at her quizzically. "I'm a bit surprised to see ya' here, Augusta, but I'm ever so glad ya' are. Thanks for helping Ma with the lad; I've no doubt he'll be a handful when he comes to. But now, I must saddle Cain and fly…"

He stepped to the stove and kissed his mother's forehead then duplicated the gesture with his father who was standing beside her, his arms loaded with firewood. Emma-Lee darted over and flung her arms around the captain's waist. He bent, cradled her face in his hands, and kissed her forehead, too.

As he straightened and turned to leave, he found himself face to face with a wide-eyed Augusta. Hesitating for only a moment, the captain put his hands on her shoulders and leaned forward to plant a gentle kiss on her crimson forehead.

He bolted out the door and across the yard without waiting for a response.

* * * *

A crack of thunder rent the midnight calm and elicited a restless groan from a fever-tossed Julius. Ma Stone wiped his flushed face with a cool, damp cloth and prepared a fresh compress for his foot as Aunt Augusta added oak twigs to keep the fire ablaze in the wood stove. The wind whistled around the eaves of the house.

Emma-Lee padded barefoot into the kitchen, rubbing her eyes with balled fists.

"What's the matter, dearie? Can't you sleep?" Ma Stone asked.

"I heard thunder." Emma-Lee looked soft and rumpled in her makeshift nightgown fashioned from one of Pap's old flannel shirts.

"Aye, sounds like a storm's blowin' up, it does," Pap said from the doorway. "I'll wager Cornelius encounters his fair share of it on his return trip with the sheriff. Provided he found him in a timely manner, they'll be on their way by now."

Suddenly, a clamor broke out in the side yard, with squawking and cackling and crowing loud enough to compete with any peal of thunder.

"Did you remember to lock the chickens in the coop for the night?" Ma Stone asked, worry lines gathering on her wrinkled face.

"Surely I did. We'll not lose another to those night-scavengin' pa'nters." Pap walked over to the sitting room window that faced the side yard. Emma-Lee followed him and stood leaning sleepily on his right leg as he peered through the thick glass.

The moon was nowhere to be seen on this black night, overcast and heavy. At first, nothing was visible except tufts of gray Spanish moss tumbling from the oak tree beside the house in the swirling wind. A lightning bolt lit up the sky, momentarily illuminating the landscape.

Pap suddenly tensed. He jerked so hard, Emma-Lee slid off his leg onto the floor.

The old man swept her up in his arms and lurched into the kitchen. "Bolt the doors and get down to the cellar! There's someone lurkin' at the edge of the woods!" He transferred Emma-Lee to the arms of an alarmed Aunt Augusta. "Here, take her, and I'll get the lad. We'll need to light some lamps and take blankets, too—'twill be a might chilly down there. Don't tarry now; no time to waste."

Everyone swung into action. Ma Stone bolted the kitchen door and ran to secure the front door as Pap pulled the groaning Julius to a sitting position on the cot. Speaking quietly to calm the boy, he explained that a change of location was necessary, and he needed the lad to help him as much as he could.

Throwing Julius' limp arm around his neck, Pap wrapped one arm around his thin waist and wrested him upright. Julius' head bobbed forward on his chest. The two tottered into the hallway, the old man half carrying, half dragging the delirious boy.

Aunt Augusta lowered Emma-Lee to her feet and piled her niece's arms high with blankets. "Follow Pap to the cellar, and be quick about it," she whispered as she grabbed the cot with both hands and began pulling it across the kitchen floor.

Ma Stone reappeared and snatched the steaming kettle of water from the stove and as many clean cloths and medical supplies as she could carry before following the cot bumping down the hallway.

Pap was just lighting the first lamp as Emma-Lee reached the top of the cellar stairs. He had left Julius propped against the wall in the hallway and descended the steps to prepare the damp, dungeon-like room for unexpected guests. With Ma and Aunt Augusta each supporting a leg and Pap grasping Julius' chest from behind, they were able to carry the unconscious boy down the steps to the cot Pap had set up beside the shelf of mango preserves and canned garden beans.

Ma Stone was getting him settled when Pap announced, "I'm goin' back upstairs for me shotgun and to find out who's trespassing in the wee hours of the night." A clap of thunder shook the house. "Stay put and bolt the door behind me. Don't be openin' that door for *any* reason, do ye' hear? Cornelius and the sheriff should be along nigh. And don't ye' be worrying about me—I'm a sly old fox, and I surely know a few tricks about me own den."

Despite protests from all three ladies, Pap did exactly as he said. They had no choice but to throw the woefully small bolt on the cellar door as his back disappeared down the dark hallway.

* * * *

Pap pulled the matchbox from his shirt pocket and lit the candlestick that sat on the small table in the hallway. He immediately went to his bedroom to get the shotgun from beneath his bed. Checking to make sure it was loaded, he gathered a handful of shells from his top dresser drawer and stuck them in his pants pocket.

Based on the cackling watch-bird racket outside, Pap figured the intruder was still out there. There was one sure way to find out. He hastened up the stairs to the guest bedroom that overlooked the side yard. Blowing out the candle so not to give away his position, he stole over to the window and slowly pulled aside the white flour sack curtains.

He stared at the yard, blinking to adjust his vision to the darkness. With the first lightning flash, he saw no movement except tree limbs, whipped by gusts of wind. *No rain yet, but it's comin'. Lord, please help Cornelius and the sheriff to get here soon. If Lox's men are out there,'tisn't likely one old man with a rusty shotgun will be able to hold them off for long.*

As the next bolt of lightning illuminated the scene for mere seconds, Pap gasped at the sight of a man in a black jacket and hat, a gun glinting in his hand, bent low, sneaking along the shrubbery lining the southern property line. Pap waited, breathless, as the next flash of light revealed another man trailing the first, and a third carrying a rifle, dashing behind the trunk of a tree not thirty yards from the house.

Panic seized the old man, and for a split second, he felt as though he might faint. "No!" he rebuked himself aloud. "God will give me strength to do what I must!"

He turned away from the window, a bit dizzy for a moment, but with his will restored. "Now, Lord, you best be tellin' me what I should do before I die of heart failure and meet Gabriel and the heavenly host at the pearly gates with a shotgun in me hand."

The heavenly host. Suddenly, he knew what to do.

His hands fumbled as he relit the candle, but the flame caught on the second try. He moved quickly across the hall to the door leading to the catwalk on the western side of the house. He set his gun and candle on the floor and pushed open the stubborn door with both hands. A gust of wind snatched the door from his hands and whipped it backward, banging on the house frame and extinguishing the candle.

Pap scurried along the catwalk, fighting to keep his balance in the strong wind. Reaching the ship's bell mounted on the roof, he gripped the bell cord with both hands and pulled. The bell's bright, cheerful peals were a startling contrast to the stark bleakness of the night.

It began to rain then, great, gray sheets of blowing rain, drenching Pap and obscuring any view below or above. Pap knew he must keep ringing, sounding the alarm to draw a host of neighbors and hasten the arrival of Cornelius if he was within the bell's range of sound.

Minutes passed that seemed like hours to the sodden old man as he kept steady at his post, the bell pealing its plea for help at this most uncommon hour. There was a loud retort from below, and something whistled past his ear. Another retort and the bell cord was jerked from his hands as the brass ship's bell was flung from its mount and tumbled down the slanted roof, end over end until it crashed on the ground two stories below.

Someone was shooting at him!

Where's me gun? Heavens above, I've left it in the hallway!

Shots struck the roof all around him and dug divots out of the house boards as he tottered across the narrow catwalk, struggling to keep his balance. Suddenly, Pap felt a sharp sting on his left forearm and then he was tumbling like the bell, falling into darkness.

* * * *

Ma Stone, Aunt Augusta, and Emma-Lee huddled at the cellar door. They heard the bell ringing and guessed Pap's intent. But they also heard the gunshots and the sudden cessation of the bell's pealing.

"Oh no, they've shot him, haven't they?" Emma-Lee looked up into the despairing faces of her aunt and Ma Stone.

"We don't know that," Aunt Augusta said, her pained expression belying her words.

"We do know that he's in God's hands, regardless of what happens tonight," Ma said, a quiet resolution shining in her watery eyes. The three turned from the bolted door and huddled together on the cellar steps, gazing at the unconscious form in the cot nestled between the canned goods.

"What do we do now?" Emma-Lee asked.

"We can't just wait here like sheep for the slaughter; we must formulate a plan." Aunt Augusta willed her practical mind to push aside the fear and horror that threatened to shut her down completely. "If those hoodlums will shoot an old man, they won't think twice about shooting helpless women to get what they want."

At that, Ma Stone clenched her lips with determination. "Then they won't find helpless women."

Chapter Twenty-one

From his position behind a huge ixora bush, Lox was startled by the first chimes of the bell, ringing from some place high above his head, threatening to destroy his mission. Mr. Snodgrass had ordered him to get rid of the boy, and get rid of the boy he would, for once and for all.

He had kept young Duckett alive a few days, thinking he could convince the boss that a few sound beatings would be punishment enough for blowing the black pearl operation, and the kid would be frightened out of his wits, out of town, and out of their lives forever. The boy had reminded him of his own younger brother—penniless, greedy, and careless. He was guilty of the stupidity of youth maybe, but in Lox's opinion, that crime did not warrant death.

Mr. Snodgrass, who was staying at the Fort Pierce Hotel for a business meeting, had a different opinion. His temper flared at Lox's display of "yellow-bellied mercy," as he called it. He demanded that the boy be dispatched before he could reveal their names and details of their lucrative business to the authorities.

"Duckett was warned of the consequences of failure," he'd sputtered, "And he agreed to take the chance. Now we must alter our plans and find another method of delivery. The police are already suspicious and have tightened their surveillance. My clients will be furious. Now, do your job, Lox, or you may suffer the same fate!"

Lox had returned to the warehouse first thing Sunday morning to carry out his orders. Instead, he'd found the boy missing and an inebriated Mack Leffers hunched in the alley, staring down the littered street toward the wharf. It hadn't taken long to sober him up with a bucket of cold water over the head, and together they had roused Leffers' cousin, Judd Griswald who, for the right price, was always available for grim, underworld work such as this.

After a hastily called conference with Mr. Snodgrass, it was determined that Captain Stone, whom Leffers had recognized as he escaped down the street with Julius, most assuredly had sought refuge in his homeport on Merritt Island. A steam-powered fishing boat was procured at the wharf when Mr. Snodgrass pulled a few strategically placed strings. Lox, Leffers, and Griswald made good time steaming north to the island.

The only hitch had been finding the good captain's home once they arrived at the Tropic docks, but a little strong-arm persuasion of Albert, the dockhand, had taken care of that problem. Albert was now retired for the evening, gagged and bound, wriggling helplessly among the sacks of fertilizer and boxes of newly delivered tinned goods in the storage shed.

And now, Lox was extremely annoyed about having to hide in the pitch black of midnight with thunder booming and lighting striking all around him. He glanced over his shoulder at Leffers, who was crouching behind an azalea bush.

Lox made a throat-slitting motion to Leffers and pointed to the roof of the house, from which that incessant bell was ringing. Leffers, in turn, stood and gestured wildly to Griswald across the lawn who could not make out his cousin's murky form until lightning split the sky moments later.

During the two seconds of electrified illumination, Griswald saw his cousin waving his gun in the air with one hand and making pendulum motions with the other. He knew what that meant: take out whoever was ringing that confounded bell!

At that moment, the clouds broke wide open, and thick, gray rain descended like a concealing blanket. Griswald, taking advantage of nature's precipitous cover, left his hiding place and boldly strode toward the front porch.

He honed in on the source of the repetitive *dong, dong, dong* that sliced through the din of the storm. Pulling the brim of his hat lower over his eyes to block the rain, Griswald aimed his rifle at the spot on the roof where the irritating sound seemed to originate.

He missed. Cursing, he fired again.

His second shot rang true, and he could hear the dissonant clang of his bullet striking brass and the bell bouncing against the shingles on its way to the ground.

Squinting, he could just make out a man's figure, obscured by the heavy rain, running along the catwalk high above the ground. Assuming it was Cornelius Stone, Griswald kept firing until his target flailed and disappeared over the far side of the peaked roof.

The rain slacked to a drizzle, and the thunder and lightning abated as if turned off by an invisible hand. A strange luminescent light brightened the sky. It didn't seem to have any particular source since the moon and stars were still occluded by the dense cloud cover, but visibility improved considerably in the purple-black light that bathed the landscape.

Lox gave a low whistle from the shrubbery beside the back stoop and signaled for Griswald to keep watch on the front porch as he and Leffers, with guns drawn, inched toward the kitchen door. With backs flat against the house flanking the door, they listened. Hearing nothing inside, Lox jerked his head toward the kitchen window and Leffers crept into position to peek inside.

He shook his head. The room was empty.

The two drenched, vindictive men turned toward the door, eying the mere slab of wood that kept them from accomplishing their murderous goal. It was time to finish it.

* * * *

Ma Stone trembled as she lay prone on the floor beneath her bed, where she'd hidden after leaving the cellar. From this position, she could watch the feet of the intruders walk down the hall and monitor the cellar door as well. There might be one intruder or ten. She had no idea what she was up against. All she knew was that one of them had a rifle and had ruthlessly gunned down her husband and was now coming after a helpless boy in her house, a boy her son had trusted her to protect.

A splintery crash from the kitchen told her the door had been kicked in. The perpetrators were obviously bold and forceful and unafraid of the meager defense that might be mounted by the inhabitants of the house. They must somehow know Cornelius was not here.

Her clammy fingers wrapped around the ivory handle of the derringer pistol she had kept in her bottom dresser drawer since Cornelius had presented it to her on her sixtieth birthday. He'd explained that a derringer was generally considered a weak weapon, but this one held forty-one-caliber bullets and could send a man straight through the window behind him. He had then taken her outside and taught her to fire it, but that had been eight years ago. Would she remember after all this time?

Heavy footsteps circled the hewn pine floorboards of the kitchen then the parlor. She could hear them pausing occasionally and pictured the intruders looking behind furniture and draperies. She heard the squeak of the pantry door and the familiar scrape of the broom closet door being opened and closed. The ominous footsteps resumed, echoing through the silent house. She saw the light flickering as they moved from room to room, carrying the kerosene lamps she'd left in the kitchen after her hasty retreat to the cellar.

Ma Stone scarcely breathed as the footsteps came closer. She felt her heartbeat throb in her temples. Clinching her jaw to quiet her chattering teeth, she counted the boots as they appeared in her bedroom doorway: one, two, three, four—two black, two brown. Two men. The enemy was only two.

She felt relief and a surge of hope. David had defeated Goliath with only a slingshot, and Gideon's small band defeated the enormous Philistine army. Surely God could work a similar miracle tonight!

She lay as still as a corpse as the pair of brown boots entered the bedroom in a circle of lamplight. She could hear the black-booted man proceed up the stairs to search the second floor. The floorboards overhead creaked as he began exploring the empty rooms.

The muddy brown leather boots walked slowly around the bedroom, leaving smudges of dirt and bits of grass in their wake. Ma Stone followed each step with her eyes as the intruder inspected every corner of the room.

After what seemed an eternity, the boots made their way back to the doorway as if to leave, but instead, halted. Ma Stone's stomach flip-flopped as the boots slowly turned back toward the bed in the center of the room.

The boots returned to the side of the bed, the worn pine planks squeaking their protests with each heavy step. The bottom of the lamp suddenly came into Ma Stone's view as it made contact with the floor. Her eyes bulged. Her pulse quickened. The boots twisted sideways, and one wet britches knee appeared as the weight in the other boot was shifted onto the worn toe. A silent scream echoed in Ma Stone's brain.

He's kneeling to look under the bed!

* * * *

Lox held the lamp high as he reached the upstairs landing. No sound. No movement. Could the house really be deserted? Mr. Snodgrass would be furious if their quest had been in vain and Duckett remained alive.

No, there had been two lamps burning and a fire in the in the kitchen stove when they'd entered the house. Someone— Cornelius Stone, most likely—had rung the bell before Griswald shot him off the roof. The kid must be hidden somewhere in the house.

Holding his gun in front of him, Lox cautiously proceeded down the hallway, shining his lamp into each vacant room. Stepping over an old shotgun and candleholder beside an opened door leading onto a catwalk, he peered out into the strange purple darkness until he was satisfied that the roof was deserted.

He reached the end of the hall and stood facing the small curved staircase leading to what he recognized to be a narrow attic door. Could Captain Stone have possibly stowed the boy in the attic?

* * * *

Ma Stone's muscles reacted instantly when she realized her hiding place was about to be discovered. She swung the delicately engraved pistol around and fired, producing a round bullet hole in the ankle of the filthy left boot, which immediately filled with blood. A howl of pain pierced the night, and two dirty hands hit the floor, releasing a black revolver that skidded across the room and into the hallway.

* * * *

Before Lox could think another thought, a gunshot rang out from the floor below. A man screamed. He turned, intending to race back to the stairs when the attic door suddenly flung open behind him, stopping him dead in his tracks.

"Didn't think ye could kill me that easily, did ye now?" a voice asked from the attic threshold.

* * * *

Reacting instinctively, Ma Stone fired another shot, this time taking a plug out of the intruder's right knee. He rolled onto his back, holding both legs and screaming obscenities, the likes of which Ma Stone had never before heard in her home.

She scrambled from beneath the bed on the side opposite the wounded man and hurried around to stare aghast as he lay writhing in agony.

* * * *.

A second gunshot rang from below, followed by a man's voice yelping in pain. Lox took a running step toward the stairs.

"If ye prefer yer head on yer shoulders, ye best halt right there, mate," the voice behind him ordered.

Lox spun around and nearly dropped the lamp in astonishment. He couldn't believe his eyes. There, bathed in the amber light of the lamp, was a shriveled old man dressed in a moth-eaten pirate's coat, brandishing a long sword in one hand and a harpoon in the other. A tall British Admiral's hat was perched atop white, wiry hair that was sticking out at all angles beneath.

Lox regained his voice. "So it was you Griswald shot off the roof?"

"Aye, 'twas me, but he didn't shoot me off the roof. Barely grazed me arm, he did, and I lost me balance. The attic window broke me fall. Reckon God still has a use for me yet."

"God, eh? Well, I think it's time for you to go ask Him about that face to face, old timer," Lox said, snarling as he lowered the lamp to the floor and cocked his pistol.

With surprising agility, Pap lunged forward and knocked the gun out of Lox's hand with a swipe of his sword. The pistol slid across the floor into the darkness of the room to Lox's left. The two men dove after the gun, each sprawling head over heels to reach it first.

* * * *

A thump and a crash overhead reminded Ma Stone that another dangerous man was upstairs and most certainly had heard the gunshots. He would likely show up any second to finish the job this one had botched.

Eyeing the intruder's gun lying in the hallway, she yanked open her top bureau drawer and extracted a brass key. Snatching the lamp from the floor, she raced to the doorway. She dropped the lamp on the hall floor, where it rocked precariously before finally settling upright.

In one frantic motion, Ma slammed the bedroom door, inserted the key, and turned it until the lock clicked. She dropped the key in her apron pocket, and lunged for the intruder's stray gun. Clumsily retrieving the black revolver, she turned to face the stairs, a gun in each quivering hand aimed at the landing.

She was breathing hard, her attention consumed by odd scuffling noises and loud thumps upstairs. If she didn't know better, she'd swear she heard men's voices. But there was no one up there except the black-booted intruder. It sounded like a mighty fight, but whom on earth...?

Suddenly, a deep voice behind her rumbled, "Drop the weapons, old woman, or die where you stand."

Chapter Twenty-two

Ma Stone froze, her outstretched hands pointing both guns toward the vacant stairs as the voice behind her rose in pitch.

"Are you deaf, woman?" the man behind her yelled. "I said drop the guns...now!"

Ma Stone slowly lowered the guns to the floor and straightened. She felt the muzzle of a rifle bore into her back. "Turn around."

She turned to face a bushy-bearded man with a nasty scar high across his left cheek that crinkled as he curled his lips into a sneering smile. Wild, unkempt hair and chipped, yellow teeth gave him the appearance of a hungry bear. Water dripped from his drenched clothes and hat, forming puddles on her newly polished floor. She couldn't believe such a thing would annoy her at a time like this.

"What were those gunshots I heard?"

In answer to his question, renewed howling erupted from behind Ma's bedroom door. Griswald stepped back and stared at the door. "Who's in there?"

In reply, a string of profanity flew that made Ma Stone's scalp tingle.

"Hold on, Cous', I'll get you to a doctor." Griswald tried the doorknob. "The door is locked. Where's the key?"

Ma Stone was at a loss for an answer. She shrugged her shoulders and held up her empty palms, hoping that she was not technically lying if she didn't actually speak.

"Come off it, old woman. You know where the key is. And you know where the kid is, too. If you don't start cooperating, you'll be the next one I pick off, and it won't be off no rooftop either!"

While he was speaking, Ma Stone's eyes grew wider and wider. Her gaze shifted from Griswald's face to a spot just over his right shoulder.

"What's the matter with you, old woman? Can't talk neith—"

His words were cut short by the clang of a cast iron skillet colliding with the back of his skull. He went down flat on his face, his body landing on top of his rifle.

Aunt Augusta stood over the fallen man, puffing and red-faced. Her hairpins had flown out from the exertion of swinging the heavy pan, and her normally tidy hair hung over her face. Her rain-soaked dress plastered tightly to her body and dripped onto her squishy shoes, giving her the uncharacteristic odor of a wet dog. She stared at the unconscious criminal at her feet and then at Ma Stone in disbelief. The frying pan clattered to the floor. She swiped at her runny nose with one dirty hand.

"How did you manage that?" Ma Stone asked. "I thought you were hiding in the closet in Cornelius' room."

"I was, but when I heard them checking the pantry and broom closet, I knew it was only a matter of time before I'd be discovered. I tiptoed to the window and had just eased it open when gunshots came from your bedroom. I knew when a man screamed that you must have used your pistol. I climbed out the window during the commotion and snuck around the house just in time to see this horrible man with the rifle run into the kitchen. So I grabbed the skillet from the stove and followed him."

"Well, aren't you the industrious one?" asked a low, monotone voice from the stairs. "Not daring like Granny here or crazy like the old geezer upstairs." Lox descended the steps quickly, his gun trained on them the entire time.

"What old geezer?"

"The one who thinks he's Blackbeard the pirate."

"Pap's still alive?"

"Who knows? I hit him hard enough to knock out an elephant." He nudged Griswald's motionless body with the toe of his boot. "Pretty much like you've done to my man here." He shoved the unconscious Griswald with his foot until the barrel of his rifle was uncovered. Pulling it free, he tucked the rifle beneath his left arm. Never taking his aim off the two ladies, he reached down with the same hand and picked up the two handguns on the floor, lodging them his pants pockets.

Ma Stone noticed a growing patch of blood and a hole in his shirtsleeve below the left elbow. It looked like the kind of deep slice a sword might make.

"Enough shenanigans. Where is Duckett?" The muscular man spoke calmly but with an intensity that left no question of his intentions.

Ma Stone took Augusta's hand and they stood together, mute.

"Maybe I should shoot one of you so the other will talk."

The ladies gasped and clutched each other.

The killer's rock-hard expression softened the tiniest fraction. "I don't cotton to killing women." He shot them a menacing look. "But make no mistake, I will if I have to. Aah, I'll find the kid myself. Now, what'll I do with you two while I'm searching?" He looked around, his eyes finally settling on the cellar door.

"What's in there?"

"It's just the cellar," Ma Stone replied. "We don't use it much any more."

"The cellar, huh? Sounds like a good place to keep you two out of the way." Lox tried to open the door. "It's bolted from the inside." He glared suspiciously at the women. "What else are you keeping in there besides jelly, lady?" He rattled the door hard. A faint moan could be heard from the locked room.

"No! Don't —" Ma Stone yelled as Lox took aim at the doorknob with his handgun and fired three shots, shattering the bolt and cracking the door. He kicked the splintered door with his foot, and it swung open to reveal Emma-Lee bending over a delirious Julius on the cot in a pool of lamplight.

"So there he is." Lox announced, a victorious tone in his voice. He motioned to Ma Stone and Aunt Augusta to enter the room ahead of him. "Don't go near the cot. Stay there by the side wall, so I can see you." The two women moved quickly down the steps and stood by the wall, still holding each other tightly.

"Please don't do this. He's only a boy," Ma Stone pleaded.

"He may be only a boy, but he entered into a man's agreement. And now he knows too much."

"What if we send him far away where he'll be no harm to you?" Augusta interjected in a nervous, high-pitched voice. "You'll never have to see him again, and you can continue your criminal activity unimpeded—"

"What if you shut up, or I'll blast a hole where your mouth used to be!" Lox's face reddened as his voice rose. The veins stood out in his neck. Blood poured from the wound on his left arm, forming a puddle on the floor. He pointed the gun at the two quivering ladies and then back at Emma-Lee and Julius.

"Who should I shoot first?" he screamed.

* * * *

Emma-Lee felt her throat constrict. Fear like she had never known squeezed her insides like a vise. The adults that had always been in charge were now helpless and in deep trouble. Julius was doomed unless she could think of something to help him.

Papa God, she prayed silently, *I know you're here. Please help me. Make me brave. Show me what to do.*

The man with the gun looked as if he'd swallowed a firecracker like the ones her brothers used to set off on the fourth of July. His eyes blazed, and the air around him fairly crackled. He might explode at any minute.

"Get away from Duckett, little girl!" the angry man shouted. "Move if you know what's good for you!"

Emma-Lee looked down at Julius. Sweat covered his pockmarked face and dampened his stringy hair. Foul breath escaped his opened mouth as he moaned, tossing his head from side to side on the cot, unaware of the trouble he'd caused the only people who cared about him or the bullet that was waiting to claim him. He certainly wasn't pleasant to look at. He'd never been particularly nice to her or anyone else that she had observed. But something about him stirred her heart to compassion. Papa God loved him anyway. And so could she.

"No," she said firmly. "I won't leave him." She sat on the side of the cot facing the killer, blocking a clear shot at the intended victim with her body.

Taken aback, Lox just stood there in a growing pool of his own blood, his chest rising and falling, and his gun unswerving. "I got no quarrel with you. It's him I want. Now get out of the way."

"No, sir. I may be small, but I'm all he's got right now."

Lox ground his teeth and took a step closer to the cot. "You must not understand me, little girl. I'm going to *kill* you if you don't move. That kid's no relation to you. Is he worth your life?"

Emma-Lee felt a calm strength fill her. She looked past the muzzle of the gun, into the wild eyes of the man with his finger twitching on the trigger.

"Are you brave, mister?"

"Am...am I...what?" the man sputtered.

"Are you able to face something that frightens the wits right out of you and do what needs to be done anyway?"

Lox simply stared at the child with the unruly red curls, her freckled face and clear blue eyes projecting an innocence he hadn't encountered in a long time.

"Well, I'm usually not," she continued matter-of-factly, as if she was carrying on a conversation in a porch swing on a sunny spring morning, "but since I've met Papa God, He's teaching me how to be brave." She turned her head to glance at Julius, who had become still and pale.

"No, you're right," Emma-Lee said. "He's not my brother or cousin or anything. Most of the time, I don't even like him much, but that doesn't mean I can't love him like Papa God does."

Emma-Lee locked eyes with the killer. "Haven't you ever loved anyone enough to be brave on their behalf, mister?"

* * * *

Lox stood stock-still. The color drained from his face. His mind was suddenly filled with a picture, a memory he'd forced himself to forget long ago.

He was twelve years old and scared to death. His drunken father was on the rampage again, busting up furniture, throwing plates and glasses from the table, screaming obscenities at his mother and grandmother, who were huddled together in the corner. His little brother and sister had run away to hide, as he usually did when his father drank too much and started terrorizing the family.

But not this time. Lox couldn't bear to watch his mother and grandmother cower any longer, staving off the inevitable beating. He thrust his thin body between them and his crazed father, shouting at him to leave them alone. His father laughed at his pathetic attempt at bravery and knocked him out cold.

By the time he'd awakened two hours later, his grandmother was dead, and his mother was a mangled mass of broken bones. He never saw his father again.

The memory faded, and the cellar came back into focus. A little girl was innocently staring at him, waiting for an answer to her simple question.

"No...yes...I don't...what am I doing talking to you? I should be putting a bullet through your puny little head!" His unsteady right arm holding the gun traced a wobbly figure eight in the air. He was confused, dazed. He had to get a grip. Taking a deep breath, he willed his muddled brain to work right.

"Will you get out of the way, little girl, or do I have to kill you, too?" His voice was quieter now, but slurred.

"You'd have *two* children on your conscience if you did that."

"I don't have a conscience any more."

"Why not?"

The loss of blood was taking its toll. Lox's knees shook noticeably, and his arm had dropped several inches so that the gun was now pointing at the base of the cot instead of at the child sitting on it. The answer came slowly and a bit garbled. "It's my job, that's all. I have to do my job. It's not my fault."

"Whose fault is it?" asked Emma-Lee, her round, blue eyes looking deep into his.

"Don't know..." Lox shook his head, trying to clear his head. Griswald's rifle that had been tucked under his left arm clattered to the floor. The noise startled Ma Stone and Aunt Augusta, causing them to jump in surprise. Lox cursed and swung his handgun around in their direction.

"No further!" he shrieked. It was becoming hard for him to speak. He swayed, struggling to maintain his balance. "Kill you...not my...fault..."

Suddenly, a gun fired. Emma-Lee cringed and screamed. The sharp, ear-splitting explosion reverberated through the cellar.

Chapter Twenty-three

Everything happened at once. Lox bellowed and toppled to the floor, blood gushing from his left calf. Captain Stone burst through the doorway, smoke encircling the barrel of a black pistol in his hand. Two other men stormed in behind him with guns drawn, one wearing a shiny sheriff's star on his chest and the other wearing a deputy's badge.

Ma Stone darted forward to kick away Lox's gun, which was lying two feet from his writhing body. Aunt Augusta shouted something indiscernible and ran to the captain, who engulfed her in his arms and buried his face in her disheveled hair.

Julius was jarred into consciousness by the blast of the gunshot and tried to crawl out of bed, his uncomprehending eyes bouncing off his surroundings like moths off a lit window. Emma-Lee did her best to settle him, speaking to him in as calm a voice as she could muster under the circumstances while pushing him back onto the cot. As weak as a newborn kitten, Julius wasn't difficult to manage, even for a girl half his size.

Ma Stone appeared at Emma-Lee's elbow and lovingly caressed her shoulders before gently moving her aside and tucking the blanket around Julius.

"I'll take of care him now, dearie. You've done more than a little girl should ever have to do. Why, you've saved his life!"

Emma-Lee sank to the edge of the cot, exhausted. The action in the cellar swirled around her like bees in a hive. She felt numb. Tears began to cascade down her face, although she wasn't aware that she was crying.

Aunt Augusta rushed from the captain's side to envelope her in a smothering hug. Unaccustomed to such displays of emotion from her aunt, Emma-Lee wasn't sure how to respond. Aunt Augusta pulled back and knelt beside the cot, holding Emma-Lee's hands and smiling through the crocodile tears dripping down her face.

"I thought I was going to lose you." Her voice was hoarse. She struggled to continue. "I realized...oh, Emma-Lee, I couldn't bear to lose you..." She lowered her face to Emma-Lee's tiny lap and broke into sobs, deep rattling sobs that convulsed her whole body. Emma-Lee could do nothing but pat the back of her aunt's head until she came up for breath.

"I prayed—more fervently than I ever knew I could—that if God would just protect you and give you the right words to say to stop that wretched man from shooting you..." she paused and sobbed again, as if the possibility caused her great pain, "...that I would trust Him with my life."

The sheriff removed the guns from Lox's pockets and shouted instructions to the deputy, who was out in the hallway checking Griswald's still unconscious body. Captain Stone now stood behind Aunt Augusta, his own eyes glistening with tears.

Aunt Augusta went on, as if there had been no interruption, speaking loudly over Lox's agonized groans and the sheriff's shouts.

"And then, you were so calm—supernaturally calm—and said the only things that could have possibly stopped that awful man. I knew it was from God. For the first time in my life I knew positively that He was in charge."

"He was, Aunt Augusta. I was praying too!" Emma-Lee cried.

"As was I," Ma Stone said, leaning over to join hands with Augusta and Emma-Lee.

"We all were," the captain said, stepping forward to place his hands on Aunt Augusta's shoulders. "I started prayin' the moment I heard that bell ringin' in the distance. We were a far piece down the road, but I knew right away what it meant. We pushed the horses hard, and as we neared the house, I heard three gunshots. My heart nearly stopped."

"That must've been Lox shooting open the cellar door," Ma Stone said.

"But where is Pap?" the captain asked, looking around the room, concern for his father etching his face.

No one answered. A long moment passed before the captain hesitantly continued. "He...he's all right, isn't he?"

A raspy voice answered from the doorway. "Aye, I'm a'right, thanks to the grace of God and a skull as thick as the Blarney Stone." They turned to find Pap rubbing a knot on the side of his head the size of a hen's egg.

Ma Stone whooped with joy and rushed toward him, hugging him mightily, as if she might never again get the chance. "If you aren't a sight for sore eyes! I thought...I was afraid that..."

"Well I had me own moments when I feared I'd not make it, but the good Lord orchestrated the whole thing so that I tumbled off the cat walk practically through the attic window, where he graciously provided me old sea farin' equipment. I was able to get in one good swipe with me cutlass before he decked me."

"And it was because of that swipe—and Emma-Lee's heaven-inspired conversation—that he didn't kill us all." Ma

Stone beamed at her husband, pride evident in her gleaming eyes.

At that moment, voices in the hallway signaled the arrival of an assorted band of islanders. The cramped cellar began filling with concerned neighbors who had been awakened by the ringing bell and gunshots and hustled out of their warm beds to come to the aid of their friends.

In filed Mr. McNamara and Elmer with their hunting rifles, followed by Tom Dinkleberry, father of Cleotis, Myrtle, and little Tom-Tom. Mr. Doogan was there, and Mr. Moses, the blacksmith, ambled in with a huge iron hook and clawed hammer. Old Amos limped down the cellar steps, a double barrel shotgun slung over his shoulder, accompanied by Toothless Jack, toting a pistol in each hand.

Funny how the cellar doesn't feel so cold anymore, Emma-Lee thought, smiling up at the circle of caring faces surrounding her.

* * * *

The next two days were confusing at best. The sheriff hauled four prisoners away—two with gunshot wounds, one delirious with fever, and one in handcuffs, sporting a whopper of a headache. Julius, Lox, and Leffers were transported to the mainland hospital under armed guard, and Griswald was left cursing behind bars at the Lotus Landing jail. State deputies began an inquiry into an alleged smuggling operation dealing in stolen properties along Florida's entire eastern seaboard.

At the cove, Ma Stone swabbed antiseptic into Pap's flesh wound from the bullet that had grazed his left forearm and packed a cold poultice on his swollen head. At first, she demanded that he rest in bed because of the myriad of bruises discoloring his back and legs from his roll down the roof. He soon began to escape when her back was turned. She finally gave up arguing with him and kept a watchful eye as he milked Beulah the cow, brushed Cain and Mable, the horses, tended the watch-birds, and puttered around the garden.

Amos alerted the children that school had been called off on Monday and Tuesday while Miss Lemstarch was home recuperating from the ordeal, details of which swept the island like a tropical monsoon.

The islanders were quick to pitch in to help. Ola May Nesmith brought over a loaf of freshly baked bread, creamy banana pudding, and a lemon meringue pie. Toothless Jack delivered an enormous speckled trout for supper on Monday and two tasty mullet on Tuesday. Mrs. McNamara and Punkin arrived at the front door with a lovely bouquet of heavenly-smelling honeysuckle blossoms, a succulent roasted duck, caramelized carrots, and three jars of guava preserves. Mrs. Dinkleberry sent Tom-Tom and Myrtle over with a crock of her special alligator stew and a round of cornbread.

Captain Stone, exhausted from lack of sleep and the stress of the rescue, cancelled his shipments scheduled for Monday and slept through the day in the cabin of the Verily, which was tied to the one serviceable Tropic dock, the other still collapsed from the twister. His mother had tried to convince him to rest at the cove, but he insisted on returning to the Verily, which coincidentally was ported a scant quarter mile from Aunt Augusta's cabin.

Emma-Lee noticed Aunt Augusta glancing out the window toward the docks countless times during the day Monday and smiled to herself when her aunt "just happened" to run into the captain on her after-supper walk. From her seat on the front porch steps, Emma-Lee watched the two wander hand-in-hand to the familiar rock ledge over the river to watch the splendid sunset.

When night fell, schools of mullet under attack by sharks in the phosphorus-abundant river produced a dazzling fireworks display of flaming streaks that lit up the river. Two heads on the rocky ledge, silhouetted against the full moon, moved close together to admire the amazing spectacle.

Emma-Lee decided it was a good time to finish her homework inside.

* * * *

Aunt Augusta and Emma-Lee returned to school on Wednesday.

"Were the bad guys really gonna kill that Duckett fella in cold blood like Pa said?" Cleotis asked during the rare discussion time allowed by Aunt Augusta before roll call.

"My father says they were only hired guns. The real mastermind behind it all hasn't been caught yet," Amy Freeman said.

"Has anyone noticed Leona and Elsie ain't here today?" Sticks asked with a sly grin. "I heard Mr. Snodgrass decided all of a sudden-like to move the family up north."

"Yeah," Louis piped up. "Nobody knows where they went, but everybody's talking about it."

"Who were the bad men snuggling?" Myrtle asked.

"It ain't *snuggling*. It's *smuggling*," Elmer said, rolling his eyes. "And it ain't *who*, it's *what* you smuggle that gets you in trouble."

"Ooh, you're so smart, Elmer!" Mary Margaret chimed in, batting her eyes.

"I don't know. I think who you snuggle could get you in pretty deep trouble, too," Theo sneered, casting a meaningful look between Elmer and Mary Margaret. Elmer socked him in the arm.

"Didja really deck one of the bad guys with a frying pan, Teacher?" Tom-Tom broke in, his young voice high pitched with excitement. "I heared if it wasn't for you, he'd 'a shot Miz Stone. Pa said you're an honest-to-goodness hero." Silence fell on the classroom.

Aunt Augusta bent her head over her desk, suddenly having difficulty making eye contact with her students. Her voice was subdued, humble. "Well, we all did our part in a very trying situation. I simply made the best use of whatever weapon I could, that's all."

Her students looked at her with a new brand of respect.

"Now, enough dawdling. Let's get right to roll call. We have much to do today." Aunt Augusta was back to business as usual.

* * * *

Captain Stone tried every position he could think of to make the stiff wooden chair tolerable as he languished in the white, sterile hospital room watching Julius sleep. He'd rushed through his regular Thursday shipping route and then skipped supper to see Julius, who was still unaware of his visitor's presence after a solid hour.

A white-clad nurse entered the room. "Mr. Duckett's not awake yet? My goodness, that medicine sure makes him sleep long and hard." She raised one eyebrow knowingly at the captain. "No doubt he'll rouse when I change his bandages."

With the scuffling and howling that followed as the old dressings were removed and fresh ones applied, the captain figured the sleeping medicine was probably the nurse's idea to keep Julius unconscious and quiet as long as possible.

"Don't let him fool you." The nurse told the captain as she left the room red-faced and huffing after the battle. "He's improving every day."

Julius, half his head and his left foot swathed in bandages, lay scowling in the center of the crisp, white sheets as the captain stepped out of the corner where he had taken refuge during the dressing change. The moment Julius saw his employer, his expression changed to something akin to amazement.

"Cap'n, what're you doing here?"

"Why, I've come to check on my second mate. How're ya' faring, lad?"

"They say I'm getting better, but you couldn't prove it by me. My broken toes and ribs are taped tighter'n a tick. Hurts something fierce." His eyes lowered to the foot of his bed. "Reckon most folks think I deserve it."

"'Tis a good thing we don't all get what we deserve. We can thank the grace of the Almighty for that."

"There you go again, talking about God like He's your best friend."

"Aye, that He is lad, and yours, too, by the simple fact that you're still here. Could've been a lot worse, ya' know."

"I know. The deputies were here plying me with all kinds of questions about the smuggling racket. Guess I'll be going to jail for a while after I get out of here. They told me what happened. You and that little girl saved my life. Been thinking on it a lot."

"And what're ya' thinkin', lad?"

Julius' head dropped and his eyes clouded. "You know, Cap'n, I used to think you were stupid for being so kind to people who didn't deserve it, and ..."

"And what, Julius? Go on and say it."

Julius took a shaky breath. "And if it wasn't for you almost getting yourself and your family killed being kind to me, I'd be dead right now."

Captain Stone moved closer and laid his hand on the boy's shoulder.

"Ain't nobody ever cared about me enough to do something like that, 'cept maybe my ma. Why would you do it, Cap'n, after I've done nothing but hurt you? You gave me a job and trusted me, treated me like a man. And I...I knifed you in the back." He covered his face with one hand and sobbed.

The captain said nothing but stayed close, patting the boy's shoulder as he wept.

Julius finally quieted to sniffles. His voice was low and broken. "How can you ever forgive me?"

"Ah, lad, that's what I've been tryin' to tell ya' all along. 'Tisn't by my own power, that's for sure, but by the power of the One who teaches forgiveness."

Julius wiped his nose with the not-so-clean-anymore sheet. "You gonna spout off again about me being a pearl in the making, ain't you, sir?" He smiled up at the captain almost shyly.

Captain Stone smiled back.

"It's all right. Reckon I'm 'bout ready to listen this time."

* * * *

Thursday and Friday seemed to pass quickly for Emma-Lee. During the Friday afternoon spelling bee, she managed to outlast Mary Margaret, generally acknowledged to be the second best speller (Elsie Snodgrass being the best). Mary Margaret went down on the word "foreign," which Emma-Lee was able to spell correctly, awarding her the distinction of being crowned "Queen Bee" for the week, much to the delight of a beaming Aunt Augusta.

What a wonderful week this has turned out to be, Emma-Lee thought, happily wearing her pasteboard crown as she packed her books to go home. Julius is going to be all right, Captain Stone and Aunt Augusta are looking all starry-eyed at each other, I'm in fourth grade with Punkin, my best friend, and I've just won my first spelling bee. How could it get any better?

Chapter Twenty-four

Aunt Augusta was in rare form on the walk home from school. She laughed over Tom-Tom's latest unfortunate incident in which he brought in a dead possum for sharing time. The unfortunate part was that the possum wasn't really dead but was only "playing possum," and miraculously revived when Cleotis poked it with his pencil.

The terrified animal rolled onto its clawed feet and hissing like a cornered alley cat, scurried beneath the nearest table, prompting Amy Freeman and Ruthie Ann to scramble atop in most unladylike fashion and release blood-curdling screams sure to be heard all the way to Georgia.

Aunt Augusta smiled and exchanged pleasantries in town square with every islander she passed and even pretended not to notice when Mrs. Nesmith slipped Emma-Lee a clandestine sugar cookie.

What a lovely frame of mind she's in, thought Emma-Lee. *Sure hope it lasts!*

The two loitered on the sandy road returning from the village, stopping to admire the flock of enormous white pelicans floating on the Indian River, their snowy plumage a striking contrast to the indigo blue of the river.

"Why don't white pelicans dive from the sky to fish like the brown ones we see so often? They're both pelicans, even though the brown ones are smaller and not as pretty." Emma-Lee watched the graceful white birds gently dipping their heads into the water to scoop food into their pouches.

Aunt Augusta angled her head, studying the magnificent birds.

"Perhaps its part of the diversity of God's creation. Just because they're all pelicans doesn't mean they're made to be the same. It's not that some are better and some are worse, they're just different. Like people. Your mother and I are sisters, but we're quite different." She watched as the majestic white birds spread their eight-foot wingspans to take flight, their papaya-colored bills flashing in the sunlight.

"Ellie was always cheerful and pretty, much like Sarah is now, but I was...not. I took everything so terribly seriously. I never found much to laugh about." She gazed off into the distance, pain reflecting in her eyes. The white pelicans grew smaller and smaller as they flew downriver.

"When I was a girl, the other children called me, 'Tweety Beak.' I used to cry in my room at night because I wasn't pretty like Ellie."

Emma-Lee gazed at her aunt in surprise. She'd never heard her say anything like this before. She wanted to comfort her, take away the hurt somehow.

"Some of the children at school call me 'Little Red Mop Top.'"

"They do?" Aunt Augusta fingered the red curls that had pulled away from Emma-Lee's thick braids at the nape of her neck. "Why, you have radiant hair. Just like my mother's. You remind me so much of her..." She smiled into Emma-Lee's eyes. "You're definitely a white pelican like your mother and grandmother."

"So are you."

Aunt Augusta snorted a short, sad laugh. "I have a mirror, child. I'm a brown pelican. I'll never be called beautiful by any stretch of the imagination."

"I think you're getting more beautiful all the time." Emma-Lee's eyes shone.

Aunt Augusta squinted at the white pelican dots on the blue horizon. "With the Lord's help, I pray it might be so."

* * * *

Arriving at the cabin, they threw open the windows to the delicious orange blossom-scented breeze and stored their schoolbooks on the kitchen table. Aunt Augusta built a fire in the stove and put on a kettle for grits to go with the crabmeat croquettes she'd planned for supper. She had just gone to her room to change from her school attire into her housedress and apron when Emma-Lee, opening her arithmetic book at the table, heard voices outside.

She looked out the front window and saw a uniformed policeman accompanied by an official-looking man in a dark suit and tie approaching from the direction of the docks. Something about the brisk steps and grim faces of the men made Emma-Lee's blood turn icy in her veins. Whatever their business, it could not be good.

Emma-Lee ran to alert Aunt Augusta just as four sharp raps sounded on the front door. Aunt Augusta quickly rebuttoned her school dress and hurried to answer the door. Emma-Lee shadowed her aunt, fending off what felt like spiders crawling through her belly.

"Good afternoon, ma'am," the suited man said. "You are Augusta Lemstarch, guardian of Emma-Lee Palmer, are you not?"

Aunt Augusta looked at Emma-Lee, alarm growing on her pallid face. "Yes, I am. Is something wrong?"

"I'm Samuel Callaway of the Division of Family Services, and this is Sgt. Kelley from the Eau Gallie police force. May we come in?"

"Why, yes, of course." Aunt Augusta opened the door wider and gestured to the seldom-used sofa and chair in the parlor. The two men crossed the floor, removing their hats and seating themselves on the sofa as Aunt Augusta closed the door and swept past them to the paisley wingback armchair. Emma-Lee stood stiffly beside the chair, her quivering body leaning heavily on the upholstered arm.

"Ma'am," Mr. Callaway began with a glance at Emma-Lee, "Due to the nature of our visit and the sensitive issues we need to discuss with you, it would probably be best if the child were not present for our meeting."

Aunt Augusta turned her pale face to her niece. "Emma-Lee, why don't you play outside for a while?"

Thoroughly alarmed now and with one last beseeching look at Aunt Augusta, Emma-Lee retreated to the back porch. A dark sense of dread hung about her like a cloud. She felt as though her heart had suddenly turned into one of Pap's lead ship anchors.

Closing the door behind her, she pressed her eye to the chink hole in the pine board just to the right of the doorframe, careful to draw no attention to herself. If she turned her head just so, she could see most of Aunt Augusta and the left half of the man in the suit sitting on the sofa. Their voices drifted out the open window.

"What is this about, gentlemen?" Aunt Augusta asked even before the back door had clicked shut.

"I'm afraid we have some bad news for you," Mr. Callaway said, a faint tone of sympathy tempering his brusque manner.

He pulled a paper from his inside suit pocket and consulted the print there. "Our office in Eau Gallie was notified by telegraph last evening that your sister, Elnora Lemstarch Palmer of Miami, was pronounced dead upon arrival at the Miami Hospital at one o'clock a.m. Thursday."

Aunt August gasped, her hands involuntarily clasping her chest over her heart. "No, it can't be! Not Ellie! What on earth happened?"

"There apparently was a domestic argument that grew somewhat, well, physical, and Mrs. Palmer fell—or was pushed—over a coffee table, striking the back of her head on the stone hearth."

Outside on the porch, Emma-Lee felt her world crumble around her. *Mama! Not Mama! Mama can't be gone!*

"Furthermore, the coroner determined that there were suspicious bruises and contusions present on the body, presumably from the same source. Fenton Palmer is now under arrest, and an investigation will be made pursuant to a charge of manslaughter and possibly murder."

"Murder!" Aunt Augusta shook her head. Tears dripped down her stricken face. "I told Ellie something should be done about that man's temper before something terrible happened." A shudder shook her thin frame. "And now it's too late." She broke down in sobs, her face in her hands, as the two men sat very still, waiting.

Emma-Lee sank to her knees on the porch in numb disbelief. *Papa's in jail for killing Mama? No! Please, Papa God, make it go away...*

"What's to become of the children?" Aunt Augusta asked as she shakily stood and crossed the room to retrieve a white handkerchief from her handbag on the kitchen table.

"They are now in custody of the Division of Family Services in Miami, ma'am, until all the relatives are notified. A Mr. Jonathan Palmer of Atlanta, the brother of the defendant and a well respected attorney, has volunteered to take the boys and raise them with his own two sons."

"Jonathan, yes, he is a decent man, much more so than Fenton ever was," Aunt Augusta nodded, dabbing her eyes. "And his wife is a lovely woman and a dedicated mother. That will be a suitable arrangement, I think, but what about the girls?"

Mr. Callaway and Sgt. Kelley exchanged looks. Mr. Callaway cleared his throat. "Miss Sarah, the eldest, has requested that you be asked to take the girls permanently, Miss Lemstarch." He paused to take in Aunt Augusta's response, which was stunned silence. Her swollen, unblinking eyes stared at him.

"Miss Sarah specified that we should clearly state, as you're making your decision, that she has already made arrangements for a job and living accommodations in Jacksonville beginning in June. She will need lodging and tutoring only until the end of the current school term. Therefore, we are really only talking about taking custody of the baby and Miss Emma-Lee, to whom you are already caretaker."

"But that was only to be temporary! Where would I put them all? My house isn't big enough for more children! Poor Emma-Lee has to sleep in a closet as it is."

Through her peephole, Emma-Lee watched her aunt pace the living room floor, wringing her hands in a fretful fashion. The pieces of the little girl's broken heart throbbed at the obvious struggle of the woman who had become more than just a caretaker to her, the woman she had grown to love and respect. But did Aunt Augusta feel the same way about her? Was the bond they had forged over the last eight months strong enough?

"Please, Papa God, please let Aunt Augusta want us," she whispered.

"Miss Lemstarch," Mr. Callaway's efficient voice entered the void, "you certainly don't have to take the girls if it's too much of a hardship. They can be assigned to foster homes or perhaps another relative will step forward. We can send out inquiries immediately."

Aunt Augusta stopped pacing directly in front of the picture on the wall of two little girls. It was the faded daguerreotype of her and her little sister, Ellie, taken in a nearly forgotten time long ago. She shook her head, wiping tears from her eyes.

"We were so happy and carefree then. We simply took it for granted that the love and security our parents provided would always be there."

Aunt Augusta's thin lips quivered, and her eyes brimmed once again with unshed tears. Her gaze turned to the table, where among the schoolbooks, Emma-Lee's little stuffed bear, Cap, lay forgotten from the early morning. She picked it up and rubbed the soft fabric against her cheek. The worry lines furrowing her forehead and carving fissures into her granite-like cheeks gradually eased, transforming her face and relaxing her rigid posture.

Emma-Lee felt a flicker of hope spark inside her.

Aunt Augusta faced her visitors. "No, Mr. Callaway, inquiries won't be necessary. Of course, I'll keep my Emma-Lee, and the baby, too. And Sarah for as long as she can stay.

We'll all sleep together. Or I'll build a room onto the house if I have to. I couldn't possibly give up Emma-Lee when I love her as much as I do. I'm sure I'll grow to feel the same about the other two with time." She nodded with assurance. "I believe God will provide."

Emma-Lee's heart leapt at the words she had longed to hear: *My* Emma-Lee. Aunt Augusta had said, "*My* Emma-Lee." The truth sank in. She was loved. She was wanted. She belonged. The island would be her home. Warm relief, mingled with the sharp pain of loss, poured down upon her like a spring hailstorm.

"Very well, ma'am," Mr. Callaway said, nodding. "We will need you to travel to Miami at your convenience to make funeral arrangements, sign the necessary papers, and bring the other two girls back with you. In the meantime, Miss Sarah is taking care of the baby as well as any mother would, and they are comfortably accommodated."

"No, I won't leave them there any longer than necessary. I will arrange teaching coverage immediately. Nannie Mae doesn't understand, of course, but Sarah must be devastated, as Emma-Lee will be—losing their mother and father at the same time." She shook her head remorsefully. "I know from my own experience how catastrophic it is to suddenly become an orphan."

She walked to the window and looked down the road toward the docks. "Mr. Callaway, Sgt. Kelley, might I ask you to assist me in performing a small task?"

"Of course, ma'am, anything we can do to help..." Mr. Callaway said as Sgt. Kelley nodded.

"I presume you came over by police boat from Eau Gallie?"

"Yes, ma'am."

"And you're to return to the wharf there?"

"Indeed, we are."

"Would you be kind enough to book passage for Emma-Lee and me on the freighter Verily for Sunday morning? That's Captain Stone's day off, but I suspect he will be gracious enough to transport us across the river in time to catch the nine o'clock train to Miami."

"Of course, that will be no trouble at all," the sergeant said. The men stood and walked to the door. Aunt Augusta followed and opened the door for their exit.

"Oh, one more thing." Aunt Augusta looked a little embarrassed. "Captain Stone should be in port at Eau Gallie this time of the evening. He is my...a good friend, that is...a friend of the family's," she took a quick breath," and I would greatly appreciate it if you could spare a moment to personally deliver the news to him about my sister and my decision to take the children."

"Certainly, Miss Lemstarch, as you wish." Sgt. Kelley put his police hat back on with a smart snap and nodded his farewell.

"Here is my card," Mr. Callaway said. "Please feel free to contact me for any reason concerning arrangements. I will notify the authorities in Miami that you're coming. I'm very sorry for your loss." He donned his hat and started down the dusty road with the sergeant.

Aunt Augusta closed the door and sagged against it. She didn't hear the soft swish of the back door opening and closing. Suddenly, two little arms wrapped themselves around her waist from behind and squeezed with surprising strength. She loosened the arms and turned to kneel, face-to-face with her niece.

The two, pain-wracked and weeping, fell into each other's arms, drawing comfort in the sorrowful embrace that tethered their hearts as never before.

Chapter Twenty-five

"Are you ready to go then?" Aunt Augusta stood by the front door Sunday morning in her long-sleeved white blouse accented by the sapphire broach at her neck, black skirt and sensible black hat. She held her brown leather valise in one hand and in the other, her traveling satchel stocked with reading material, wrapped soda biscuits, two boiled eggs, baked mullet, several tangerines, and a wedge of cheese. It was ever so much more practical to take lunch than to buy food on the train.

"Yes, ma'am," Emma-Lee responded, stumbling into the living room as she struggled to carry the worn carpetbag Aunt Augusta had loaned her for the trip.

"My goodness, child, are you taking everything you own? Remember we'll only be there a few days and then we'll have all Sarah and Nannie Mae's things to bring back, too."

"I know, but I want to take presents to Michael, Archibald, and Dexter since they're going to live with Uncle Jonathan and"—her voice broke—"and I want them to remember me." Two blue eye-shaped pools of tears appeared on the earnest face beneath the yellow travel bonnet.

Aunt Augusta dropped her bags and leaned down to look directly into her niece's face. "Oh, my dear Emma-Lee, I know this has been immensely hard on you. I know it all too well. But believe me when I say your brothers will *never* forget you; you don't need to take them presents."

Her heartstrings were tugged as she recognized the child's misery, and her strong will melted like lard in a skillet. "Very well. Show me what you're taking them, dear."

Emma-Lee set the carpetbag down at her feet and opened the clasp. There, resting atop a wilted lace handkerchief embroidered *E.L.P.*, her nightgown, dresses, and undergarments, were her stuffed bear, Cap, the small bag of marbles Captain Stone had brought her, and a cigar box containing the slingshot Pap had made for her tenth birthday. She'd included in the box a handful of smooth, round stones she had collected from the riverbank.

"I'm taking Cap to Dexter to hold at night for when he misses Mama. The marbles are for Michael. When I was home at Christmas, he showed me his marble collection, and I told him about mine. And the slingshot is for Archibald. He likes to shoot things."

Aunt Augusta couldn't help but smile although her eyes welled with tears. She was touched by the selfless generosity of the child who would give her most treasured possessions to her brothers at a time when she truly needed the reassurance they brought herself.

"Are you sure you want to give these away? They're your favorite things."

Emma-Lee nodded solemnly. "That's why I chose them. I only have three brothers, and I won't see them again for a long, long time—maybe never. I want to give them the best I have."

She hesitated, then reached into the carpetbag and dug her small hand down through her belongings, searching for something. She brought up a wrinkled paper folded into fourths and held it out to Aunt Augusta.

Aunt Augusta slowly unfolded the tattered paper that had obviously been opened and refolded many times. It was a crude drawing of a house and a crooked tree and lollipop flowers. Seven stick figures were bunched around the tree. Two of the figures were larger than the rest, one with a triangular bottom that was apparently a skirt; the second had a rectangular-shaped top hat perched on its head. The other five figures were smaller but varied in size, two with triangular skirt bottoms, and one particularly tiny figure sitting on the ground.

"That's a picture of our family. I drew it when I first got here and kept it hidden under my bed. I used to take it out and look at it every night before I went to sleep, so maybe I would dream of home." Emma-Lee gently took the drawing from Aunt Augusta and refolded it into a small square. She carefully inserted it back into the carpetbag and closed the clasp.

"I don't need it anymore. The island is my home now. I'm taking it to Papa. Maybe when he's sad at night because he doesn't have a home or family anymore, he can look at it and dream about the happy times."

Aunt Augusta found she couldn't speak properly. She simply nodded and reached out to take the carpetbag. She swallowed hard. In a strained voice, she said, "why don't we trade bags? I'll take your heavy one, and you take my lighter one. It's much easier when we share the load."

In mutual silence, they gathered their luggage and walked onto the front porch in the whispering light of early morning. Together, they descended the steps. Treading the sandy road toward the docks, two islanders of like mind admired the golden sun as it rose through the mist hovering above the Banana River in the east.

* * * *

As Aunt Augusta and Emma-Lee stepped onto the dock, Captain Stone hurried down the weathered planks to help them with their bags. Behind him on the deck of the Verily, Franklin, the first mate, halted in mid-stride, his arms loaded with wood and sweat beading on his ebony forehead in spite of the coolness of early morning.

"Do you need my help there, Cap'n?"

"No, Franklin, I think we'll be fine."

"Aye-aye, sir. I'll be in the boiler room preparing to cast off." He disappeared down the steps into the hold.

The captain looked more serious than Emma-Lee had ever seen him. He took both cases from Aunt Augusta and the travel bag from Emma-Lee. "The two gentlemen stopped by night 'afore last to tell me the sad news. I can't tell ya' how sorry I am for your loss, both of you." He looked each of them square in the face, his brow knitted with concern.

"Thank you, Cornelius." Aunt Augusta's voice sounded small.

"I have something important I need to talk to ya' about 'afore we cast off and I get too busy." He turned and led the way to the end of the dock where the Verily waited, gently bobbing up and down with the current. He hop-stepped from the dock onto the deck and deposited the luggage beside the cabin door before turning to help the two ladies onto the freighter.

He clasped Emma-Lee around the waist and lifted her across the small gap between the dock and the boat, her sunflower-colored traveling dress and matching bonnet gleaming in the sunlight. As he set her down and turned to take Aunt Augusta's hand, the cabin door opened, and Ma Stone and Pap stepped out on deck.

"Ma, Pap, what are you doing here?" Emma-Lee asked, surprised. Ma reached out to her as she crossed the small distance to where the little girl stood and enveloped her in a tight, grandmotherly hug. Pap followed and wrapped his arms around both of them. Emma-Lee felt snug and safe within her little cocoon of love.

"We're so sorry about your terrible loss, dearie. We've been praying for you ever since Cornelius told us about your mother," Ma Stone said, misty-eyed.

"Aye, lassie, 'tis a terrible thing. But ye have the faith to see ye through it. And we'll be here whenever ye need us to help ye along." Pap's voice was husky with emotion. He knelt on one bony knee and put his hands on Emma-Lee's shoulders, looking deep into her eyes.

"'The Lord giveth, and the Lord taketh away. Blessed be the name of the Lord.' Remember that, lassie. A fella in the Bible called Job said that after he'd lost his family and everything else he had, too. 'Tis easy enough to bless the name of the Lord when He giveth and life is sweet, but the mark of a true believer is when she can bless His name though the bitter times, after her very lifeblood is taken away."

Emma-Lee nodded and wiped away the tear trickling down her cheek. She would think about that and hold it close in the dark nights to come.

Ma Stone and Pap offered Aunt Augusta the same soothing hugs of comfort and words of encouragement and then backed toward the cabin door, as if purposely removing themselves from the gathering.

"No—Ma, Pap, stay," Captain Stone said. "I think you should be here since you're a big part of this."

He gestured to Aunt Augusta to sit down on one of a pair of wooden chairs that had been brought from the cabin for this purpose. Aunt Augusta, looking completely puzzled, complied. The captain sat on the chair facing her.

"Augusta," the captain said in a stiff, uncomfortable voice. "I don't really know how to say this." He looked like he wished the river would rise up and swallow him.

Ma Stone smiled at Emma-Lee and motioned for her to come stand beside her. She wrapped her arms around the little girl as they stood quietly watching the scene before them unfold.

"After my route yesterday, I docked here in Tropic and spent the night with my folks. I hope ya' don't mind that I told them about your sister." He reached out and took her hands in his." I want ya' to know I think 'tis a wonderful thing you're doing, takin' in the three girls. It didn't surprise me a' tall that you'd come to that decision, bein' the charitable, noble lady that ya' are."

Aunt Augusta's eyebrows lifted, and two rosy spots sprouted on her cheeks.

"But I also know your heart is bigger than your house, which was a fine enough dwellin' for a single lady, but woefully small for a family." His eyes flickered toward the horizon as if to gain strength before retraining on Aunt Augusta's face.

"A family's truly a blessing, it is, and lately, I've thought quite a lot about what a magnificent blessing it would be. What I'm tryin' to say is," he took a deep breath and dropped down onto one knee, "I'm asking ya' to marry me, Augusta, and allow me the blessing of sharing this wonderful family with ya'."

Aunt Augusta gasped and sat stock-still, her gray eyes round in amazement and her thin lips forming a tiny circle.

"Ma and Pa have offered to have us come live at the cove with them. There would be plenty of space if we fixed up the attic as a room for us; Emma-Lee and the baby could share my old bedroom. Sarah could have the guest room while she's here, and it'd be a place to call her own when she comes to visit for holidays and the like."

Aunt Augusta stared, speechless, as the captain rambled on.

"We've talked it over and prayed about it, and it surely feels right. You'd be closer to the school than ya' are now, if ya' want to continue teachin', and Ma and Pap could watch the baby while you're away. Or ya' could stay home with Nannie Mae, if you'd rather." He stopped abruptly, as if he realized he'd been running like a detached train car out of control.

"Well, what are ya' thinkin', Augusta? I know the idea is kind of sudden-like, but I wanted you to know all your options before you go to Miami."

The always-in-control schoolteacher was unable to respond. Emma-Lee noticed that the lone black feather extending skyward from her sensible black hat was quivering in a most unusual way. The back of her aunt's neck was the color of ripe strawberries. Emma-Lee looked up at Ma Stone, who smiled back with a wink.

After an awkward pause that seemed to stretch into the realm of forever, a strange croaking noise finally issued forth from Aunt Augusta's opened mouth. She cleared her throat and began again.

"I think...it certainly is a most generous offer, Cornelius, both from you and your parents." She nodded in the direction of the small huddle of people at the cabin door and attempted a nervous smile, which faded quickly. "However," she swallowed hard, "I would never be able to forgive myself if I accepted such an arrangement without one condition."

In the stunned silence that followed, even the screeching seagulls overhead seemed to cease their perpetual racket to listen.

"And what condition would that be, Augusta?"

Emma-Lee thought the captain's face looked pained, like he was sitting on a tack. His chest stopped rising as he held his breath.

Aunt Augusta took her time about answering.

Gradually, the crow's feet around her eyes crinkled, and her lips stretched across her teeth in an awkward, teasing smile. "The condition is...that my fiancé first tells me he loves me before planning my entire future."

The captain's chest swelled with much needed air, and he looked mighty relieved.

Emma-Lee glanced up at Ma and Pap and found them both smiling broadly.

She, too, smiled as she pulled Ma Stone's arms around her tighter and felt warm inside as well as outside. It was strange to feel such intense joy and sorrow at the same time.

Like that man, Job, she had lost so much. Mama was gone. She might never see her brothers again. Papa was lost to her now—maybe she'd never had him to begin with. But she still had dear Sarah and baby Nannie Mae. And now, God had given her a new family and a new home on the island. A seed of hope stretched its warm, tender roots around her heart.

The seagulls circling the boat scattered in squawking protest as the fresh morning air was suddenly rent by a booming voice with a charming Irish lilt, "'Tis all too true, Augusta! I love ya' now, and I'll love ya' forever!"

"Blessed be the name of the Lord," Emma-Lee whispered, meaning every word.

Debora M. Coty

Acknowledgements

It's such a privilege to thank those who made this book possible. I begin with utmost gratefulness to Robert Robinson, who graciously shared with me the beautiful memoir of his grandmother, Kathryn Harrison, whose early pioneering childhood on untamed Merritt Island was the inspiration for this story. Also of great assistance in describing a nearly lost land, was Life and Adventures in South Florida, (published in 1906) by Andrew P. Canova, Robert's great-great-grandfather.

A debt of gratitude goes to the work of Vernon Lamme, whose 1973 Florida Lore stories, "not found in the history books," were compiled over half a century of reporting in numerous Florida newspapers and recorded on MyFamily.com, Inc. Mr. Lamme's tales of homesteading life on Merritt Island provided fodder for many of Emma-Lee's exploits.

Heartfelt thanks to my editor, Sheila Cragg and to my friends, supporters, and early readers, Austine Keller, Terrell Clemmons, Cheryl Barber, Ann Currie, Cricket Coty, Cindy Hardee, and the Foster family, Gloria, John, Elizabeth, and Emily (special thanks to Emily for loaning me her name and lovely countenance as a model for Emma-Lee).

Thanks also to my parents, Adele and Frank Mitchell, who have been my most ardent supporters since the day I was born and filled my life with security and love.

My deepest love and gratitude go to my husband, Chuck, without whose wisdom, guidance, editing skills, patience, and technological expertise, Emma-Lee, Captain Stone, and Aunt Augusta would have never become flesh and bone.

Debora M. Coty

Break It Down
Creative Writing Instructional Questions

Chapter 1

The use of symbolism is a valuable literary device. What do the following symbolize?

 a. Mama's handkerchief
 b. Wasps
 c. The man in the black hat

Write one-sentence descriptions of each of Emma-Lee's family members based on their reactions to her leaving. Set these aside and after finishing the book, look back at these descriptions to see if your first impression was accurate.

Chapter 2

Very little dialogue is used in this chapter; give examples of the effective use of interior monologue (thoughts) to illustrate Emma-Lee's feelings.

Write two paragraphs about something in your own life that, like Emma-Lee, made your "insides turn hard" and want to simply turn and walk away.

Chapter 3

How are sensory descriptions used (involving the senses: taste, smell, touch, hearing, vision) to make you feel you're in Emma-Lee's shoes?

From whose point of view (POV) is the story written at the beginning of this chapter and when does it shift to another POV? (Hint: POV is the character viewpoint; which person's lens the reader views the story through.)

Debora M. Coty

Chapter 4

Where and why is narrative summary used? (Hint: Narrative summary is a secondhand report like a narrator speaking in a play.)

Give two examples each of concrete and figurative language in this chapter. (Hint: "a cloudless, turquoise sky" (concrete) versus "This must be what the gates of heaven look like" (figurative).

Chapter 5

How is Aunt Augusta's backstory introduced, and in what ways does her past explain her present behavior? (Hint: backstory describes a character's background prior to the beginning of the story.)

What purpose does Emma-Lee's flashback of her family at the beach serve? Why do you think the author waited until chapter 5 to introduce this information?

Chapter 6

What can you surmise about Captain Stone's romantic experience by the doorknob scene? Aunt Augusta?

Which approach is used in this book: first person, second person, third person, or the omniscient perspective? (Hint: first person is an intimate sharing of firsthand experience; second person is the author speaking directly to "you," the reader; third person is telling a story about someone else; omniscient is from an overall POV (like God's perspective), which provides a broad overview.

Chapter 7

Point out three aspects of character development in this chapter. (Hint: character development means just that—action that defines who a character is.)

Cite two similes and two metaphors used and explain the difference. (Hint: similes use "as" or "like" in comparison, i.e. "like an echo from a tunnel"; metaphors are analogies that liken ideas by word pictures, i.e. "the reflection of the sunset on the water created a huge basin of shimmering pink jewels.")

Chapter 8

Study the stylistic devices used in this chapter. When are poetic speech, exclamation points and italics used to move the story forward without being distracting?

Name at least two instances when cliché's are avoided by creative figures of speech (freshening an old turn of phrase with new imagery, such as "a snowy day in June").

Chapter 9

Point out "show, don't tell" passages in this chapter (action versus narration).

Find two examples each of the use of ellipses and dashes. (Hint: ellipses are used for gaps, dashes for interruptions.) Now write two of your own examples of each.

Chapter 10

Name two aspects of plot development in this chapter. (Hint: plot development propels the story line forward.)

How is the use of dialect effective in the porch scene? Write your own scene using dialect to define your character's personality. (Hint: More is not better; dialect must be understandable to the reader and should be used sparingly.)

Chapter 11

Three different POV's are used in this chapter. How do you know from whose lens the scene is viewed? Why use more than one POV?

Explain the use of active voice versus passive voice in the wagon scene. (Hint: active voice is *doing* the action; passive voice is receiving the action, i.e. "The rocking wagon threw Aunt Augusta against the captain" (active) versus "Aunt Augusta found herself thrown against the captain by the rocking wagon" (passive).

Chapter 12

Name five examples of sensory adjectives used in the Thanksgiving scene. (Hint: "buttery creamed potatoes" makes you imagine the smell and taste of the food.)

What do you learn about Julius? Does this knowledge make you view him in a different way?

Chapter 13

Write a brief essay explaining what impresses you most about the story of Lady and Tomcat. Has God ever sent someone to help you find your way?

Would you describe the ending of this chapter as a "cliff hanger"? Why are cliff hangers excellent chapter endings?

Chapter 14

How is the recurring theme of courage addressed in this chapter?

Do you think abbreviated sentences and short paragraphs create excitement and move the action along faster? Why?

Chapter 15

In the bedroom dialogue between Emma-Lee and Aunt August, locate three examples of the use of "beats" (brief descriptions of physical action that pace dialogue and show the reader what characters are doing; beats also help limit character attributes such as stating "Emma-Lee said" or "Aunt Augusta said" too often). Example: "Aunt Augusta sank down on the bed beside her niece."

How is Aunt Augusta changing? Write a half page comparing her metamorphosis to someone you've observed changing in your life. (It can even be you!)

Chapter 16

Double meanings are a literary device often used in fiction. What does Sarah say in the carriage that has double meaning?

How is body language used to convey unspoken feelings in this chapter?

Chapter 17

In what way is the Palmer's Christmas tree a metaphor for their family?

Which subplot is ascending toward climax in this chapter?

Chapter 18

How is the intensity of the confrontation between Captain Stone and Julius driven by the fast-paced delivery and use of "white paper" spacing? (Hint: white paper means fewer words were used, leaving more white paper than black ink visible.)

What example of foreshadowing did you see concerning the black pearls? (Hint: foreshadowing lays the groundwork for plot twists to come; look back in chapter 12 for a clue about pearls.)

Chapter 19

List five sensory descriptions that add excitement and depth to the warehouse scene (using the five senses).

Locate ten power verbs that replace –ly adverbs (adverbs ending in "ly") to better "show, not tell." (Hint: "He *stole* across the outer room" instead of "He walked *slowly* across the outer room."

Chapter 20

Using your own words, explain Ma Stone's tapestry perspective of life.

Find three examples of placing –ing phrases in the middle of a sentence rather than at the beginning (strengthens the sentence and appears more polished). Example: "...her agile fingers pushing the needle through the tapestry..."

Chapter 21

Write one sentence explaining the symbolism of:
    a. The pitch black of midnight
    b. The purple luminescent light
    c. The ringing bell

Why is it okay to jump between heads (change POV) eight times in this action scene? How is it formatted so the reader understands the POV is changing?

Chapter 22

How is Emma-Lee's confrontation with Lox in the cellar foreshadowed by previous events? (Hint: involves the courage theme.)

In two paragraphs, compare Lox rationalizing and de-personalizing murder as simply part of his job to a time you rationalized sin in your life.

Chapter 23

Two subplots have just climaxed; despite resolution (tying up loose ends), the reader gets the ominous feeling it's not over yet. What is the key sentence that implies there's more to come? Why is this a good page-turner phrase?

How was the grace Captain Stone shared with Julius foreshadowed? (Hint: see chapter 15.)

Chapter 24

In three paragraphs, explain the brown and white pelican metaphor. Which did Aunt Augusta consider herself? Emma-Lee? Which are you?

How have all previous clues concerning Emma-Lee's mother and father paved the way for the ending? Did you see it coming?

Chapter 25

All the intertwining subplots have now been resolved; pause right now and name them. What would you have done differently if you'd written the story? (Answer: the three subplots are Emma-Lee's quest for a home for her heart, love transforms Aunt Augusta, and Julius discovers grace.)

Debora M. Coty

Billowing Sails, the sequel to *The Distant Shore,* is now underway. Want to be involved? Brainstorm plot ideas for Emma-Lee, Captain Stone, Aunt Augusta, Julius, and Sarah. Where would you take them from here? Submit up to five of your plot ideas (one for each character) via my website, www.DeboraCoty.com, and a brand new character named after the winner will appear in *Billowing Sails!* It could be you!

References for study questions

Strunk, William, Jr. and E.B. White, *The Elements of Style.* New York, © 2000, 1979, Allyn & Bacon.

Browne, Rennie and Dave King, *Self-Editing for Fiction Writers.* New York, © 2004 by Renni Browne and Dave King.

If you liked The Distant Shore, you might like the following inspirational romance available now from Vintage Romance Publishing:

Copper Star
Suzanne Woods Fisher
ISBN: 978-0-9793327-4-6
Inspirational Romance
Trade Paperback

After participating with theologian Dietrich Bonhoeffer in unsuccessful plots to assassinate Hitler, Louisa is sent to "wait out the war" in the dusty mining town of Copper Springs, Arizona, to be sponsored by Robert Gordon, a friend of Bonhoeffer's from his year of seminary in the United States.

Grateful for a safe haven but anxious to return to Germany, Louisa finds herself trying to adjust to American life in a family with problems of its own: Robert's wife had mysteriously disappeared, leaving him to cope with the special needs of their four-year-old deaf son, William. This mischievous boy soon finds an ally in the well-intentioned-but-overly-helpful Louisa, who recognizes the intelligence behind his silent pranks. But Robert? Louisa irritates him, challenges him and intrigues him.

Reviews

"Fisher has a knack for sweeping us up in the small triumphs and tragedies of her characters, which echo in surprising ways the often overwhelming dramas being played out in the world around them." --From David Kopp, co-author of **The Prayer of Jabez** (Multnomah Publishers)

"Ok, it is all your fault! I didn't get anything done today - laundry and dirty dishes are piled up, but I just couldn't put down your book. I kept saying just one more chapter... I loved it!!!! I feel like I'm getting to know a new family and have a window into their life. I don't want to stop getting to know them now. I want to find out what happens to Louisa!" --From Linda Danis, author of the bestselling **365 Things Every New Mom Should Know** (Harvest House)

Available now from all major online retailers and your favorite bookstore.

CPSIA information can be obtained at www.ICGtesting.com
Printed in the USA
LVOW041654220912

299899LV00001B/1/A